SAFE HOUSES

Lynne Alexander was born in Brooklyn, New York, in 1943. She studied English and art at Hunter and City College, and then at the University of California in Berkeley, where she moved in 1964. She studied harpsichord in Berkeley and Amsterdam, after which she performed and taught professionally in the USA, Britain and Holland. She ended her career as a harpsichordist in 1981 and turned to writing fiction, while doing various office and research jobs. Lynne Alexander now writes full time and lives in Lancaster with Oliver Fulton, who teaches at Lancaster University.

LYNNE ALEXANDER

──

SAFE HOUSES

A KING PENGUIN
PUBLISHED BY PENGUIN BOOKS

Penguin Books Ltd, Harmondsworth, Middlesex, England
Viking Penguin Inc., 40 West 23rd Street, New York, New York 10010, U.S.A.
Penguin Books Australia Ltd, Ringwood, Victoria, Australia
Penguin Books Canada Limited, 2801 John Street, Markham, Ontario, Canada L3R 1B4
Penguin Books (N.Z.) Ltd, 182–190 Wairau Road, Auckland 10, New Zealand

First published by Michael Joseph 1985
Published in Penguin Books 1986

Made and printed in Great Britain by
Richard Clay (The Chaucer Press) Ltd,
Bungay, Suffolk

To
Lillian

AUTHOR'S NOTE

This is a work of fiction. Although Raoul Wallenberg's name has been used, as well as certain recorded facts concerning his achievements in Budapest and his subsequent disappearance, it is not – nor is it intended to be – biographical. It is a story narrated by two characters who are fictional, and whose version of events is imaginary. In particular, what they have to say should in no way be taken as evidence that Wallenberg ever had a mistress in Budapest, or a daughter by her. I do not for one moment assert that he had. It is a fictionalized Wallenberg, therefore, who finally emerges from these pages.

Indeed, nothing in this book should be taken to discredit or diminish in any way the real Raoul Wallenberg. His heroic public deeds and his private life will remain, I trust, undisturbed and undistorted by anything I, or my characters, have said.

Furthermore, nothing in this book should be taken to discredit or diminish in any way the real Raoul Wallenberg Committee of the United States, who have worked unstintingly on his behalf. I wish to thank the Committee for their generosity in allowing me access to their files.

Part I

1956

Gerda

1

Who is he, where is he? Handsome, brave, blond, kind? Was he, is he? Every time she opens her mouth a question mark falls out. She drives me to my green chaise, to the toilet, the television set, the window – any escape hatch will do – yet there she is right behind me, poking her pointy nose up my tail. Sniff sniff. What does she want from me? Simple, she wants to know who her father is. Was.

I demur. I am frigid on the subject, I'm not in the mood. I will not be poked into action. Leave me, I say, but she hunts and hounds me; she pins me down with a claw but I shimmy free. When she's older, maybe, we'll see. "*When will I be old enough?*" she interrogates. When? Do I look like a Gypsy fortune teller?

This scratching for information gets on my nerves. Why should I tell her? *What* should I tell? What's wrong with a little mystery between friends to make life interesting? To withhold is to excite. Besides, what's in it for her, what prize at the end of the line? The mere fact of paternity. Big deal. She won't find him, whoever he may be. Forget him, I say. I try plugging her hole with a chunk of Velveeta cheese but it's too tight, it won't go in. She eats nothing. I eat it myself, I pop it in my mouth and swallow it down. If I'm lucky she'll starve before I pull a Daddy out of a hat.

All right, so why not tell her a story, any story? Your father was a poor tailor, a brave soldier, an honest seller of insurance policies, a Rabbi. He died in a concentration camp because he wasn't concentrating when they asked his occupation. There's a resemblance, especially around the nose. But why not tell the truth? Because the truth complicates. What is truth, anyway? One leads a rich and varied life, naturally the memory isn't always crystal clear. One makes a choice. One tells – What else? – the best story.

So we wait a year. She turns her attention to other business. She's a scholar. She grows into a string bean. No more questions about fathers. All of a sudden fathers are out of business. She has a crush on teacher's pet who comes up to her crotch. I see them walking home from school together like Mutt and Jeff. Good luck. Who am I to interfere? I mind my own business. I don't go for shrimps, myself.

One night I'm listening to the late news on the radio. The Russians are invading Budapest. So what else is new? Imre Nagy, the Hungarian leader, is crackling helplessly. "We plead to the strong and free nations of the West to help Hungary in its hour of need. We are down on our knees, the Russians are already at our doors. We are falling." What can I say? Get up, Nagy, don't get your nice clean pants dirty. And don't waste your breath begging. It was on the cards Hungary should fall to the Russians, so enjoy the vodka. Listen, they're playing Schubert's *Ave Maria*. Beautiful. I'm far away from everything, now, the Russians can't touch *me* with their tanks and their meat hooks. I work, I pay my rent and nobody tells me what to do. This is a free country. Eat your heart out, Imre.

I pace up and down smoking cigarettes. It was different in my day when the Russians were the Great Liberators. And I was the Great Beauty. I threw flowers to them, the gift of my famous smile I gave *gratis*. Not now. Now if they should make me a proposition I'd say: Go stir your tea with it. I was free then, I came and went with whoever I pleased, but I'm freer now between these four walls, with those bars across my windows. I'm safe. Safe enough to talk. So there you are: you want a story, I'll tell you a story.

"Put away your books, sit down and listen," I say when she comes home from school. "You're always pestering me to know who your father is, now I'll tell you." News of the Russians rumbling through Budapest has brought it all back. Inspiration. I blow a family of smoke rings, close one eye and sight her through the loops. How far away she looks, how insignificant, sitting on a patch of worn embroidered roses, her skinny arms hoisted up like a puppet.

Then she grips the rocker's arms with her ten transparent wishbones, rocks back and forth. Her jaws click as she works on her bubblegum, nourishment for the day.

"All right," I say. "Are you ready?" She gulps and nods, stops rocking and chewing; maybe she's swallowed the wad. I never did. I either spat it out or gave it back to them in a kiss. Here, a present from you to me to you. Hah! She makes me laugh with that prune face. How tempting to give it to her right between the lips: force feed the goose. Are you listening? Your father also had a shriveled rump and a pinched nose. He wore silver granny glasses, elevator jackboots, a swastika *schmatta* around his left arm. How does that go down, my dear?

But come, how could I feed her such poison?

I'm no beast. Look how she sits there blinking and rocking, trusting as a baby waiting for a nipple. Come, allow me to be generous. Let me give her a choice. Here, my dear, in my right hand I give you for a father the little Nazi coward, afraid of his own shadow, Adolf Eichmann. In my left I give you the balding but beautiful champion of the Jews, the gentle Gentile Raoul Wallenberg. Which will you have? Take your pick, you may be lucky in the draw. Your chances are fifty-fifty, even Stevens. Ready? I close my eyes and see those last days in Budapest, the thick snow, black ice. I shiver. "Why is no heat coming up?" I ask. "It is," she says. "Listen." I hear the sizzle but I prefer to operate by touch. I always have. I put my hand around the *eau de nil* pipe. Ah, the familiar feel of a cold pipe warming up. This to me is home.

I remember when she was born. I looked down into the wrinkled face expecting a reproduction in miniature of the Swede's face – the wet brown eyes, the thick lips, the square jaw. No such luck. What did I see but the thinnest lips and nose in babydom, pale blue eyes fit only for putting behind cold silver spectacles? I wanted to drop her in the nearest scrap bucket and run but the nurses said all babies are born with blue eyes, they will change. So I waited and watched. Sure enough, by the time she was two months old they were already like the Swede's: big round malted balls, her only decent feature. Could be she's a composite, a freak of nature? One egg fertilized by two in the last

5

unchronicled battle of Budapest. Excellent. I could try that one on for size: you're half-and-half, a mongrel. How do you like that? Wait for the penny to drop. Hah!

Such a waste. With an ounce of imagination she could have made him up for herself – a great artist, an actor, a lover, a warrior, a god; anything she chose. But not her. All she can do is chew gum and rock and wait for a gift from heaven. Or me. I look into the meatball eyes and what do I see? The final solution. So I tell her of Gerda and Raoul, both beautiful and brave, who worked side by side in Budapest; who met at the Majestic; who rescued Jews and brought them to the safe houses. How well we worked together! Of course, I don't go into too much detail about the off-duty jobs we did under the satin bedspread. But there you are, we must protect our young. I talk on – once I start, why should I stop? I am warming to my subject and as the eyes play on me I wonder how I could ever have doubted. Of course – *of course* she's his.

I get to the part when I deliver him to the Russians and take my leave. "What do you mean, it was risky to walk so quickly on the ice *in your condition*?" she asks.

"It means I was pregnant," I say.

"Oh, I see."

"What do you see?"

"I'm not sure," she says, closing the eyes and rocking again. I'm getting seasick.

Okay, so I have to spell it out for her, put two and two together. Connect the dots, fill in the colors. Look, dummy: "I did a quickstep off the ice and left Budapest before the Russians could get their hands on me. When I got to America – nine months later, conveniently – I dropped the baby at the feet of the Statue of Liberty. You, my dear, are sitting in her saddle shoes."

The eyes click open like a doll's, she stabs herself in the breastbone. "You mean me?" she says. "Raoul Wallenberg is my father?" I demonstrate my best Mona Lisa smile. She is overcome, rocks back and forth with the cushion in her arms like the orphans at the Jewish hospital in Pest. Ask me no more questions, I'll tell you no more lies. Rella, you see, after Raoul. The eyes have it.

2

We are identified by a carved stone above the main
doorway: The Bridge Arms, Brooklyn Heights' finest.
Rella is propped against the skirt of the building. I watch
her from my ground-floor window. She in turn is watching
a little boy blowing a bubble, as round and pink as one of
those luscious cheeks hidden inside his pants. Hers are
more like a newborn baby's – chapped and shrivelled and
covered with fine black hairs between the crack. Who
would ever guess her age? When I was eleven I was already
a big strapping girl – and already a beauty. When the bubble
pops she turns tail and runs in to me for protection, that
nose of hers twitching like a frightened rabbit's. God only
knows how she ever grew such a specimen. If only I could
hire a blackbird to do a snip job!

"How strong are horses?" she pants.

"Why?"

"You said Wallenberg – Raoul – was as strong as a horse,
with nerves of steel."

"So?" Raoul is it?

"So, they make bubblegum out of old horses. We learned
that at school."

"Don't believe everything they tell you at school. Old
horses never die, they only fade away." For such a
simpleton she has a mind like a pretzel. Somehow she has
managed to make this contorted association between
Wallenberg, old horses and a lump of pink bubblegum.

"But why did the Russians arrest him? I don't understand. Weren't they on the same side, against the
Nazis?"

"Arguably."

"What do you mean?"

"The Americans helped him out."

"How?"

"They financed his rescue missions."

"But what's wrong with that?"

"Don't they teach you about the Cold War in
school?"

"Yes, but I thought that was between the Russians and us."

"Brilliant. So figure it out for yourself. If he was heavily supported by Yankee dollars, then he was not to be trusted by the Russians. Worse."

"How worse?"

"They might suspect him of spying."

"Was he a spy?" she whispers, protecting her chest with her elbows.

"It depends on what you mean by the word spy," I say, and walk away.

It's too late to take him back. The father is now adopted by the daughter. She protects him by crushing him against her sprouting rosebuds. You can see by the dead-fish glaze around the eyes how much in love she is. With her own supposed father, no less; for shame. Whose Raoul is he anyway?

3

She materializes with a library book two times the width of her chest, opens it to a full-page photograph and points.

"Look what I found. Do you know who that is?" she asks.

"Benito Mussolini," I answer.

"Don't be funny. You know perfectly well who it is."

"Then why ask me?"

"Because he's dead. I thought you might want to know."

"What should I know? I never said he was still alive."

"You led me to believe it."

"What?"

"Nothing." She bites her non-existent lip, marches off to her room for a good cry. As if I killed him.

So this is the way it ends, crushed between the fat thighs of a library book. Dead? Really dead? I flip back to the beginning of the book, to a picture of a fancy hotel with shutters on the windows, window boxes filled with geraniums, gas lamps, an outdoor café. Elegant people lounge in wicker chairs: old goats in goatees and bow ties with fat cigars; beastly women in straw hats and ankle strap shoes. The Hotel Majestic, where Adolf Eichmann lived while supervising the deportations. Where he had drunken orgies and was the victim of loose women. Very accurate – but for a price, Adolf, for a price. Budapest, it says, was sophisticated, happy-go-lucky, vulgar, naive, corrupt. Budapest was a willing ally of the Germans by secret pact; when they realized what was going on it was too late. Don't I know.

Death marches? Deals? Rescue missions? So-called liberation, siege? All this I know. When the Russians entered Budapest, I read, Szalasi, the Hungarian Fascist, fled to an evacuated university on the outskirts of the city where he held seances with the beyond through the services of a Scottish medium. I didn't know this – very interesting – but other services, yes, those I remember. And after that? The Russians fought the Germans and the Hungarian Fascists, and the Jews hid themselves and hoped they would kill each other off. "It was during this period also that the heroic Raoul Wallenberg is known to have lost his life," it says. Known? What is this baloney? I rush to knock on Rella's door. The nose is not improved by misery.

"Dry your eyes. He may be dead – I give you no guarantees – but he didn't die in the siege. That much I can tell you."

"But it says so in the book."

"Don't believe everything you read. There were witnesses, others besides myself, who saw him leave Budapest to go meet Malinovsky in Debrecen. That was on January 17, 1945. On the way, the Soviet secret police arrested them. Next day they were put on a train to Moscow and it was bye-bye Raoul Wallenberg. That was the last we knew from first-hand evidence. The siege went on until the end of February. Raoul was not killed during the siege, he was in Russian hands by then. This is a fat book of lies. Take it back to the library and tell them what they can do with it."

"But why should they say he died then if he didn't?"

"Because it's a convenient story, it suits everybody: the Russians, the Swedes, the Americans. If he's dead, they can stop worrying about him; such a nuisance. Even at the time of his arrest, the Swedish Ambassador – Sodaworks, some name like that – said he believed Wallenberg had been killed by the Arrowcross during the siege, when all along he had a letter in his pocket from the Soviet Ambassador saying Wallenberg was safe in Russia and would soon be returned."

"But he wasn't."

I shrug. "Then where is he, what happened to him, why didn't they send him home like they promised?"

"They liked him too much to let him go. They're keeping him in cold storage."

"You mean they took him prisoner. He might still be there like that?"

"Who knows?"

"But still alive?"

"It's possible, anything's possible. They say prison life is excellent for the digestive system; you can live forever in there."

This is too much for the delicate lamb chop. Her eyes turn to *ptcha*: warmed calf's foot jelly. Just like mama's. The kind of woman who would wait forever for a man.

"Don't you want to try and find out where he is, if he's still alive, if they're ever going to release him?"

"Why?"

"Because." She holds the picture of him up for me to see, lined up with her own ghost face. "Do I look like him?" she asks. "Same eyes," I say. "Just like wet meatballs flecked with Quaker oats." She smiles, plops herself down on the bed to moon at him. Traces the eyes, lips, square jaw with her finger, caresses the knot of tie around his neck, presses her dry lizard's lips to his cupid's bow. Papa.

4

The butcher's shop is her second love. Italian, Jewish, Polish – it doesn't matter so long as it's the old-fashioned kind with sawdust on the floor and blood on the walls. To her it is better than live theater, this transformation of animal to dinner portion. This is where the supermarket fails her. She says it is more like a hospital, with the patients lying in undrained beds, covered over with tight plastic sheets; there are bright blue-white lights overhead and it is very very cold.

The curious thing is that she will not touch – to eat – a piece of meat herself. Especially meatballs. ("You said his eyes were like meatballs.") You see how literal-minded she is. Perhaps she draws nourishment through the eyes like a voyeur. Like my customer the Peeping Tom. Every other week he comes to report on the goings-on at the Casa del Re dancing school. Always the same story, little girls in tutus, lifting their legs, bending over. This to him is exciting. He says they remind him of stuffed *dermas*, good enough to eat. With a similar drooling expression Rella describes three-inch thick rib chops decorated with paper skirts. No thank yóu, I prefer my meat naked.

Schultz, the Jewish butcher on Melrose Street, she informs me, sells fish on one side of his shop, meat and poultry on the other. He flaps back and forth, pale as his chickens. Meanwhile Rella stands there staring at the dead fish. She notices gobs of blood in the corners of their gaping mouths. This too excites her. (She herself might have been dragged from the bottom of a river.) According to her, Schultz's latest acquisition is a live catfish which swims around in a wooden tank next to its dead cousins on the slab. A monster with long whiskers like whips. She worries that it is confined in such a small space, and that it knocks itself against the sides of its wooden tub. Would she prefer it to be laid out on the ice block? At least it's alive and kicking, I tell her. This comforts her. She claims it's the ugliest creature she has ever seen (Perhaps that's why she's so attracted to it?) but this Schultz thinks the world

11

of it. "You see that fish?" he asks her one day, noticing she spends her life staring down at it like it's her long-lost brother. "That is a really old fish. But smart. I bet you didn't know a fish could be smart, young lady?" So the old yellow cock has a twinkle in the eye. Rella shakes her head. She could use a few lessons in survival from that ugly catfish.

From Schultz I get soup bones so big they hardly fit into my pot. Plenty of healthy marrow in there. One of my favorite late-night treats is sucking on those bones. But even better are the chicken feet; nowhere else can you get feet nowadays. What I do is chew on the bones until they splinter so I can suck out the grainy pink marrow. Then I suck on the toes, one at a time.

Rella's true passion is the Italian butcher shop on Pacific Street, run by three brothers named Gnocchi (pronounced Nyucki); I know them well. They are always coming to me with dried blood under their nails, strips of meat in their ears and private parts. To tell the truth, I do not distinguish one brother from another; one uncircumcised gnocchi looks very much like another from my point of view. Rella gets a different perspective. Tom, she says, is the serious one. He trims off the outer layers of fat and gets down to business. Tony sings Italian arias. John, the comedian with the handlebar mustache, does the death-defying butterfly cut, lighthearted but precise. All three brothers wear blue and white striped aprons. Why death-defying, I ask, and she says, "One false move and he slices off his hand." To her the shop is part music hall and part three-ring circus.

She sits on a bench with her sneakers half buried in sawdust. What does she like best? She considers the belly slices, foreribs, chump chops, ox hearts, tripe. No. "Veal cutlets," she says, "thin ones." "Okay, you got it," says Tom, pointing at her with his delicate slicing knife. Already she is wriggling with excitement. He brings from the back of the shop a triangle of upper thigh which is hoisted on his shoulder; he eases it gently onto his thick butcher's block. He stares at it, smacks it a few times like a playful lover, then flips it around with his knife until he gets the exact angle of operation he desires. He sets his sights. "Are you ready?" he whispers to Rella, instrument poised over the lump of quivering flesh. She nods. "Okay, here we go," and he inserts the point of his knife just under the tough orange outer skin. Once he starts, the entire strip comes away and he tosses it into a bucket at his feet. "Soap," he says, not looking up from his work. The next layer, very rough and white, he pokes away in thick clumps, using the knife as a jabber. "Sausages and lipstick," he mumbles, deep in concentration. Now he is getting down to the quick; the final layer of fat close to the meat itself, dense in texture. He removes that. Now the meat is pink and smooth, every fluff of fat removed, like Rella's virgin scallop. "Palest pink is always best," says Tom, giving the lump one last affectionate slap before turning the job over to John.

John lifts his filleting knife off its hook, sharpens it on the leather strop, rolls up his sleeves, ripples his muscles and flashes his teeth. He shaves off an eighth-inch slice. Not thin enough. He slits the cutlet horizontally, three-quarters of the way across, folds it open and holds it out across the palms of his hands. A mere sixteenth of an inch thick; a work of wonder, she says, just like the transformation of a caterpillar into a butterfly. He pounds it flatter with his mallet. He flashes his teeth again and throws the completed pile of scaloppinis at Tony, who plops them onto a piece of white butcher's paper, breaks into *Un Bel Di*, tosses them up and down, catches them on his paper behind his back and presents them to Rella. She claps and the brothers bow, linking arms together. Bravo, bravo. "What animal do they come from?" she asks. "Moo, moo," says Tony. "Very small baby. Delish." He kisses the tips of his bloody fingers. Good boys, these Italians, they know how to handle a nice piece of flesh.

It was different in Budapest. I remember the sausage shops with their white tiled floors and breast-high marble counters along the walls; they were more like cathedrals than butchers' shops. The sausage lover went to worship, he held up his fat fingers (two, three, four)–words are superfluous at such moments–to indicate his appetite and make a blessing like the Pope. These thin snakes, known here as Frankfurters, always came in twos, like lovers. One was too thin to satisfy: it would slide in and get lost. But there were so many others to choose from: brown, red, black; short and thick, long and thin; curved or straight; marbled or smooth. The men would stop their own eating and stare as I slid one of those steaming black leathery wursts between my red lips. As I bit down it exploded between my teeth; the delicious juice ran down the corners of my mouth. I wore the stains like the decorations of an aristocrat. The girls behind the counter would stamp their feet with jealousy, pretending they were freezing on the duckboards – and who can blame them? Yes, it was different in Budapest.

5

Now she must find out: is he really alive? Is he a prisoner? Where? Does he share a cell or is he in solitary? Does he eat? Will they (whoever *they* may be) ever release him? She writes to organizations around the world and awaits answers. Such questions, of course, have no answers; there is only guesswork. It is rumored, for example, a certain Swede was observed in a Soviet prison – and it is assumed to be him. But they do not know. Even I do not know what became of him after the Russians took him, since I left Budapest in something of a hurry. Let the rest of them track him down. Where is he, she asks, over and over again. I do not know. Somewhere.

That it should lead to this. I imagined I was giving her the gift of a father safely disappeared, and what do I get? A nuisance, the object of a game of hide-and-seek. No international agency will bother to write to a lovelorn Pinocchio, I say to myself, but I am proved quite wrong. They do – see, here is a letter from the Red Cross in Geneva saying there is evidence to suggest he is still a prisoner in the Soviet Union; that he is not only alive but, so far as they can tell, quite well. And she is not alone in her concern for him.

This resurrection I need like a hole in the head. It makes

my toes curl up to think of a world full of little virgins like
Rella knitting woolly stockings for his cold prison tootsies,
praying six times a day for his release. What do they know
of prison, or release after eleven years? What do they
know about Russian stubbornness? If he is alive – if – he
will be used to it by now; to him it will be home. And so I
say let him be; leave him in peace.

When I was Rella's age, the boys were already lining up
outside my house; my mother had to throw cold water
down on their heads to dampen their enthusiasm. Such a
waste. If I were in her shoes, I would be whispering sweet
inspirations into those boyish ears (How about some long-
stemmed roses for Gerda?), twirling their ducks' asses
around my little finger. But not Rella, with her one-track
mind. What boy would interest himself in such a bag of
bones? Of course she is now oblivious, she is in number
seven heaven. What does she care about ordinary boys
when her Raoul may be alive? She traces and colors his
photographs and tapes the finished masterpieces up on her
bedroom wall. Raoul the pin-up. Perhaps I should encourage her artistic tendencies; one does not need to be
beautiful to have an eye for beauty. Look, for example, at
the deformed Toulouse Lautrec. She traces and colors my
photographs, hangs them next to his. Such a handsome
couple.

Her nostrils are trimmed with the color of trichinosis
pork. Happiness, yes. She is like a happy sardine, flipping
around with those silvery grey teeth; it is quite painful to
witness. Perhaps I am just not used to her behaving in this
unusual way. I am more used to her dragging herself
around like the oldest fish from the bottom of the sea. But
now she washes and brushes her greasy strings, she wears
socks that stay up on her stick legs, she eats an entire
peanut butter and jelly sandwich, including the crusts, *and*
licks her fingers. This is life – no, this is hope. Raoul
Wallenberg is alive and well!

Her interest in life blossoms like a Judas tree. Can she
have the canary I once promised her? Why not? A good
idea, I think, maybe she'll fall in love with it, and forget all
this nonsense. Ah, but I am quite wrong: the bird *is* him.
She names it Raoul. She sings duets with it *à la* Jeanette

MacDonald and Nelson Eddy. She models her triple A bra; he whistles out his little yellow heart. He walks sideways along the bottom of his cage. He jumps on his swing and blinks. She sticks her cuttlebone through the bars and murmurs to him: alive and well. Peep, peep, he replies.

6

Budapest, Brooklyn – the men come to me wherever I am. I remember how it was the first day I arrived on Riker's Island, late in 1945. I stood at the back of a long queue behind old women with their bundles and shopping bags and their thick legs and *bubitschkas*. They were the refugees, not me. I wanted to run from their Yiddish voices and their unpronounceable names. I had to get away. So I thrust out one leg – I wore a pair of black suede shoes with four-inch heels and ankle straps, no stockings. I waited until a particular pair of official blue eyes became fixed on the leg and then I shot my head sideways and flashed my famous smile and beckoned to him with a finger. He dropped what he was doing like a hot *wurst*. When he came up to me, I took hold of his hand and placed it on my belly. Then I leaned against him and whispered in his ear: "Fetch a doctor, quick." I threatened to drop the baby on his feet. That was when the rest of them came running. I remember thinking how ugly Liberty was when viewed from so close – and how green. But she gave me an idea. When they asked me for my papers I rolled my eyes up to heaven and went into labor. I gasped the name Gerda Green and fell into a pair of strong arms. Papers, what papers?

I had all the help in the world. A Jewish refugee organization found me this apartment, paid my bills, filled my cupboards with tins of tomato soup and red Jell-O. A laundry service brought clean diapers every other day. I didn't lift a finger, only right and left nipples to satisfy Rella's appetite. They sent a nurse to help care for her. A Jewish woman alone with an infant was first priority. And such a lovely young woman. To be without a man, they said, it's a sin.

Not that I was. It didn't take long to make friends. First there were the delivery men. Then I discovered if I put my fine profile out the window other men would come running, just as they had always done before when I swiveled my ankles in front of the Majestic. Now they begged for the privilege of doing my errands – poor lovely swan stuck at home with that ugly duckling. I was doing them a favor, accepting their mountains of groceries; how could I turn them away? Some of them only wanted to talk; one brought his chess set and taught me to play. He was amazed at how quickly, and well, I learned. He stared at me with his watery old eyes and told me I had the face of a goddess and the brain of a god; never on this earth had he encountered before such an unholy combination. I think he was a little afraid of me. I beat the pants off him.

During that first year I lived from hand to mouth, mouth to hand, and other variations on this theme. I stopped worrying about going out in the world to earn a living. Why should I bother, when my living was coming to me? My admirers paid my bills, brought an endless supply of food, clothes, jewelry, perfume. I could have opened my own gift shop. The rich ones brought extravagances – for example, a pair of nymph and shepherd lamps, a Chinese vase, a crystal chandelier, a set of leather-bound Encyclopaedias Britannica for Rella. The best gift of all was the portrait of me painted by an artist admirer from Greenwich Village. In it, I am looking over my right shoulder – which is bare – straight into the eyes of the viewer. The eyelids are drowsy; the eyes underneath are a cloudy green. The cheekbones, chin and shoulder are in highlight while the neck is in deep shadow. The lips are curved slightly upwards at the corners. The hair is like a burning bush. He called it a characteristic pose. It was mounted in a gold frame and hung in a place of honor over the green chaise longue, which a dealer from Grand Street brought to me, also a gift. I had my walls painted green with bright white mouldings and ceilings. I put up large mirrors with complicated gold frames. I put a salmon satin bedspread across my bed – delivered from Macy's – to make me feel quite at home. It could be Budapest, if you don't go outside. Which I do not.

I have been inside for eleven years, same as Raoul. Why should we leave our safe houses now? What would be gained? What more could I want, having everything here at my fingertips? I have a radio, newspapers, television to inform me about the outside world. Rella does my shopping. I have a window looking onto the street, fresh air comes to me from the East River, my friend the tree whirls it around like a big green fan, straight into my apartment and up my skirt. I have what is known as a prime apartment, rent-controlled to boot. I have flowers galore – my admirers bring me bouquets which I embrace like long-lost lovers. Animals? What use to me are animals in zoos, so neurotic they don't even remember how to perform the sex act. This is nature? She can have it, with my compliments. I have a moose's head (complete with antlers) mounted on my wall, a gift from a Canadian big-game hunter – one of my best customers. He follows me with his shiny popeyes; I keep them nicely polished.

Grass? My apartment is carpeted in pale green, wall-to-wall. I wiggle my toes in the thick pile, imagine cool wet spring grass, wild daffodils, sunshine, snowy slopes in the distance. I threw away those black suede shoes with stiletto heels. The suede was worn thin, the heels dangled. They were no more use to me in my green playground. I bunched them together in the sixty-nine position, wrapped them in newspaper and threw them in the dumb waiter. Bye bye shoes, I said. Maybe some bag lady got a kick out of them.

If feet could sigh with relief, mine did. I am no Cinderella's ugly sister, after all, that I should have to force my feet into puny glass slippers. They retired gracefully onto their pale green woollen pasture, swishing their tails, nuzzling and nibbling and spreading sideways until no pair of shoes could contain them. I became the Barefoot Contessa of Brooklyn Heights, my chiropodist's dream. Goodbye corns, bunions, verrucas, ingrown toenails, warts; hello to a pair of feet smooth and broad as butter beans. While I was at it, I also threw away my underwear, except for a few essential items of black lace. I freed the bosom and gave liberty to the body, as someone once said.

Yes, I am as free as Liberty herself, maturing nicely in my cool green cave.

And Raoul? There will be no green wool between *his* toes. Such lovely long toes. I can remember taking them to my lips, ready to suck them one by one. But he stopped me. Wait, he said. *I* was the beautiful chicken, I must allow him his delight, his privilege. You see, I was doing him a favor. That's how it was between us.

7

Come out, come out. Who does she think she's talking to, Twinkle Twinkle Little Star? She would like to shoo me out; O-U-T, OUT. To her it is a way of celebrating: he is alive. All right, I say, I'm glad he's alive – if he's alive – but not enough to do a rumba in the streets like Ginger Rogers. One learns so much more in private about people: the messages in the eyes, the bare feet, tattoos on the arms (flowers, hearts, numbers); the size and shape of the plumbing. Such variety, who needs to go into the streets to shake hands? What do I miss? Nothing.

She would like to slide her arm through mine, conduct me on a tour of the city. Look look, she would point: skyscrapers, derelicts, ladies from Kansas – it bores me to think of it. She would waltz me to the end of the block to see the river, boats coming and going. I demonstrate how I see all this from my window with a swivel of the head, but it doesn't satisfy her. I ought to have a close-up view from the Brooklyn Bridge to the Statue of Liberty, complete with raw wind up the poop. I tell her it's too cold out there for someone who wears no bloomers. Inside I breathe better.

She tries to entice me to Macy's, to the Empire State Building. One hundred and two stories up in an elevator and we can view the entire world from the top. The elevator moves slowly, my nose is tickled by the fly of a hat, a bump in the pants is shoving at me from behind; I'm suffocating. No thank you. Or we can go to a movie, sit on the end of the back row for a quick getaway. Travel by subway. Drink sodas at Schrafft's, eat cream cheese and walnut sandwiches at Chock full o' Nuts, squashed between dumpy ladies spreading their knees under the counter. This, to her, is fun, a day out. No, I tell her, it lacks a certain glamor. What about Central Park, does that have glamor? Oh no, I say. But she wouldn't recognize it if she shook hands with it in a bedroom suite at the Ritz.

But what about the supermarket – now there's a brilliant idea. Certain glamor. I float down the aisle, pinking like a virgin bride, to the accompaniment of piped-in music. I pluck items from the shelves like wildflowers from a hillside in the Alps – Moosabeck Sardines, Skippy Peanut Butter, Heinz Tomato Soup – all these wonderful things I put into my very own basket. Sausages you want? A fat clerk in a dirty apron wrapped up under his armpits scratches his crotch and looks me up and down. Come with me and I will show you a sausage you will not forget so soon. Dribbling like Schmidthuber. This is celebration?

What are these dark plottings of hers? She brings me a picture book about deserts. Does she imagine I will develop a sudden lust to go hitch-hiking across the country? I can think of better things to do with my thumb. She is so limited; her world so small. My four rooms are bigger, to me, than any desert. Here I lie on my green chaise and the world grows around me. This is the desert for me. Like magic the sky turns velvet blue and the stars come out. And then it's daylight and bright red-orange flowers burst into bloom in front of my eyes. I remember the night I wore my red dress at the Majestic, how I must have resembled such a flower. The truth is it takes imagination to be really free. I sit in splendid isolation on my bathroom throne and see the world: a sunset over Death Valley, the Danube in spring, a cell in Vladimir prison in winter. It's all there before me: present, past, future.

Look, a total eclipse of the moon. My neighbors are lined up under my window, men and women moaning like death marchers. Have they never seen a disappearing act before? It looks to me like the moon's being smothered with a black fishnet stocking over its face, bleeding to death, oozing red out the sides. My neighbors ooh and aah. The mixed excitement, pleasure and pain of witnessed torture. Ask Adolf about that.

"Will the moon ever come back?" asks Rella the Bleeding Heart.

"Guaranteed, watch," I say. And then, later, when the moon pokes her shiny nose out of the sky again, I say, "There, you see, what did I tell you?" Ooh, aah. Magic.

Making moons reappear is easy; fathers can be a little more tricky. I tell her she's asking for trouble, celebrating too soon can bring bad luck. What does she know? Nothing – no facts, only guesswork, dumb hope. The grass may have long since grown between his toes. Not me, I tell her, count me out of the whoopee. I got what I wanted from Raoul Wallenberg and took my leave like a lady. Up above the world so high, like a diamond in the sky. Wink wink.

8

The future is a skinny chicken slaughtered in the kosher style. I remember grabbing for one as it flew past me without its head; only a tailfeather came away in my hand. Next time on its blind journey round the coop I got smacked with its blood. There was no third time around. I went over to where it had collapsed and picked it up: dead at last, thank God.

Luck, another illusion: here today, gone tomorrow. One day music, the next, silence. Why? Where is the little bird's song? He's gone, disappeared, victim of a loose thread hanging down from a lovely flowered cover. Rella's Raoul – her little yellow bird – inspects the loop, thinks yes, a new swing, a new game; why not try? It's too good to resist. He sings one last sweet song and sticks his head through the loop. He pushes the swing away with one foot – Look, a new trick, I can hang by my neck! – and then he hears the snap of his own fragile bones.

Rella runs to the toilet: all that peanut butter she's been eating.

"He's dead," she croaks, looking greener than usual. "What should we do with him?"

"Buy him a plot in Forest Hills Cemetery and invite the Salvation Army along to play." Her skin is stretched like a tambourine's. She thinks I'm cruel, but not at all. I could have given her a good smack and a rattle: "Eat him for lunch," I might have said. Hallelujah!

She wants to know how such a thing could have happened. How? Maybe he dreamt about her in her triple A bra and got so excited he jumped up and down and got his poor little neck caught in a loop. Which happened to be dangling from his cover. An accident, pure and simple, these things happen. "Look at it this way," I suggest, "maybe he's better off dead than in that stinking cage. Think of him in heaven, free as a bird." She bites her lip. "What if it was suicide?" she wants to know. Ha! No, a bad move to laugh now, I turn away to light a cigarette. She reaches into the cage with one of her chicken-bone hands and lifts the bird out; cradles it in her palms and offers it to me. I shrug. "Take him down to the river. He'll have plenty of company."

After flinging the bird in the river, she goes for a consoling visit to her Italian butcher friends. A little distraction from her troubles, maybe a sing-song. But not today, a sign in the window reads: Death in Family – Closed Until Further Notice. The shop is dark. An old man appears in the next doorway. "Psst, you wanna know what happened, girlie?" Oh, I should have guessed something was up. He didn't sing a note of *Madame Butterfly* that night, not a note. Just sat on the edge of the salmon satin bedspread with his head in his hands like a crown roast. No matter what fancy tricks I tried it hung there between his legs like a canary with a broken neck. "Found floating in the river," cackles the old cock. "Which one?" she whispers. "Tony. *Un Bel Di*." Ha ha.

They say bad luck comes in threes. What next? A letter for Rella from Geneva. She won't mind if I open it. So far the score is one dead canary and one dead butcher boy. Two down and one to go: which one? Raoul's feet, like his other appendages, were elegant. The mailman's are square and hairy. "What's a little bad news between friends? Forget it," he snorts. I can feel the satin bedspread against my cheek, then his rough beard. This one must go.

Rella comes home from school, starved and chirpy. Dead butcher, dead bird – who cares? So long as *he*'s alive. I let her eat her peanut butter and jelly sandwich, then I hand her the letter. She sits in her rocker, moving her lips, a backward reader.

Dear Miss Green:

You will be interested in some new information which has only recently come to our attention. The Swedish Government was delivered of a note from Andrei Gromyko, the Deputy Foreign Minister of the Soviet Union. The note refers to a report, supposedly written in 1947, by a Col. Smoltsov, head of Lubianka Prison's health service, to Viktor Abakumov, Minister of State Security. Here is the note which is quoted:

> "I report that the prisoner Wallenberg (sic) who is well-known to you, died suddenly in his cell this night, probably as a result of a miocardial infarction. Pursuant to the instructions given by you that I personally have Wallenberg under my care, I request approval to make an autopsy with a view to establishing cause of death.
>
> P.S. I have personally notified the minister and it has been ordered that the body be cremated without autopsy. 17 July. Smoltsov."

Gromyko's letter ends by saying, "The Soviet Government presents its sincere regrets for what has occurred and expresses its profound sympathy to the Swedish Government as well as to Raoul's relatives."

If the above information is to be believed, it is of course tragic news. But there are questions to be raised. Both men (Smoltsov and Abakukmov) are now dead, so there is no corroboration to their story. Furthermore, there is no original copy of Col. Smoltsov's note or even a photocopy and that is unusual for

23

the Russians with their penchant for exact documentation.

These so-called facts are therefore not entirely credible, so that we may continue to be hopeful that Wallenberg may still be alive and well somewhere in the Soviet system.

W. Unde.
Assistant to Director of Information
International Red Cross

"What's a myocardial infarction?" she asks, looking up. Her teeth are coated with peanut butter.

"Look it up," I say, stalling for time.

She reads from the dictionary: "A sharply limited region of necrosis and hemorrhage in an organ, resulting from obstruction of the local circulation by a thrombus or embolus." Terrific. "What does that mean?" she asks, blinking.

"It means heart attack."

Boom, he grabs his chest, falls to his cell floor, spewing blood over the Lubianka Prison. Her imaginary papa—gone. He is joined by Tony the butcher, dragged from the river, his apron still stiff with the blood of animals. A dead canary lies at their feet, a gob of black blood on its orange beak. The moon slides across the Moscow/New York sky; it too is bleeding to death.

"Listen," I say, "can't you read? It says right here he may still be alive and well somewhere. They're hopeful, see. The Russians are lying, can't you understand? They think by saying he died everybody will forget about him and stop poking their noses into Russian secrets." But no, she can't see. She looks like the rape victim of a Nyilas gang, dumped on the edge of the Danube, poked for good measure with the tips of their bayonets and flung into the icy river to freeze.

He could whistle like a canary. I remember how he prepared his lips, wetting them with his tongue, making a neat hole for the notes to fly out. Different from the shape of a kiss.

She's giving up, letting him go. She waves. He's gone,

floating out to sea with the rest of the bodies. Those American songs he learned to whistle in Michigan, they got on my nerves. *Bye Bye Blackbird*.

Jack

1

Where am I? Who am I? I feel so strange to myself. I look in the mirror. My eyelids are drooping down like the shades of a bakeshop window; I can hardly see the chocolate butter creams inside. I test my cheek with a finger to see if I am fresh. The finger sinks in, the flesh is tender. There are eggy pouches under the eyes. I conclude the face is stale, like an elderly puff pastry filled with soured cream. This is not the way it should be. *Schaumrolle* – the word comes to me from far away – should be light and sweet. I run my finger underneath the eyes and along the nose and then I lick it. It is too salty for cream.

How did I get to this place? Where are the other inmates? I do not recognize anyone. There are bars only on the ground floor, where the beautiful woman lives. She pokes her head from her window, like a princess in a fairy story looking for a lost prince. There is also a skinny girl. People are coming in and out of the building, locking their own doors behind them. I too have my own key. Yale, it reads on its flat yellow face. How should it be that I have a key to my own cell?

There is a small suspicious bump on the left side of my doorway; what can it be? I examine it but the hall is very dark and my eyes are not so good at their job. I believe I can see the tablets of Moses rolled into a miniature scroll, like a toy for a child. Why have they put the Ten Commandments on the doorway to my cell? I do not think I am a Jew. What about the doors of my cellmates? I pad quietly down a flight of stairs in my slippers to cell number 12B and feel for a scroll there. Yes, Mrs O'Brien, she too has the Ten Commandments! I smile to myself in the dark but Mrs

O'Brien opens her door and looks very angry with me. She puts her hands on her hips and asks why I have my nose in her door. I say I am only feeling for her scroll. We are lucky here, protected. Look, I say, God protects us. This is a safe house, just like ... But I do not remember. She pushes her fingertips into my stomach, as if she too is testing for something, and yells words at me I do not understand. Nutcase. What is this – a suitcase for nuts? Perhaps it is an expression meaning a casing for nuts? Ah yes, this I understand. I bow to Mrs O'Brien and excuse myself, shuffling backwards across the hall. I will apologize for my intrusion by making her a present of a nutcase, then she will forgive me. A strudel filled with the best grade of walnuts from California, stuffed into a rich delicate casing. I will leave it outside her door, with a card saying "Nutcase."

But she doesn't like to accept it. I find the poor orphan nutcase sitting in front of my own door, untouched. It smells very good. People are putting their noses out into the hallway to sniff. A small piece of paper sitting on its stomach reads, "Keep your presents, Nutcase." I do not understand but I will eat it myself.

She is not the only one who does not like me. The other inmates of this prison also yell for me to go away. They tell me they don't like my accent, the children are sticking their tongues out. The grown-ups talk amongst themselves or move away when I come near. I have no friends in this cellblock. And yet I am free to come and go. There is no jailer to tell me what to do. I feed and clothe myself. There is such a variety of goods in the shops, it is like a dream. Each month I put a little yellow key into a gold box in the hallway and inside there is an envelope with a cheque addressed to me. I take the cheque to the bank and sign my name on the back and they give me money – enough to buy whipped butter, fresh eggs, flour, nuts; it is like magic. I show a small card with a picture on it. The name under the picture is Jack Baum. Baum means tree; this much I know.

The trees are my friends, they do not call me names or push me away. They are standing guard up and down the streets. They are the people's protectors, and therefore privileged. They are allowed visitors any time of day or night; I stay as long as I like and say what I like. The trees are free to answer me. The food, they confess, is terrible – poor and indigestible, poisoned by noxious chemicals. They cannot breathe and they are becoming stooped and shrunken; their branches die and fall off. Their seeds are growing into pollarded dwarves; where should their roots go – where? I do not have the answer. Should they enjoy a burst of new growth, large men wearing bright orange hats come and saw them off with a noisy machine. They do not know what their crime has been.

This is also my case. I have been in prisons for most of my life but I do not know why. It must be where I belong. But this steepled building, these people roaming the streets in colorful uniforms – how did I get here? Where is here? Last winter a boy threw a snowball at me and shouted, "This here's America. If you don't like it you can go back where you came from. We don't like nuts." So I think I must be in America; I must be free at last. The ball of snow landed inside my coat collar and melted next to my skin. It was very cold oozing down. How should I go back to where I came from? Where is back?

But I really cannot understand this hatred – almost an obsession – against nuts. Nuts are so good, so innocent. Who could be bothered to hate a nut? They make wishes come true, especially if you find two kernels in one shell. Then you eat one of the kernels, make a wish and throw the other kernel over your left shoulder. The wish always comes true. I love to eat nuts. I nibble them in the street, fresh from their cellophane bag. It is one of the wonderful things about freedom. Look, I can eat nuts in the streets – cashews, filberts, pecans; mmmnn, delicious.

But wait, let me think. Yes, now I remember. The devil also carries a bag of nuts: the bag is black and the nuts are stolen. He goes about the countryside collecting them and putting them into his bag because he wishes to steal their magical powers; he is a jealous devil. When he gets them trapped at the bottom of his smelly bag they cannot escape. Then he puts them to work for him – evil work – although they themselves are goodness itself. Nutcrack Night it is called, when he stalks the streets with his stolen fruits, up to his devilish tricks. Perhaps that is why they do not like nuts here, why they look on me with suspicion for eating them in the street. Do they think I am *he*? Can that be my crime?

2

Hallowe'en. How hallowed when the entertainers are unholy –giant pumpkins with jagged mouths, lit up from the inside, like the peaks of hell; ghosts, skeletons, witches hanging in the shop windows doing the dance of St Vitus? See how eager they are to get out and do their mischief; it is indeed giving me goose's flesh. But how serious is this frightening business? It is to be an occasion for dressing up, this much I understand. But what kind of costumes? I like dressing up very much. So far I have pretended to be an artist, a sailor boy and a businessman. Each time I play make-believe I think perhaps I will find out who I am. I would like to dress up too, but I must learn the rules of this game called Hallowe'en. I do not want them to laugh at me; I must not look too queer.

I ask the trees but they do not know. For them it is a time of becoming un-dressed, for the weather is getting windy and cold and they are losing the last of their leaves. They say it is to be a full moon soon and then they will be exposed in all their nakedness; they will not be able to hide in the darkness. I assure them it is a temporary condition but I myself would not like to be without clothes in the street at this time of year. I should like a warm costume.

Who will inform me? I think of asking the woman who lives behind the bars –she is called Gerda –but each time she looks from her window and smiles at me I feel a curious chill of the spine which causes me to turn my back to her and hurry away as fast as I can. No, I will approach these boys, they will tell me.

"What is the meaning of this holy day?" I ask. "Why are people dressing up? Is it for everyone or only children? Why are the costumes in the shop windows so ghoulish? Who are they trying to frighten? Why should good little children pretend to be bad?"

29

They are slapping their knees and dancing up-and-down. What is so funny? The tallest one puts his face close to mine and says in a voice which is itself frightening: "There *are* no good guys, stupid, that's the point. You're supposed to be as bad and as scarey as possible. Y'know scarey? Yeah, that's right, the worst thing you can think of."

Then a smaller boy says, "It's to frighten away the evil spirits, the devil. Ever heard of him?"

"And death," says an even smaller boy.

Then a bagel-faced philosopher says, "Yeah, that's how it is. You're good inside but you're dressed up to look bad. Got it?"

I say I would like to be an angel with wings; wouldn't that be a good idea for chasing the devil away?

"You, you?" they shout in chorus, doing their up-and-down crow dance again.

"No, listen," says the leader, "you gotta be something bad–real bad, understand?" And after a private whispering amongst themselves they decide I should be a devil with a long tail. A little fat, red devil. Perfect, they agree. But I am not sure. There are so many possibilities hopping around in my head. I must go away and think. As I am climbing the stairs of the dark hallway to my apartment, I hear bells ringing–bells bells bells coming from every church tower in the city. What city? I do not know. But I know they are ringing to frighten away the evil spirits and the harmful ghosts: the giants, dwarves, forest women; the devils with their black bags filled with nuts. From what forest? I see only darkness and I smell a damp rotting smell. Then I see mourners walking around a graveyard carrying burning torches and then, afterwards, people sitting in a candle-lit dining room eating soul cakes. They are honoring the souls of the dead. This, I remember, was another kind of holy night, far far away.

Here it is different. Of course, now I understand. It is to be an orgy of evil; a simulation of hell. Yes, I like it very much, pretending; it is good fun. And I have such a wonderful idea! Yes, now I am decided. I will make myself a costume so terrible it will frighten Lucifer himself.

"Well, well?" The boys dance round me, follow me down

the street in a tail as if I were the Pied Piper. I sing: "Jack be Nimble, Jack be Quick; Jack jumped over the candle stick." They add the rude words: "And burnt his balls." But I do not mind; I know they mean no harm. They want to know what my costume is to be: the devil or ... how about a pumpkin, a little fat pumpkin, waddling from side to side. And they laugh and laugh, holding their own thin sides. Soon they will not laugh.

"It is a secret," I tell them. "A very special secret. A surprise. You must have patience."

By now I am quite excited about my plan. I have bought a pair of tall black boots; the brown shirt and trousers hang in my closet. The rest of my costume I must construct myself: I buy a tin of black shoe polish, a small piece of black material, black thread and a needle.

I spend my evenings sewing. I sit in my armchair with the moon keeping me company; it is very bright. I am drinking a cup of Ovaltine; this I like very much, it makes the bottom of my stomach warm, also my toes. It is a complicated shape to sew and, as I am not very skilled with a needle, I am often pricking my finger. Then I suck the blood and I am again reminded of evil creatures. But mine will be worse, much much worse, than any blood-sucking vampire. Just wait.

I buy myself a thimble. Now I sew late into the night and the thimble protects the soft pads of my finger. I sew, and as I sew I see pictures in my mind. I see a scene in a warm bright kitchen. Three people are sitting at a table – two parents and a child. There is a cake in the middle of the table. Baked into the cake are a coin, a ring and a thimble. Whoever gets the coin will be wealthy, the ring shall marry, the thimble shall never marry. The fat child, I remember, bit into the thimble and cried, but he loved to eat cake. Holy Night was then a time for telling fortunes.

Now all is different. Americans are having fun, preparing for Hallowe'en. I am having fun, sewing my dreadful costume, giggling to myself. Oh, it will be such a surprise! I am sure no one else has thought of such a costume. I will be the most terrifying sight on the whole block, a beast. The devil will take one look at me, drop his black bag and melt away into a red puddle. I will rescue the nuts. The people will be free of him; they will thank me, slap me on the back. They will say: "Good work, Jack," or some such thing. From now on no evil will come to us. We will be safe and I will be a hero and a saviour, like the Swede. The Swede – what am I talking about? I sew and sew, stitch, stitch, stitch. Three more stitches to the end of the bar and I tie a knot and break off the black thread. So, it is finished. Yet to see it there in my lap makes my hand tremble; that I could have sewn such a thing. Shame on me. The wind howls at me and I am frightened. Am I doing the right thing? I must be brave. I finish my cocoa and go to bed. I must rest and be strong for tomorrow's *divertissement*.

I am excited but also very nervous. I tell myself it will be a success. Slowly I put on the costume: shirt, trousers, boots (they are too tight, they squeak at me like prison mice). I put the black polish on my hair and comb it straight across the forehead, just so. Then the mustache – such a terrible smell – and finally the armband. I look at myself in the mirror, but I must look quickly away again or I will faint. No. Yes, I am sure it is right to do evil for the sake of good. Please God, forgive me, for what I am about to do. And I march down the stairs, boots high, saluting as I go.

Gerda

1

I'm leaning out my window, minding my own business, when what should I see but a middle-aged man skipping and sucking on a lollipop. He's decked out in a child's sailor suit–short pants, middy blouse, little round hat, the whole get-up. Holy Moly. He has hairy twig legs and a round belly, just like Humpty Dumpty. But with each skip he seems to rise up in the air and float down again. Yet he doesn't break, he's no egg man. How can something so round be so light–even lighter than a balloon, a bubble? I'd like to reach out my hand and catch him.

He pauses from his skipping and sucking. His hat tumbles off his head and tries to escape, rolling further and further away from him. When he catches up with it he pounces like a fat cat: aha! Caught! He smiles and skips, his horn-rimmed glasses bouncing on his nose. Big nose, big sausage–this could prove interesting. Come here, Fritz Wurst, tell me your name. As he comes closer I hear his private sing-song: "Tchack be Nimble, Tchack be Qvick, Tchack tchumped over the candle . . ." And on the word *stick*, he jumps with both Schmoo feet from one hopscotch box to another without touching a crack. Bravo! He swivels his head without moving his feet; he is safe. Ah. He smiles. He bends over to pick up his hat again and one of his *matzoh* balls drops out of his shorts. Hello there.

Who is this Nimble Jack? From where does he materialize? I yell for Rella to come to the window, to put on her glasses. (Oh sick frog, spare me the sight!) You see, not all spies can be stunning.

"Inform me, who is this nut?"

"Oh, him. He's new in the building. He has the apartment up in the turret. His name is Baum – Hanny or Hanno, I'm not sure, some name like that. They call him Jack. I think he comes from Europe, maybe Hungary like you."

"Not with that accent he doesn't," I say.

"What accent?"

"German. Just listen."

He stops so close to the window I catch his eye and wink, but he turns his back and waddles over to the tree, a few yards to the right. He lifts his cap to the tree. "Good day," he says. "My name is Hanno. And how are you today?" He puts his head to one side to listen and his cap falls off again, but he doesn't seem to notice, so much is he concentrating on the tree. He raises his eyebrows. "You are wounded, weak? You are losing your leaves? You say someone is nibbling on them? Who can this be?" He listens again, his ear touching the bark. He laughs, reaches down and examines one of the many dropped leaves at his feet, pats the tree's trunk. "Now listen to me, my friend, it is quite normal you are losing your leaves; it is the cycle of nature. Every year it is happening to you, don't you remember? What has become of your memory? Soon it will be winter, very cold, and all your leaves will drop off until you are as bare as a *torte* without icing. But not to worry, I am only giving warning. It should not last forever, this naked phase of your life. Inside of yourself you will be quietly gathering together your energies and feeding yourself with thick saps for spring. And then you will grow magically a whole set of lovely new leaves – beautiful and green with delicate veins through which your sweet food will be running. These old ones will be dropping off. That is good; they are of no use to you any longer, you must let them go." He reaches up and pulls free a dangling leaf. "You see?" he says. "Say bye-bye." And he flaps one of his clumsy hands in a wave, sticks his lollipop into his mouth and skips away, backwards.

I watch his feet: flat as cardboards. Not feet to rest your cheek against. Feet to trip you up. Feet to play deliberately dumb or without memory. Feet to make false steps, walk in the wrong direction. Feet to turn on their heels and run away. He sticks his lollipop back in his mouth – it is the round kind with chocolate goo in the middle. Hey Fritz, where are you going? Didn't they teach you never to run with a lolly in your mouth? Wait a minute, come back. How 'bout a suck for Gerda?

2

Hallowe'en. I wonder what he's doing on such a night, up in his attic with the moon nosing into his windows? An interesting specimen, this Jack. A little crazy maybe, but those flimsy legs of his are attractive, the feet make me laugh. I imagine dressing up – since it's a night for costumes – like Theda Bara: white face, aged-steak-colored lipstick, teased hair, raccoon rings round the eyes, trailing black gown, pointy teeth. Such a fetching witch. Come in, Jack, come in, make yourself at home ... Then when he's sitting pretty in Rella's rocker I swirl around behind him and pounce, sink my teeth into his soft neck. Such an easy prey, I could have him with the snap of two fingers; a whistle and he'd come, as fast as his little legs could carry him. But better to handle with care; bubbles can break, disappear into nothing. No, I'll wait. But will he come? So far he pretends not to notice me, but I know it's only a game; it can't last. Eventually he will. One day he'll be skipping along and he'll bounce right up over the bars and into my lap. They always do. Watch the spikes, little Bubble.

I'm sitting at my make-up table, applying Velvet Rose to my upper lip, when Rella the ghost materializes behind me. My hand jumps. "Look what you made me do," I say, spitting on my finger. "What do you want now?" As usual she wants to make a nuisance of herself just when I'm getting ready for work. She wants to watch me do my face. Why not? Beauty should be a part of every girl's education. I was born with it; she'll have to learn about it.

"Want to hear a song?" she asks.

"Don't bother me, I'm busy," I say. But then I think, why not? "Sing, sing your heart out, my little ghost," I say, waving the lipstick like a baton. And so she sings, and I listen with one ear, the one not covered with a tangle of hair:

> Mother mother mother pin a rose on me
> Two young fellows are after me,
> One is blind and the other can't see –
> Mother mother mother pin a rose on me.

I turn to look at her: not a bad little voice. "You should go for singing lessons," I tell her. "It could make all the difference. Marlene Dietrich is the ugliest woman on earth but she knows how to use her voice. Plus a little make-up helps. Let me see, suck in your cheeks." How much further can they sink before they disappear? "Come here, let's see if we can make a beauty out of you." I trap her between my legs. I have no rose to pin but I cover her ghost's skin with Sultry Tan, rouge her cheeks with Flame and draw her a mouth with Velvet Rose – the color of the long drapes at the Majestic. The eyes will do as they are. Let the blind boys look on her now and be fatally struck with Cupid's bow. "There now, let me see you, stand back." But no, the make-up only makes things worse. A shrunken clown's head. "Go wash," I tell her. "You're more convincing as a ghost."

It is such a relief to get back to my own face. I smile, wide; those glorious teeth sparkle against the dark lips. I lick them with my tongue, all around, twice over, to make them look still wetter. "Well?" I ask her when she comes back from the bathroom, smudges of Flame all around her mouth like a syphilitic. It is the first time she has smiled since the news about Raoul. She says I look like a movie star, a princess, a queen. She has never seen me more lovely. So? With such a mother, why does she mope around over a missing father?

She wants to know if she will ever look like me. Don't make me laugh. At her age my face was already my fortune. I was well aware of that precious commodity, beauty. Who can resist it? Not even Jack-be-Nimble. Like I tell her, I was a dream baby. People stopped my mother in the street as she pushed me in my carriage, photographers begged her permission to take my picture. I was the winner of a baby beauty contest. The prize photograph is up on the wall, just to the left of my dressing table, in its oval gold twist frame. The photographer was a miserable crook – my mother had to pay for the enlargement and the frame. But even so, it was worth it. I travelled lightly from Budapest but for that photograph. A hundred times I swore I'd leave it behind, give it to someone in return for their hospitality, but at the last minute I couldn't bear to part with that sepia angel. Just observe how the round head is framed first by its crocheted bonnet, then by the round hood of the baby buggy. Even the popcorn stitches along the border of the layette are round, also the eyes, nose, cheeks – the hands of the baby beauty are like bunches of small ripe bananas peeking out of the sleeves. They don't make them like that nowadays. Rella stands with her squashed bat's nose touching the glass, running her hands over its surface like a blind one. I tell her it will not improve her profile, but all she can say is, "Is that really you?" To which I reply, "Who do you think it is, Winston Churchill?"

Such infant roundness, of course, is rather boring. More interesting is the photograph, on my dressing table among the perfume bottles, of Gerda at twenty-one. The eyes are no longer wide open, nor the cheeks so plump. No, here is the essential face, trimmed of all excess fat and gristle like a lean lamb chop. Observe the svelte nose, the even teeth, the high cheekbones, the strong chin, the prominent collar bones. I remember fearing they looked like a yoke for farm oxen, but I was reassured they were a sign of great beauty. But wait, look once again at the cheekbones, don't hurry, notice their fine structure, the hollows beneath; not even Garbo had cheekbones like that. As for the ears, well, that upsweep accentuated them; if my hair had been down they would have been quite hidden. Don't mistake me, they are no elephantine appendages.

I brush my hair up from my neck and ears, pin it on top of my head in a frizz. I lean back, put one hand behind my head, tilt my chin up. My kimono falls open. There is more flesh now, but the neck is still good, the collarbones are still quite harness-like. I put my nose to the glass, turn my head. With one finger I trace the undulating coastline from temple to chin, stopping only for a moment to brush the soft patch just in front of the left ear – the hairs which are always escaping treatments: short and silky like the hair at a child's temple. The place he loved to stroke.

But it is time for us to turn our tricks. The beggar ghost Rella will go out into the streets with her tin UNICEF can hanging from a wrist as thin as two fingers. I throw a white sheet over her head and cut two holes where her eyes are. I feel them blink at me from behind the sheet. If pathos ever pays, she may one day be a rich woman.

I am just making my first customer of the night comfortable when she comes flying back into the house and flaps around the bed with her white sheet, a demented creature. Ghosts should be more discreet. But she is pulling me by the foot, insisting I go to the window to see what's going on outside; the whole neighborhood is out there, she says. My first instinct is to kick her for disturbing me while working, but she is well trained; I know she would not do this for nothing. I leave my client dangling, wrap myself in my kimono and go to the window. I pull up the shade. There on the pavement is Adolf Hitler munching on an Oreo, his smeared shoe polish mustache jumping up and down. The little boy at his side is gazing up at him in amazement. "*Ach, ziss iss un fantastiche kipfel*; my compliments to the chef," says Adolf and pats the little boy on his head. He giggles and runs away.

The Führer goosesteps across the street, climbs the stoop of the first brownstone and raps hard on the door. When the woman answers with a smile ready on her lips (Was she expecting a fairy princess?), he clicks his heels and gives her the Nazi salute: "Heil Hitler, Trick or Treat!" The woman disappears for a moment then returns with a pail of water which she pours smartly over his head. He runs down the stoop as if he has been burnt, crying and spluttering in German. People are beginning to shout at him: murderer, shame, madman; go home; obscenities. An orange hits him in the stomach. He falls to the ground, doubled up. "I am wounded," he cries, holding himself. Like an incontinent dog, a puddle is forming around him. He crawls on all fours back across the street to the foot of the tree and wraps his arms around it. "Vhy does nobody give me any treats?" he howls up to the top branches; the moon lights him up, a convenient spotlight. When the police arrive he tries to scramble away but his legs don't work properly in those ridiculous flyer's boots. Two big cops – friends of mine, as it turns out; I motion to them to take it easy – support him under the arms and drag him to the car; his legs are like boiled *flanken*. He is crying, "I am only trying to frighten the evil spirits. I do not mean harm. Please don't lock me up again. Please."

My heart bleeds, Adolf, but I predict you'll be away for a long time. Not a crime you get away with on a New York street. Too bad, you blew it, little Bubble. We could have had a nice time together. *Auf Weidersehn*, Jack.

Part II

1966

Jack

1

For my sin they called me Adolf: hey Adolf this, hey Adolf that. They described to me what I had done, sparing no detail in the cause of waking my stubborn memory. They must be speaking of another person, for how could I have done such a thing? But I was, after all, in a mad house. They would not have put me in such a place if I had not done something mad. So it must have been. They told me I was getting my "just desserts," though it is so sad to think of a dessert as a punishment. Why should this be so? They tried to prove it to me by dragging me down to the storeroom late at night to see the evidence: boots and swastika armband. I told them I believed them and begged them to leave me alone – I did not want to see these things – but they were always egging me on, trying to get me to repeat the foul deed. I believe, though I do not like to say such a thing, they would have liked a Führer strutting in their midst, to lead them on to some kind of imagined victory. I disappointed them. Eventually they gave up trying to reconstruct me. Even my own name flew back to me. Hanno, I told them. What kind of name is that? They were incapable of, or unwilling, to call me such a crazy name. One of the young social workers came to my rescue. Jack she suggested, the American equivalent of Hanno. Jack, Jack? The word bounced back at me like a ball of elastic dough. But eventually I would become used to it. It was, after all, an improvement on Adolf.

I had little else besides *the deed* in my memory – that is, the story of the deed I am said to have committed when they put me away. The memory of a previous life was very much absent. When they strapped me down to give me

43

shock treatments, I prepared myself by imagining I was standing before a shop window in a foreign city. It was no ordinary shop, however, with its windows framed by polished mahogany, its etched glass doors, its gold-lettered sign. Yet what did it sell? A black window-shade concealed its mysterious wares. Ah, but that was no secret, could be no secret, to anyone in possession of that most important piece of equipment, the nose: it was a bakeshop. When they turned on the juice–for that was the expression, although it felt dry and crackled in my head–I saw an attendant in a starched white apron lean forward into the window and pull up the shade, snap. It gave me a fright for a moment but then, there before me, was a display of cakes and pastries so beautiful as to make my eyes water. And then it was all over. Down came the window-shade once more. Darkness. I remembered nothing.

Of certain basic facts about myself I was aware: for example that I was a foreigner, of German extraction. I could hear my own voice as others heard it, but what did it mean? The significance was absent. Somehow I had made my way to America (from where exactly on the map I did not know) and found my way to a certain apartment building known as The Bridge Arms, which had a noble tree growing in front of it, and which was located in one of the five boroughs of New York City, in an area called Brooklyn Heights. I had rented a small apartment high up under the roof tiles and there lived an uneventful life for but a brief time before (so I am told) perpetrating the dreadful deed. Of the people in the building, I could recall only two–a woman who lived on the ground floor, and her very thin daughter. The woman looked from her window quite frequently, but I had the impression she never actually came out. The child I had seen many times carrying shopping bags larger than herself.

From the hospital window there was a view only of bars and a brick courtyard, but they allowed me to work in the kitchen, mixing batters and doughs. There was nothing beautiful about the hospital kitchen, but it was some occupation. The diet was very bland, so I was forced to limit my repertoire to milk custards, rice puddings, biscuits, bread puddings, and so on. It was uninspired but it kept my hands and eyes busy in the bowls. It was a kind of view. The kitchen staff were amused with me. They patted me on the back and made comments like, "Hey Jack, you take to baking like a fish to water. How come?" I did not understand this remark (I am no fish, I thought), but yes, there had been something familiar about the big kitchen and the steam on my spectacles. I remember pressing the stomach of a gigantic bowl of dough to see if it was properly risen, and in the shadow of the belly button made by my forefinger I saw another of those teasing pictures – of a cake iced with a sort of chocolate mirror, twirling round and round on a silver cake stand. But the dough *was* properly risen: it jumped back in answer to my touch and the mirage of the chocolate cake disappeared.

After ten years the hospital doctors became convinced I was convinced I was not Adolf Hitler. They decided to risk releasing me, partly because they actually believed I was reformed, but also because policy had changed and more crazy people were being integrated (as they called it) back into the community. Not even an Adolf Hitler would be denied a second chance. So I was released, wearing clothes too small for me from the hospital's charity box. I had gained weight, perhaps from drugs, perhaps from too many rice puddings. I should have liked a new blue suit to wear, it might have been slimming. And I should have liked a friend to re-introduce me to that new world which had been my old world for such a brief time. But I knew no one. I walked up Ocean Parkway from Avenue Z to Avenue A, like a backwards child saying his lessons out loud. It was a street as wide, though less luxurious, as some other street in my memory which I could not identify. A horse track ran down the center, on either side three lanes of cars went in opposite directions and beyond these were rows of trees and houses. Were the horses fed on tranquillizers, I wondered? How did they keep to their own lane, not to be upset by such terrible traffic noise? Perhaps they pretended to trot down country lanes. The trees would also have to pretend. They appeared sad, stoop-shouldered, exhausted. Their fruits lay scattered on the ground; I avoided stepping on them as I walked. When I came in sight of the Brooklyn Bridge, I knew I had found my way back.

There was the building with the noble tree and the woman called Gerda who used to look out the window. Those things I remembered and so I cherished them. Somehow they had been etched on my memory like the glass doors of that mysterious bakeshop.

Still she looked out her window; now she had a dog beside her. Was it the same woman? I had remembered her as an over-glazed French tart, the kind with rows and rows of shiny overlapping fruits – plums, peaches, even cherries when in season. It had made me dizzy to look at her; to tell the truth, I was perhaps a little afraid. French tarts were not to my taste; I was quite sure they would give me a bad case of indigestion. But while she had been painted and rather angular around the face, now she looked softer and risen, like a boiled yeasted fruit dumpling, filled with steamed apricots and drizzled with butter, cinnamon, nutmeg – good enough to eat. Yes, it was the same woman, Gerda, but she also had gained weight. Yet the shell, emptied of so much glistening fruit, was still beautiful; that any child could tell.

They told me I should consider myself lucky – fresh as I was from the loony-bin – to have landed an apartment in the same building as well as a job nearby. I was to be a maker of bialys and bagels. Hot Bagels, Hot Bialys, said the brightly flashing sign over the shop: plain, onion, poppy seed or egg. You know of the bagel but what is a bialy? Well may you ask. It is a kind of roll, not unlike the bagel, but without the hole and still heavier in density, and the color of a prisoner's face. Altogether an insult to the great bread family. However, the bialy master was kind to me. "So who isn't crazy nowadays?" he asked, putting his arm around my shoulder. "So long as you can make a decent bialy, my friend, I ask no questions. It's a deal?" Yes, it was "a deal" but he would never become my friend because I would not worship the bialy. He pressed bags full of these heavy creatures into my arms each morning for my breakfast. I ate them – it would have been a waste otherwise – but each night I dreamed of light buttery creatures – the brioche, the croissant, the *Kaiserschmarren*. Where these memories came from I did not know, but I woke up feeling I had been unfaithful to the lumpen bialy.

My boss had given me a uniform of white trousers, white jacket, white shoes, and soon it became a habit with me to wear this uniform at home. With my first salary I bought a small set of white dishes. I thought, little by little I will draw the clean outlines of a life. I realized, one day sitting at my kitchen table, my environment was completely white—white walls, white eyelet curtains (I had myself sewn them with white cotton), white tablecloth, white dishes and white teapot, white tea towels. And there was I, white Jack. It was not the antiseptic white of a hospital, no, but the white of a mountain top which, while covered in thick snowy icing, is still discernible, the hard edges and angles of rock beneath making clear shadows. The linoleum, which had been the color of thick country cream splashed with red, yellow and green dots, I painted over with white deck paint.

I worried, but no one seemed to remember me or my horrendous deed; at least, no one referred to it. Few of the original tenants remained from that time and those who did were polite. No one spat in my face or screamed or laughed at me. They may have despised me behind my white back, but that I could not know. They called me Jack—"Good morning, Jack"—a fine healthy American greeting. I was grateful they could accept a momentary aberration and forgive. Like my kitchen, I could be renovated. I would have to wash my white floor every day.

2

Empty as I was of history, so my bedroom (a dark room facing the courtyard) was full of an assortment of hoardings, such as empty toilet paper tubes, milk containers, orange skins piled one inside the other like cupcake papers, used tea bags heaped up into wet and dry hills, empty cans along with their jagged tops, and used razor blades. A hedge of old newspapers was fast growing up around my bed. I cannot say why I lived like this except that I was somehow comforted by these crumbs and relics; perhaps out of these old tin cans would come a familiar smell? Silly, you say, and you are right, for the thought of myself peering into an empty can of S&W green beans is quite embarrassing. What could I hope to find in there? Nothing, I had scrubbed it so well.

However, I prowled around my room at night with my nose in cans, picking up orange skins, looking with one eye through toilet paper tubes as if they were telescopes. But it was not stars I looked for. I sniffed, I probed; one day, I believed, a story would come to me, something would remind me and, as in the funny papers, a bare lightbulb coming from nowhere would appear over my poor be-nighted head, and I would shout "Eureka!" and greet my long-lost memory. In the near-darkness my cluttered shelves looked like a miniature landscape of mountains, caves, buildings, even crenellated castles and trees. By half closing my eyes I could make these objects appear real. And so I went on evening journeys, floating – on my bed – down the Danube, and watched and waited for an element of scenery to hail to me and claim me for its own.

My apartment was located at the right shoulder of The Bridge Arms, in a circular turret well articulated from the low browline of the roof. From the street below as I looked up it appeared to me to have half popped out of the rectangular body of the building like a piece of toast or a child's Jack-in-the-Box, and with such an expression of surprise as if to say, "Where am I?" and "Who am I?" This turret looked down onto the street with two enormous dark eyes surrounded by white arches; a pointy hat, decorated in dull green fish-scales, sat on its head; and between the two window eyes, a sort of broad stone nose hung over the parapet in the shape of an angel with its wings spread out. There was no mouth visible, as if the clown Jack was still hiding under the roof ledge, afraid to come out. One day, perhaps, tired of feeling himself an asymmetrical and inappropriate addition to an otherwise square and serious structure, this Jack might sink in shame so far down into the neck of the building that he would be gone into his box forever. I should not blame him – battered as he was by wind and rain and the ridicule of people below – but where would I be if he disappeared?

Such a strange building – who could have designed it? To what purpose? Square, half rough brick, half smooth stone, single bulging turret, styles mixed up like a tipsy cake. Perhaps the architect himself had been a mad chef. To enter, one mounted five steps and walked under a horseshoe-shaped archway which leant forward overhead as if pushed out by the interior air. It was a building which seemed to eat and disgorge people; we did not walk simply in and out. But it was a gentle, toothless Jonah, who did not chew but snoozed with his great mouth open onto the street while the eyes of my turret kept a careful watch. The inside lobby, with its vaulted roof, was painted the color of shiny cream, with panels of bittersweet brown. It reminded me of the chocolate glazed sponge called *Rehrücken*, which means saddle of venison. I had somehow a memory of this fanciful cake, long, dark and fluted.

This hallway felt safe to me: children played there on rainy days or hot days, young people held onto one another under the stairwells, old ladies knitted soft garments, sitting in their folding chairs on the chocolate and cream tiled floor.

But after the darkness and closed space of the hallway my apartment was to me the perfect expression of light and freedom. It was like a white ceramic bowl filled with sky and sunshine. In the turret room itself there was little furniture, only a simple white dining table and two chairs. I had painted the parquet floor white. White shades could be drawn to cover the windows at night. I had a fine view. The skyscrapers of Manhattan winked and twinkled at me like giant slabs of *Sachertorte* decorated with magic sprinkles. During the day they wore a more modest white icing, like *Nusschnitten*, and the sun glinted off their smooth angular shoulders. In the foreground I could see the Port Authority Pier with its containers and crates of orange and blue, like children's blocks, and what seemed like toy trucks and cranes beetling around. Between the two boroughs ran the East River, which I could just see with its tugboats and rusty ships going up and down. The tugboats frequently had to rescue the big ships. And I could see the Brooklyn Bridge squatting rudely over the river, with overhead wires blurred into a bridal veil.

My eye was first struck in the morning by the tree. I was able to look down on its branches and observe how they leaned in this direction or that, like the partings of a person's hair. It was fine to be so high up, to greet the tree and to see so much of the world. I was reminded of other cities in which I might have lived. Yes, there was something about the river particularly. This was a working river, always full of the motion of feeding such a great city, the piers sticking out like hungry tongues. The other river, I was somehow sure, had been more peaceful and had been sated with small meals. I seemed to recall an image also of bridges, but they were light and they flew gracefully over the river. But alas, I could remember no more. I was like a fluted *Gugelhupf*, going round and round, with a hole in my center: this was my empty core, my lack of memory. Nevertheless, I was beginning to feel a bubbling inside myself, like a yeast and sugar mixture. This was hope. I would be patient and wait. Perhaps something, or someone, would soon come to me.

3

Ten years ago she did not have a dog, I remembered that. This dog spent a great deal of his time looking out the window, his muzzle wedged between the protective bars. I observed the animal with his long shiny teeth, his tongue which dripped saliva onto the pavement, his fur which was black and shiny and tipped with a dusting of cocoa. Except for one of his ears which had lost its power of erection, he looked a perfect specimen. From the size of his paws, he was certain to be still a puppy, but already he filled the window frame. It was a cosy fit when he and his mistress Gerda looked out together; this was the time, it seemed to me, he fulfilled his purpose in life. On one occasion I observed him nearly attack a man who made a gesture to pass an envelope through the window. He was an excellent protector. But with me he was very peaceful, his breathing became easier, and little by little he seemed to smile; that is to say, his features formed themselves into the muscular imitation of a smile—the raised eyebrows, the forehead wrinkled into thick honey and velvet folds, the mouth pulled back and lifted at the corners, showing the black saw-edged rubbery inner lip. Thus could he cock his head to one side, asking silent questions or sharing unspoken knowledge. In my capacious apron pocket I would find him a bialy and offer it to him, and he would take it with some urgency but great gentleness. After concluding our encounter I would lift my hat to him and walk on my way. Occasionally a whimper would escape from him but most often he allowed me to leave him with no recriminations.

I recognized the daughter one day at the supermarket, the crêpe-thin girl grown into a crêpe-thin woman. She was standing at the pet foods section, choosing nourishment for the dog. But did she not eat herself? Was not her mother—Gerda—well-fed, indeed over-fed? As she reached up for a particular brand of dog food, she reminded me of a single vanilla pod waving around in a glass jar. I wheeled my cart close to hers and said, "You are choosing for your dog? He is very handsome." I do not remember exactly what I said, but it sounded in my own ears obvious and impertinent. Had she been the kind of young woman with eyes painted like chocolate doughnuts—the kind who crack gum with the ferocity of distant mortar fire—she would have tossed a head set and lacquered in the high round shape of a Jubilee doughnut, and shouted at me in a coarse voice to mind my own business. She might have called me a rude name. People said such young people were fresh, but it was hard for me to understand how anything fresh could be in bad taste, except perhaps the bialy. Yes, those girls could be fresh as bialys, that would be an appropriate description.

But this one was otherwise. Just to look into her eyes was to see two cream puffs coated in still-wet dark chocolate. If I could take the time to search around in them I might find the part of me I had lost. This was my impression. But who should be talking about losing things? I noticed when she looked for something on the shelf she craned her head forward on its thin stalk and peered too closely; perhaps she needed spectacles. And that reminded me of mine – those heavy horn-rimmed frames, caked in their hinges and crevices with dough and dumb memories. I should have liked something light and silvery and hardly any weight at all on the nose. Perhaps they would be an aid to remembering.

I explained how I had been away but that I still remembered her from when she was a child. She nodded, avoiding my eyes and with a hand guarding her mouth. The dog was called Vitez, she said. Vitez, Vitez? "It's Hungarian. It means Hero," she addressed her cart. Such a name, it pricked me like a whisk of sharp birch twigs. My head began to buzz out of tune with the fluorescent lights of the supermarket. I had to close my eyes and lean against the castles of dog and cat food. A castle, yes, there had been a castle of lemon-and-cinnamon colored stone and they had put prisoners into it. Who? I opened my eyes and beheld toilet paper rolls, labelled Soft, Super Soft, Fluffy Soft, Gentle Soft, Facial Soft, Snow Soft. Soft as the snow in Budapest, I thought, covering so many dead bodies. I shook myself back to the present (it was clearer at any rate than the past) and noticed my thin friend had disappeared. As I started to go around a corner with my wagon, a woman with a mountain of groceries with a tiny child perched on top like a cherry crashed into me. I apologized and backed off, hurrying away to find Rella, for that was her name. There was something I wanted to ask her. I passed an army of red white and blue soldiers – soap powders – and other items which for some reason reminded me of Swedish flags. I hurried on, and found her once again at the pet accessories section. I stared. There were wet and dry shampoos, rubber mice, rubber bones, flea collars, flea sprays, flea combs, bells, ribbons, rubber pork chops, jewelled collars, coats, brushes, vitamins and aspirins. Before my nerve should be lost I asked her if she would like to come up to my apartment for tea one day. She looked me straight in the face, her eyes wide open, and smiled. Her teeth were like whole cloves.

4

The Bridge Arms was not blessed with an elevator. Therefore, in order to make her visit, Rella must climb four flights of stairs up the right wing of the building. Then she must pass through a low doorway and climb another stairway, narrow and circular, up to my turret. I hoped she would not lose her way, become dizzy, or bump her head. She knocked and I went quickly to receive her, knowing she must be quite out of breath. She was not very strong. She inserted herself into a dining room armchair, stiff as a meringue. I was afraid she would crumble before my eyes, so I busied myself with making the tea. She lit a cigarette and began to look around her. She put her hand above her eyes and made slits of them. I thought it must be like waking up in a snowstorm for her to enter my room. Perhaps she needed dark glasses to shield her from the glare of so much whiteness. But she smiled gently and said she liked the room; she had never seen anything like it before. She ran her hands appreciatively over the white tablecloth. She was afraid of getting it dirty; what if she should spill her tea, or some ash from her cigarette should fall on it? I assured her it could easily be laundered, so she was not to worry. But she was not yet entirely comfortable at my table. Perhaps for her a table was an ordinary object, a thing which wears a plastic cloth with sticky patches and rocks when you lean your elbows upon it; a careless, unkempt thing? Yes, I think to her this table – this whole room – were too beautiful. Something was giving her pain. To me, on the contrary, this stark purity was suddenly not enough, and I was unnerved by its simplicity.

Visions of something more elaborate danced in my head. I imagined an enormous high-ceilinged room in which the whole of one wall was covered by a molded gilt mirror reflecting the other walls of Italian marble and a sprinkling of people, blurred but well-dressed, in top hats and silk scarves, which they removed as they sat down at their magnificently laid tables. Candelabras sent off triple shooting stars of light. The tables too were of marble but were discreetly covered by white damask cloths. They were set with fluted porcelain, ornate silver, heavy napkins folded and embroidered with the initials HM. In the center of each table stood a silver cake stand whose base was wrought in the figure of a naked goddess. Each goddess held a god-like creation – cakes like dark satin, or the wigs of eighteenth-century gentlemen, decorated with rosebuds and seashells and crystallized violets. I shook my head; where might I have seen such a vision? Perhaps in a magazine. Whose were the initials HM?

But my reverie was interrupted by the ringing of the oven timer. I opened my eyes to the present, feeling quite confused; then I remembered. It was time to reveal my secret, and so from the oven I took the strudel, golden light and flaky, and from the refrigerator I removed the whipped cream puffs. More than ever these smooth round objects with their warm chocolate coats and interiors of thick snow reminded me of her eyes. As I put these delights down in front of her – arranged in happy harmony on a white porcelain plate – she opened those *Indianerkrapfen* eyes and blinked and blinked until they began to melt and a colorless substance like extract of almond fell heavily down her face. "Are these for me?" she asked, pointing at herself, and when I nodded the tears fell faster. What was my crime? Did I serve her snakes, worms, horrible things? I looked with new eyes at the rich confections and then at the sapling I had expected to devour them – and only then did the truth dawn. I was mortified. This was no snake in the habit of swallowing whole pigs. I scolded myself for my insensitivity and stupidity. I removed the offending objects to my side of the table. (Could she even look upon them without feeling sick?) No, it was quite wrong, I realised; she would have to be exposed slowly to the joys of the coffee table. She asked, "But where did you learn to bake such things, they look so professional?" Where indeed. "I do not know," I said, and it was quite true. "It comes to me the way it comes to some people to sit down at a piano and play beautiful music by ear." But was this true? Her question disturbed me. Where did I learn? Who taught me my sweet music?

We changed the subject. Rella spoke of the dog Vitez and

his inauspicious beginnings in life. During his first week he chewed on a loose plug and received many volts of electricity through the mouth. "How he howled," she said; and his teeth chattered, his eyes spun around and he lost control of his bowels. Gerda was quite furious with him. Rella wrapped him in an old blanket and carried him to a veterinarian who "fixed him up" but for one ear which, she said, as if concluding a fairy story, ever since then had refused to stand up. So the flopping ear was the mark of his unfortunate experience; perhaps also the quizzical expression which, I imagined, contained within it the memory of pain but not an exact understanding of what had produced it, or why. The expression said, "What happened to me? Something, but what? If only I could remember!" And that, I concluded – also like the ending of a fairy story – was what Vitez the dog and I had in common.

For a long time after the accident he was not himself. He hid under the couch and whimpered when the garbage men threw lids around, jumped at the sound of a car horn, and shook at the roar and vibration of children roller skating on the sidewalk outside. Gerda diagnosed his case as a nervous breakdown and prescribed chicken feet and chocolate doughnuts; she allowed him to sleep with her. A lucky dog, I thought.

Gradually he recovered and the question of his going out was eventually posed by Rella. "Out, where out?" cried Gerda, outraged, looking to left and right for the source of this mutinous inspiration. "Dogs are not like people," Rella told her. "They need their freedom." "Freedom? What is freedom?" Gerda bellowed back. "It is all in the mind. He lives here with me like a prince, what more could he want?" Rella replied, "He needs to smell things, other dogs, and get some exercise." There was a silence and then Gerda said, "All right, you want to take him out, go ahead, take him out, but do not blame me if anything happens." What would happen? Rella immediately began to wonder, and then imagined the worst: Vitez pulling away from her and getting hit by a car, Vitez stolen by dog-nappers, Vitez fighting with another dog, attacking – or being attacked – by a small child, Vitez picking up fleas, worms, distemper. She regretted ever making the suggestion. But Gerda stood with her hands on her hips, watching as Rella fumbled with the collar and leash. Vitez's eyes showed he was aware of Gerda's disapproval directly behind him and so did his tail, which would not make a demonstration of outright excitement; he was allowing himself to be taken out, nothing more. But Gerda made things easy for them both. She held open the door and said, "Go," with the authority of an SS *Kommandant*. And so they had no choice but to go out together into the dangerous world.

They stood on the outside step, both of them blinking and panting after their ordeal with Gerda, unsure of what next to do. Rella stepped down first, urging Vitez with a tug of his leash to follow. He went, hesitating, to the gutter and there lifted his leg. He sniffed. His nose began to lead him, here and there, along the curb and around trees. He lifted his leg quite naturally wherever he could manage to insert himself. He forgot Gerda and they headed for the river, and eventually for the open bridle path of Ocean Parkway.

Vitez ran and Rella flew behind him, holding on with all the power of her thin arms. He skidded and kicked up dust and often enough wrapped his leash around trees, people, benches. But it did not matter; nothing mattered as they grew more confident and forgetful in their explorations. Which was when the horses, with no warning it seemed to Rella, came up behind them and frightened Vitez so that he escaped with his leash from her grasp. She stared at the three lanes of traffic going in each direction and imagined him crushed and swept along, to Manhattan or Coney Island; there would be no remains for Gerda to mourn. So she had been correct in her warning. But when the last of the horses passed by, flinging dirt and excrement with their hooves, Rella noticed the shaking paws of Vitez showing from under a bench not a few yards away; he was hiding from the horses. She crept up to him and took hold of his leash, moving quietly as a shadow so as not to frighten him again. Then she put her arm through the loop of his leash, to make sure she would not lose him again, and coaxed him out from his hiding place. Eventually, by mutual consent, they turned towards home. Vitez led the way, sniffing his way back over familiar territory, crouching low to the pavement like some kind of reptile, pulling harder and harder as the signals of home became stronger. Now his only thought was a return to safety and Gerda; his outing had ended in terror. Rella feared any moment her arm would come out, like a cork from its bottle, or she would be forced to fly. A woman walking a white poodle remarked to her, "These dogs'll pull ya guts out if ya give 'em a chance." Rella imagined Vitez trailing her guts behind him like an unravelling ball of wool; I imagined candy, in the softball stage, making threads.

Gerda was triumphant at her window. She went to the door to allow Vitez back in. In his great need to return to her he practically clawed the door down. He had had his lesson. She ignored him for a time, but then she comforted him with a caress of his floppy ear and soon his breathing returned to normal. She allowed him to lick her feet. Vitez would not go out again; clearly it had been a great mistake. He must be content with his window view on the outside world, a hint of the lady dogs inviting him to love and the gentlemen dogs inviting him to do battle. It seemed to me a recipe for great sadness and disappointment, but he bore it bravely, Rella said. For a time he followed her to the door and she had to push his nose back inside as she slipped herself out. Then, for a time, he stood by his leash and licked it. Was this to encourage it (Perhaps it was the leash all along rather than Rella with the power to take him out?), or was it to lick away the sadness the leash must also be feeling? Rella did not know. His solution to the problem, eventually, was to turn his back on these potential enemies, the leash and the door; they might at any time betray him again. He would stay close to Gerda, the only one he could trust.

He was at peace with himself and the world. He carried out his duties as Royal Lion to Gerda with such a vengeance it began to look like an uncomplicated act of devotion. It was also a matter of pride, it seemed to Rella, that he would no more dream of going out now than he would of chewing on one of those loose plugs. I myself was less sure, thinking of him looking out of that window and what would happen if those bars should ever fly away. But he was quite sure; he followed Gerda everywhere. What was the point of going out now? He could not remember. I thought to myself, this is how we are alike. This is why we can have long conversations without speaking. This is why words are unnecessary between us. Rella said, "He thinks he's a human being, he goes to the toilet, he tries to talk. He doesn't remember who he is." Just so. I ate another cream puff and began to think about this strange woman, Gerda, who always wins. I began to imagine I had seen her somewhere before. But where? I invited Rella to come again for tea.

Gerda

1

They have released him. Welcome home Adolf, Jack-be-Nimble, whatever your name is. So you are cured, free to walk the streets in a coat down to your ankles, a hat to your nose; *le tout ensemble* the color of boiled liver. Never mind, what does it matter how you look? Congratulations, my friend, you made it. But – tell me – what became of the old Jack? Did you leave him behind? He made me laugh. Every day a new personality would jump out of the front door – artist, baker, sailor boy, Napoleon. What next? It was better than the television. Of course it was the Hitler routine got you into hot water, a little too much of a good thing, Jack, but that's the risk one takes when the imagination is allowed to run free. Poor Nimble Jack, so they have turned you into a normal man – how dull. This is what ECT does? Scrambles brains, fries memories to a crisp? They deserve a medal. Then you get your walking papers: bye bye, Jack, go join the rest of the crazies loose in the city; you'll fit in perfectly. You look like you're still playing Trick or Treat in your grandfather's overcoat, but why should they care? They give you a few pennies and a few words of wisdom. Such generosity. Now behave yourself, they say, or you'll be right back in the old padded cell before you can say Jack-be-Nimble. And they slap you on the back and shove you out the door. Watch your step, Jack.

Where to now, my dear? You're quite lost, don't even know what city you're in – Vienna, Budapest, Moscow? Ah, it comes to you, you're in New York City, land of the brave and the free. A memory comes to you, of a face. You point yourself uptown, your legs seem to know where they want to go. Or is it in the brain, some small fold where the shocks didn't reach, that a certain memory was kept safe? Of a face somewhere near the Statue of Liberty. That's right, Jack, keep going, it won't be long now. Yes, she looked out of her window. She was so beautiful – you remember – you couldn't go too close, even to say hello could be dangerous. But you must see her again, perhaps live near her again; why not? Just the sight of her could heal your poor cooked spirit. Your little legs churn faster and faster, making butter. You're almost there, Jack. You think she might not be there – she could be anywhere by now – but there she is, still looking out of the window, smoking a cigarette. Bad for her health, you wish she wouldn't, but how dare you say such a thing to her face? You wouldn't want to make her angry, would you? She has acquired a German Shepherd dog for her protection and they make a handsome couple, framed by the window. Pretty as a picture. You notice she's a bit fuller in the face than you remembered, but just as beautiful, perhaps even more beautiful. Yes, Jack, you have come to the right place. By some miracle your old apartment up in the turret is waiting vacant for you. Don't thank me, Jack, these things can be arranged. No one else would live up there under the sky – so exposed, such hard work getting there. So you see, it's right what you have done on your first day out, come to me. They all do, sooner or later. You'll need time to find your feet, as they say. Then we'll see if you can find mine.

He's dressed in white shoes, white trousers, white apron; the stockings and underwear, I would guess, are also white. On top of the little mushroom body is sitting a smaller mushroom head in its baker's hat. So sanity after all does not last long: today a baker, tomorrow Teddy Roosevelt. He is carrying in his arms two grocery bags and a white dish rack, which he holds in place on top of the bags with his chins. Soon, I believe, he will begin to skip and sing a little song – how does it go? Pattycake, pattycake, baker's man, bake me a cake as fast as you can. But no, I smile at him and he is so flustered the dish rack falls to the ground and bounces even closer to my window. Dangerously close. What will the overloaded double-decker mushroom do now? He is trying to bend down with the two bags in his arms and hook the dish rack with his little finger. He's getting redder and juicier in the face all the time. Vitez is barking at him. His hat falls off. "Just a minute, Mr Baum, I'll send my daughter out to help you." He huffs and puffs into his grocery bag but doesn't reply. Rella reaches him in time to rescue a dozen eggs from tumbling out as he is bending to retrieve his silly hat. "Here," she says, pinching the material between two fingers and lowering the hat onto his head. She crowns her Knight. "Please," he says, shooting his head forward to receive it. I hear her tell him she'll help him upstairs with his bundles. He says please, not to go to any trouble. She insists it's no trouble at all. Round and round they go, bowing and scraping and dancing their way up the front stoop. Once again his hat tumbles down behind him and Rella chases after it. She'll be chasing men's hats for the rest of her life. Not me, Jack. When your hat lands at my feet, I'll say: "Welcome home, Mr Baum." The honor will be yours.

"Well?"
"Well what?"
"So you saved the hat and dish rack of a gentleman in distress. Such a hero – heroine, excuse me. You see, it runs in the family."
"It wasn't heroic. I only helped Mr Baum up to his apartment, it was no big deal."
"Mr Baum, Mr Baum. Jack-be-Nimble, you mean."
"I don't think you should call him that."
"Why not? Look at him, already he's impersonating a baker. Soon he'll be skipping along the street, just like old times, in his sailor suit with his hairy legs sticking out, singing 'Tchack be Nimble, Tchack be Kvick,' in that accent of his. It won't be long before the men in white coats take him away with a dish rack sitting on his head. A flattering *chapeau*, no?" Obviously not. She crosses her arms over her chest, bunches her lips together into a wrinkled *pupik*, and shakes her head.
"You don't understand. He isn't impersonating anyone. He *is* a baker. He got a job making bagels and bialys in that

new store on Fulton Street. That's his new uniform, it isn't a get-up, they gave it to him."

"Oh? This is interesting. But how did he get such a job – did he ever bake before in his life?"

"I don't know, I guess so. He said he worked in the kitchen at the hospital."

"What about before that, did he tell you about that?"

"I only walked him up to his apartment, I didn't get his life history. Besides, I don't think he remembers much of anything."

"Better luck next time, maybe he'll invite you in. Don't give up hope. But I would advise you to try fixing yourself up or he might not see you." This line of conversation annoys her. She raises her eyes to the chandelier, my pre-Raphaelite lamb chop. Don't talk about the birds and the bees, we cover our ears. What else should I talk about? Food? The bagel, for example? Another glorified hole.

Protection, always protection. Don't hurt his feelings, don't make fun of him. Oh she is soft, soft as a prune. I can smell them stewing. The *Obersturmbannführer* and his men at the Majestic would order them for their breakfasts. My father would blow his nose into the stewpot and then ladle out monstrous portions topped by pints of thick cream. Then on his way out of the kitchen he would whistle and curse through his teeth that they should only be stricken with the terrible trots. And then he would bow to their faces. I remember how the juice ran down their chins onto the white tablecloth. Except for Eichmann, of course, that fastidious little picked bone. It was believed by everyone at the Majestic that he never shat, which explained why he was that bilious green color. A miracle, after all those prunes.

2

They collide in Gristede's: the baskets of these two maladroits lock together in a passionate embrace in front of the paper products. The collision causes a tremor which in turn causes a whole shelf of toilet paper rolls to come down on their heads like a volley of Jewish curses. They manage to free their baskets. They knock heads bending to pick up the liberated rolls. He is sorry. "So sorry, please forgive, how clumsy of me," he mumbles. She covers her mouth with a hand like a slice of fillet of sole. Then he smooths his white coat over his stomach and clears his throat. Bows. "Please, will you do me the honor of joining me for tea later this afternoon?" he says. Her mouth drops open. Was it rehearsed and ready to drop from his tongue or was it a sudden inspiration, brought about by the world falling in on their heads? Who knows what disaster will strike next? Better not waste time, grab the opportunity. Bakers don't grow on trees. She nods her head like a dumb one, then ditches her basket and runs out the store. So much for Vitez's dog food and my chicken livers.

"So you're getting dolled up for the Mad Hatter's tea party?" I say. The dress she has put on makes her look like a spear of dill pickle, good for sucking. She quivers with anger; how can I spy on her like this? Oh, she would like to pretend it means nothing to her to be invited by a man – even a rolled roast of a man old enough to be her father – to tea. She gets such invitations every day of the week. She drops the dress and puts her old dungarees back on; they flap against her legs like flayed skin.

For ten years she has been depressed – ever since the Soviet allegation of Raoul's death. At first her hair fell out in clumps. Then her teeth went black. She acquired the habit of putting her hand over her mouth whenever she spoke, which was not often; and when she smiled, which was still less often. I warned her it drew more rather than less attention to her mouth, but she only shrugged. She lived on Cokes and coffee and the hard skin around her own fingernails. She sat in her rocking chair and rocked until one day she didn't even have the strength to do that, so she just sat. I acted quickly by pouring a quart of milk down her throat. She gagged and spat and the milk made a terrible mess all over my green carpet but some of it trickled down her throat and saved her. Another rescue mission completed; who else would have done my errands?

After graduating she wanted to get a job, but who would hire her? How could such a ghoul become a Girl Friday, a Waitress, a Personal Assistant, even a Library Clerk? For such jobs a woman needs looks; and if not looks at least a set of teeth; and failing that a shining personality. She had none of these. One must be able to smile at people to get anywhere on this earth. People would take one look at her mouth and lose their appetites, their desire to read. But even so, I thought, there must be something she could do to make herself useful, to earn some money. I might not be in a position to support her forever. But what? And then it came to me: she could clean office buildings, preferably at night. It would suit her to work alone, she would be less conscious of her looks. I pictured her going to work in the middle of the night, alone in one of those big buildings in Rockefeller Center, trailing around with a damp mop. Her sneakers would make no noise on the glistening marble hallways. She could imagine the handsome executives who worked there during the day, the beautiful secretaries. It would be a thrill for her to creep about the corridors of power. It would be easy work, nothing to do but empty ashtrays and flush a few toilets. She could take a quick peek in the files, learn a thing or two. But no. I concluded, after all, it would be too dangerous. She could be attacked along the way—in the subway or in a dark alley or by someone locked in the building, waiting to pounce from behind a closet door. You don't need to be attractive these days to invite attack; even old women with dugs down to their knees get raped. She might get trapped in the elevator. No, it was too risky, out of the question.

The next day the superintendent of The Bridge Arms asked if I knew anyone who might become his assistant. Perfect. "How about Rella?" I suggested, and he laughed. He said a skinny malink like her couldn't lift a mop. I said,

"Don't be so sure. You can't judge a book by its cover." By the time I had finished with her she had flesh on her bones and a twinkle in her eye. He believed he was hiring a lady Charles Atlas.

She does a good job. Skinny as she is, she heaves garbage cans around, hauls heavy buckets of water up and down stairs. How does she do it? She eats the crusts of sandwiches I leave over; she pecks like a chicken. No wonder the skin on her legs is scaled and dry. Do you know her knees are fatter than her thighs? Can you picture it? The camps were full of girls like her. But she lives. She sucks on sugar, drinks sixteen cups of coffee a day, with milk–plenty of vitamin D. She lives for her job, for me; what else is there?

She works in the middle of the night, when everyone else is asleep. A peaceful time. It's quite safe, even down in the cellar. I'm right here to protect her should anything go wrong. On her first night she asked if she could take Vitez with her for protection, but I refused on his behalf. Imagine. Do I need to remind her of that disastrous occasion when he was separated from me?

I tell her there is no such thing as a perfect job; you take the bad with the good; I should know. Besides, what is there to be afraid of? A few cockroaches, an insignificant mouse, a family of starving alley cats? She should have lived through the war in Europe, then she would have the right to be afraid. Rats, nothing. She talks about the boiler as if it were Adolf Hitler himself breathing down upon her, reaching out to cuddle her in his white hot pipe arms. He would get more satisfaction from a water bug.

Alone in the hallway in the middle of the night, she is busy slooshing her mop around, covering over the Coke and urine smells with ammonia. She stops for a moment and leans on her mop like Step'n'Fetchit. Suddenly the walls come to life. They are painted tan with a dark brown design in the panels, like some of these newfangled ice creams she brings me–Jamoca Almond Fudge, Chocolate Ring-a-Ding, Marble Swirl, Cocoa Cake. Only she imagines fictions, melodrama. She sees people running away from some unspoken danger; they are screaming in terror. Perhaps she watches too much science fiction on the television. What can they be running from, these imaginary victims, here in this ordinary American apartment house lobby? She flies into me with her mop to tell me she hears screams. No, I tell her, you're only scaring yourself; it's nothing, only brown paint in a suggestive design like ink blots. I myself would see other things in it. I push her out again to face the bogeys. She shakes her mop as if it were her own head. The screams stop, the walls change back to innocent ice cream and the building is coated in the silence of a chocolate dip. I go back to my beauty sleep. All safe in this house.

3

At first the old people complained it wasn't right for a frail young woman to do such a dirty heavy job, but now they say the building never looked so clean. They're used to seeing her around in her Big Mac overalls with her hair tucked up under a baseball cap. Young woman, they call her, but who would know to look at her? Her breasts are like two pink Hershey's kisses glued to a Monopoly board. The other evidence is more damning: no period, no crotch hair. Yet–Who knows?–maybe Nimble Jack will take pity on her. Touch her with his magic rolling pin and wake her up. Maybe he has a taste for sucking pink chocolates.

"So?"

"So what?"

"So anything. What's he like, your nimble friend, what kind of apartment does he run?"

"Very unusual," she says. "One room is like a storeroom, very dark and stuffed with all kinds of garbage–only very clean garbage. He keeps old teabags, toilet paper tubes, orange peels, all stacked up neatly on shelves around the walls. In the middle is his bed. But the kitchen and dining room are like a whole other world. That's the turret room. He's painted everything white, even the floor. White curtains, white shades, white tablecloth, white dishes. I think it's really beautiful. You should see it."

"I don't need to see it. What you tell me is enough, it sounds like a hospital. What did you have for tea?"

"He baked an apple strudel and chocolate cream puffs. All by himself. Only I couldn't eat anything. That upset him. Here, he sent a cream puff for you."

"So he is fond of chocolate. How nice. What else did you talk about?" I slipped the cream puff into the refrigerator for later.

"I don't remember, nothing in particular. I told him about Vitez and he told me a little about his stay in the hospital. He can't remember anything that happened to him before that. He doesn't even know where he learned to bake so well."

"It's called amnesia."

"I know," she says. Smartass.

I put Jack-be-Nimble's present on a plate and examine it from all sides. Then I pick it up and gaze into the smooth chocolate dome with its fat wrinkled neck and sink my teeth into it. There's a crunching noise: I think of Schmidthuber. Underneath the chocolate skull is a membrane of jam, then cupcake, then cream. I'm up to my false eyelashes in it. Jack-be-Nimble, Jack-be-Quick – ah, Jack, you are no mere bagel man. You may bake for me anytime. Fill me with cream. Delicious.

Jack

1

The young woman Rella came to me again. This time I made an offering of *Vanillekipfels* – vanilla-flavored crescents made with unsalted butter and roasted ground almonds. She should not be overcome by too much richness or elaboration, but even these simple flowers were too much for her; she was quite immune to their charms. "I'm just not hungry," she said; perhaps she did not understand the meaning of the word? Yet I would be patient. One day, I dreamed, perhaps she will be busy mopping the halls, with the smell of filthy water and ammonia in her nose. Suddenly the aroma from my kitchen drifts down to her like a long-lost memory. She stops what she is doing and allows her nostrils to fill up, like a dog who has not been out of the house for many years. She cannot continue her work, it is no use, she must have a sniff and a nibble. She creeps up to my door and taps. I am already waiting with a tray of freshly baked *Haselnuss-Schnitten*. Close your eyes, I say, introducing one to her lips.

We sat at my white table in my white turret room. She took from her pocket a rather worn photograph and passed it across to me – this was no simple confection she showed, but a heavily iced and decorated concoction. The face was hard and cold, though perhaps capable of melting, like a perfectly shaped ice cream cone. It was a posed picture; the eyes of the sitter looked to the stars. On her head sat a hat like a Charlotte mold – tall with fluted walls and a hole in the middle, out of which grew a feather. I handed it back.

"Do you know who that is?" she asked.

"No," I said, munching thoughtfully.

"Gerda, when she was young. Isn't she beautiful?"

"Yes," I said, still preoccupied with my cookie. They were quite tasty, as I remember.

"She was born in Hungary, in a city called Budapest. That's where she lived until she came to this country. Have you ever been to Budapest?"

I hoped she would keep talking. I listened, nibbled softly on another cookie, pushed the others absent-mindedly around on their white platter until an engaging flower pattern came into being. I closed my eyes and the corners of my mouth turned upwards like one of my own *kipfels*. This was quite pleasurable. An early spring bud uncurled itself in my memory. I saw before me a porcelain espresso coffee machine. Yes, I could see it quite clearly, the deep milky white surface with its strawberries, roses, butterflies, little bees deep down in the rich soft glaze. It was a porcelain garden. I ran my hand over it and felt its smoothness. Yes. But when I opened my eyes I saw it was Rella's hand I was stroking. I was so ashamed I did not know what to do. "Please forgive me," I said, and then, "Yes, I believe I have been to Budapest." But who was this speaking? I did not recognize my own voice. I got up and took another batch of *Vanillekipfels* from the oven and put them, one by one, onto a wire rack to cool.

"Gerda lived at the Hotel Majestic. Adolf Eichmann stayed there too," she said.

"I'm sorry," I replied. "I remember nothing."

"Don't worry, Gerda remembers everything. She can remember for both of you."

I closed my eyes again. I saw something – a scene from a painting in a museum, though it eluded me with its surface of cracks and misleading highlights. I felt I must look very deeply into it to understand, just as one must taste well beneath the icing of a cake to reach its true essence. Then it came to me. I said out loud, "I see a dinner party taking place at the Majestic. It is in a grand room with a high ceiling so that the people appear by comparison minute. It is lit by candlelight, but I begin to discern a few splashes of bright color – a red dress, a patch of red sky, a curious object on the table, perhaps a wedding cake. A man is rising from his chair, holding up his wine glass to propose a toast, perhaps to the happy couple, I do not know ..."

Rella rose from her chair and leaned across the table. I saw her eyes were very like those of the man in my imaginary painting, the one evidently proposing the toast or about to make a speech.

"Don't stop," she urged. "What is he saying?"

But it was no use, the words of the man had receded. I told her the painting was now quite silent, the figures were frozen in their actions, especially the thin man in military uniform wearing silver spectacles behind which were eyes red as the devil's.

"Eichmann," she said, like a sneeze. "But the woman – do you know who the woman is, in the red dress?" I said no, I couldn't see her because her back was towards me.

"But the man proposing the toast – do you know who that is?" she demanded of me rather urgently. Why was she doing this to me, and what was I to say? I opened my mouth and – like the pie with four-and-twenty blackbirds – I began to sing. Who was this speaking?

"Oh, that was the man called Wallenberg, the Swede; everyone knew about the Swede. He rescued a hundred thousand Jews. He held up his glass and said, 'Let us drink to the end of Nazism,' and the woman in the red dress clinked glasses with him and said, 'Hear, hear.'" And then my mouth closed down hard and I bit my chirruping tongue.

"Wait, keep trying," Rella coaxed, massaging my arm, but a black curtain had dropped down over the scene. I was exhausted from so much looking into the past.

"I am sorry," I said, dropping back into my chair like biscuit dough from a spoon. "I remember nothing. Nothing."

I closed my eyes once more and saw before me a four-tiered silver cake stand, going round and round under sparkling chandeliers like a carousel, filled with the most heavenly confections; the names came to me like painted smiling horses: *Taccherln, Makronen-Schnitten, Ischler Tortschen, Aprikosenblattergebäck, Faschingskrapfen, Gugelhupf.* "What did you say?" I asked, as dumb as the *kipfel* I cradled in the palm of my hand and held out to Rella. It seemed at that moment a thing of substance but, like my memory, it too could be nibbled away. Perhaps she was weary of refusing,

I do not know; but she took a small bite, no more than a crumb, and I was pleased to see the crack of a smile. "So," I said. "Was that so terrible?"

She chewed and swallowed enough for someone who has eaten a dozen such cookies, and then she said, very quietly, "I know you won't believe me, but the man in your memory, Raoul Wallenberg, was my father."

"Father? Was?" I replied stupidly. She bowed her head like a heavy, chocolate-covered cherry on its stem.

"Yes, he died of a heart attack in a Soviet prison in 1947. When I was two years old," she said, and the liquid from her eyes spilled down her cheeks.

"I am so sorry," I said. I would have liked to warm her hand in mine, but I dared not. I reached for the last *Vanillekipfel* instead.

2

How the onion flakes escaped I do not know. They flew, round and about, not onto the bialys – where I had aimed and where they belonged – but into my trouser cuffs and apron pockets and onto my shoulders; a few flakes landed on my nose like snow. My hands had always behaved themselves, kneading and folding, sprinkling the flakes and seeds precisely where they belonged. Why could I not control them now? Because of this strange idea of Rella's: Raoul Wallenberg her father? Could this be? Naturally, it was difficult to turn the whole of my attention to the bialys, especially when I could not remember who this Wallenberg was or how I came to say the things I had said about him. I seemed to know about him; but how? I brushed at my nose and shoulders and then when I looked down at my kneading board I saw not so many small lumps of dough but faces – round and pale with little bits of onions for eyes, or even two poppy seeds. This first batch of the day were oddly shaped and featured because the seeds and flakes had scattered so wide of their mark. Poor orphans. I felt the jelly bun eyes of my boss observing me, so I decided to start once again. I picked off the stray features and knocked together the two dozen dough heads, squashing noses and cheeks with the palm of my hand. The renewed lump of dough was again smooth and featureless. I threw it up into the air and let it fall with a smack, and then I flattened it again and brought its edges up and around and over again, working air into the dough until it shone like a giant buttercup. Buttercups – where had I seen them? I imagined myself walking in a wood, tripping with my clumsy feet over a tree root and falling down with my nose in a clump of buttercups growing in a patch of dark moist earth like a black forest cake decorated with yellow candles. I shivered, feeling the wet chocolate earth but reminding myself of the warmth of the bakeshop. I formed a batch of ordinary bialys and slid them into the oven and turned my back on them.

One had escaped. It looked up at me. Whose was this bialy face with the sad poppy eyes? I told myself I must stop playing pat-a-cake – baking is a serious business – but the face seemed to speak to me, to say, "This is no game, you *must* remember, it is of vital importance." Oh dear. My stomach turned over like an upside-down peach cake; would it be something dreadful? Oh, but I must be brave, I told myself. Yes, I *must* remember. I squeezed my eyelids together, feeling the heat rise up to my scalp. This is how it must feel to be baked in an oven of 400 degrees, I thought. Droplets of sweat, like pickle brine, formed on my forehead, broke, coursed down my face and eventually trickled into the corners of my mouth. It was then I tasted the truth: it was in the year 1955, just before my release. We were together, by some mistake, in a prison cell in the Corpus II wing of Vladimir Prison. He begged me to make contact with the Swedish diplomatic mission, and tell them about him. He had been imprisoned since 1945 (as had I). "If you forget my name," he said, "just say a Swede from Budapest and they will know who you mean." The next morning they interrogated me and made me swear I would not talk to any other prisoners about Wallenberg, or else they would put me away for life. But why was I there? "There are no reasons," he had said. "We are political prisoners."

Round and round I went, asking questions: what were these political crimes of ours? What were we doing together in a Russian prison – a Swede and a German? Was he really Rella's father? How could this be? I felt quite faint with dizziness. I began to think more on dates. How could he have died in 1947 if I was with him in 1955? No, it did not make sense; it was impossible, quite absurd. One of us must be wrong. I wiped my forehead with the hem of my apron. Perhaps I imagined the whole thing. Then I heard a clanging noise and the smell of burning which turned out to be my poor neglected bialys gone too far and one of my colleagues throwing open the oven doors to release them. They were burnt black, reminding me of the charred remains of other things perhaps best not remembered, and my hand shook as I removed them from their incinerator and slid them into the garbage pail under my work board, where they sizzled and hissed at me, and clung together before expiring. Suggestions of a past life were beginning to come back to me. Now I was not sure I did not want to give back the gift of memory, but there are no returns, I knew, on such gifts. I apologized to my boss – a man with numbers tattooed on his forearm – who was most sympathetic. "Go, take a walk, you need the rest of the day off. Go, you will feel better tomorrow. It could happen to anyone."

3

I took my first steps in little white shoes. I fell, picked myself up, and fell down again. I learned to toddle. I was fed rich memories with a silver spoon which caused me to spit up a cheesy cake on my white bib. I gurgled for joy and clapped my chubby hands. I stuck my fingers in my mouth and wailed. I played with the mucus where my mustache might have been. I slept with my knees curled to my chin and my fist in my mouth. I fell asleep clutching my piece of white blanket with its satin edge. And when I woke up I looked over the side of the bed and saw a pair of white shoes, American size twelve, on the floor beside me. I sat up and put my feet into them; then I stood but I did not fall over. I shuffled across the floor to the mirror and saw myself, as bowl-bellied as a teapot. When I tipped over, what would spill out? Memories, and more memories.

The miracle had happened, the clotted nozzle of a pastry bag – my memory – had opened up. Oh, I thought, let me squeeze the bag and let the waves of piped whipped cream smother me in billowing sweetness.

And so there I sat surrounded by my new-old memories, my *souvenirs de jeunesse*; my kitchen walls were papered with them, my empty cans and orange skins were full to their brims. On each square of toilet paper was etched a picture. Even the skin on my arms and chest bore tattoos. My kitchen cupboard was well stocked with little round boxes, big square ones, lumpy bags – enough memorystuffs to last a lifetime. But what kind of cake would they make? I required directions for putting them together and a practised hand to shape them into edible form. As if in answer to my question, in the middle of the night I heard a tap on my door. I went, with some trepidation, to open it and found there – How to say it? – my memory in the form of my old self. I was nervous; how does one greet oneself, a stranger, after so many years? Now let me look at you properly, I said. I stepped back to look at him. He had no waist, like me, and his baker's apron smoothed him into a squat, slope-shouldered loaf, and while I suspected him of harboring razor blades and madness under his apron, he had a kind face. Ugliness and beauty, captivity and release, these were the pattern of his features, like the dark and light lattice crust of a *Linzertorte*. Come in, come in, I welcomed him, shaking him by the hand which hung like a wooden spoon at his side; and then, rejecting false shame, I embraced him. He was so cold! I promised him we would get to know one another again, become as one. Come, sit down, I said, and tell me about myself; and I offered him a cup of tea and a piece of reheated strudel. The tea he accepted most gratefully but not the strudel. Together, he said, we would recreate *me*.

He wore a necklace of cake pans. For what purpose? Was he a tinker, a gypsy? Did he wish to sell me something? I grew suspicious. But he gestured for me to look into one of the pans, which I did, and I pronounced them typical false-bottomed cake pans, perfect for the making of sponge *torten*, but quite empty. Well? He took them from around his neck and dealt them out to me like playing cards, and instructed me to look again; concentrate, he said. I put each pan up on a tall jar so that the outer rings slipped down like so many petticoats – and there by some magic stood ten *torte* sponges containing the ingredients of my life. It was up to me, he said, to stack them in order and put the appropriate fillings in between, then dress them with icing.

He allowed me to sniff, yet not to taste. There was I as a fat Viennese cherub; as an eager apprentice in my father's shop; delivering pastries to the socialist underground in Vienna. After that the layers smelled strongly of concentration camps, prisons, madhouses, although there were alternating layers of escape and release. It was a strange cake with flavors of sweetness, bittersweetness and plain bitterness. I shook my head at the confusing melange, which I took to be an inedible failure.

But my other self said it required the filling in of details to make the mystery cake complete; nuts, fruit, apricot jam, custards and creams would improve it, he said. But what about razor blades, I asked. You remember, he replied. I nodded. Oh yes, they were winking at me so brazenly, how could I deny them? Yes yes, my sharp-eyed children, I said, there is a place for you too in my history cake. There were fillings which smacked of luxury and relative ease, others which stank of bombs and burning flesh; there were rotten walnuts and shells to break your teeth on; raw lemons sharp and stripping to the palate; onions reminiscent of bialys; and vanilla cream, to remind me of the times which were very nearly smooth and unmemorable. Finally there was I, as I am, all my layers assembled, the various fillings in between, covered over with piped whipped cream. He offered me a silver fork with which to taste. Dare I? He very kindly cut me a slice and I looked at it from all sides in the manner of the true artist. What is it called, I asked, and he replied, *Baumkuchen*: a delicate creation of many layers of the thinnest dough showing concentric rings like a real tree trunk. When you eat of it you will know yourself.

My stomach turned over but I took a piece onto my fork. I opened my mouth wide to receive it. Then I rolled the ingredients around on my tongue and felt them going down, and my eyes stung and my lips and tongue bled and my throat ached – and I thought, so this is the taste of Jack's tree. And when I felt I had swallowed enough, I put the memory cake to one side and looked at my guest, my other self, and I said: "You have worked hard, now you must be cold and hungry, let me make you a proper breakfast." By then the dawn had come creeping up behind my turret, soon I would have to go to work. I made for him *Kaiserschmarren* – pancakes of flour, eggs, butter, milk, cream, sugar and raisins, torn with two forks into small pieces, soaked in rum and sprinkled liberally with confectioner's sugar. I served them hot, with coffee. It was my way of saying thank you to the strange gentleman sitting opposite me.

As I left that morning, I felt as if I was walking through a thick slab of *Rigo Jancsi* – a Hungarian chocolate cake so dense and rich and swirled it was named after a nineteenth-century Gypsy violinist who, legend says, broke the hearts of princesses with ease and equanimity. I thought how good it was to come out of the dark tunnel, into the daylight.

4

After work, I took a subway ride to the end of the line, to a place called Sheepshead Bay. A curious name. I strolled up and down like a tourist, with my arms clasped comfortably in the small of my back, sniffing. I passed a rather strong fishy restaurant with the name Lindy's inscribed in arabesques on its red awnings. Red awnings – just like the Majestic's! A sharp wind blew across the bay, making the boats bob like toys in a tub. The water was a pale cloudy green, and choppy, like whipped cream flavored with *crème de menthe*. It reminded me of another picturesque place, in the French Alps, where my parents used to take me before the War. It was called Annecy, I believe – yes – and it had also had such frothy, mint-cream water. Across the lake, however, were mountains like brazil nuts, only huge and threatening to a small boy, and I remember being afraid they would march across the lake and gobble me up. "Don't be such a silly goose," my father had said. Oh yes, I remembered that too. You see, it had all come back. I had become, after all, like other men: a man with a memory.

I walked down 16th Street towards Sheepshead Bay, across a skinny bridge to Manhattan Beach, past the houses of rich people to where Brooklyn ends and the Atlantic Ocean begins. I sat on a bench and watched how the water played with the rocks. Just as they began to dry out another kind wave came up and made them wet again. I thought, these rocks will never dry out, not even at low tide; nor will I, so long as the waves of memory continue to baste me in their sweet syrup. I made my way (with some difficulty) over boulders for a little time and then I dropped down onto Coney Island beach. I knew it to be a dangerous place, but I was nevertheless unafraid. The winos, the yogis standing on their heads, and the seagulls ignored me; they drank and balanced and shrieked, respectively, as if hypnotized or controlled by the movement of the waves. I could not bring myself to feel threatened, so at peace was I with myself. I stepped closer to the ocean and at that moment a gigantic wave came up and barrelled towards me like a blue ceramic rolling pin. Would I be flattened into a gingerbread man, lying on his back in the sand, smiling up to heaven? No. The great wave dissolved into foam and crept to within an inch of my feet, like the lacy edge of a pancake made with lemon juice and powdered sugar. Like a crazy man I informed the waves: "You see, you cannot hurt me now that my memory is complete. I remember. I remember, I remember, I remember!"

I walked with my naked toes gripping the sand up to the boardwalk steps, where I put my socks and shoes back on my feet and climbed the stairs. The boardwalk had recently been restored with honey-colored boards set in parallel V-shaped patterns. It was like walking on wooden sunbeams.

I passed restaurants, tea shops, gambling parlors, souvenir shops, people bundled into fur coats sitting with their faces turned like rising bread up to the sun. I stopped and listened to the language, which was both foreign and yet familiar. So this was the area of Brighton Beach known as Little Odessa. I walked on.

I heard laughter, or was it screaming? When I looked up I saw what resembled an open cattle car rush out of the sky towards me. The people were grasping horizontal metal bars and I could see their tongues and teeth. At the last minute, the front car jack-knifed and kept, by some miracle, to its track laid in a pretzel bend. Someone's spectacles flew off and hovered for a moment in the space left by the retreating cars like a glass butterfly over the tracks. I did not wait to see if they would be crushed when next the cars came around. It was the infamous ride called The Cyclone. Perhaps, I concluded, it is exciting to pretend you are about to die. I walked on past the ferris wheel, from which people dangled like soup ladles from posts directly above me. I remembered such a ride from my childhood, at the Prater Amusement Park in Vienna. I had been afraid then, too. Next to the ferris wheel was the parachute and I folded my neck back to see three tiny humans bouncing up and down at the top, preparing to be dropped. A whirring noise like an egg beater began and suddenly they were ejected; would their chutes open? I held my breath. Halfway down they did so, and the three came swooping in quite suddenly for a landing. Someone yelled at them to bend their knees and then they were buried in billowing clouds of *crème chantilly*.

By that time the sun was already a thin egg wash on the ocean and a cold wind was blowing up. The people were folding away their webbed patio chairs and chaise longues, complaining to each other in Russian that the autumn sun was already too weak for their old bones, it was time to return to the warmth of their apartments. Tomorrow they would meet again for another chess game, another pinochle game, another walk with baby. I started towards home with sand in my mouth; I would make a pudding filled with ground almonds.

I met Rella in front of The Bridge Arms, preparing for

her descent into the cellar to fill the oil burner (she was by this time employed as the building's assistant superintendent). She removed the piece of sheet metal which covered the cellar's entrance and I followed her, ducking down my head and feeling with my feet the steep stairs which had no railing. It was a horrible, wet place. At the bottom of the stairs was a light switch and a heavy iron door leading into the boiler room. Rella flipped the switch and we entered and went down yet another flight of stairs past a wall populated by giant cockroaches known as water bugs, which glistened in the dim light like dates. She instructed me to run past them quickly so they would not jump or fall on my shoulders. I obeyed.

At first the heat of the boiler was comforting after my long cold walk but after a few minutes it became stifling and I hated to look into the face of the furnace, which seemed to me like a monster with red glowing teeth and a hideous laughing mouth. It was Rella's job to give water to the monster through a funnel, and although I did not understand the function of the water, I knew without his twice-daily drink he would dry up and have some kind of attack. And so it was required of her that she come down to this horrible place every day and stand beside that creature to make certain he had digested his drink. It was ninety-seven degrees and I could not breathe. I asked if I could be excused for a moment, as I felt rather faint and in need of air. I invited her to come up to my apartment later, after her chores, for a cup of tea and perhaps a little something to eat. I explained I had something very important to tell her. And then I escaped from that murderous place.

What would I prepare? I must work quickly, as she would soon be with me. I lined a mold with a light biscuit dough and filled it with a custard, ground almonds and sour cherries. This was an improvisation based on the *Malakov Torte*. I licked my fingers before placing the mold in the oven, in a pan of water. When she came in I poured her a cup of tea and set a place before her. I explained how my memory had come back to me, how good it was to belong to myself again after so long. She said, "That's nice. I'm so happy for you," but she did not look happy. "Yes," I replied, "now I am complete," and I leaned back in my chair and smiled. "I am full-full of memories," I said, chuckling and patting my round stomach.

"But how did it happen?" she asked, and then-her mouth puckered like the forked edges of an American apple pie-"*What* do you remember?"

"Oh everything, everything," I said, waving my spoon in the air.

"Tell me," she whispered, as if frightened to hear.

And so I began to talk. I talked until my throat was quite sore; I might have been shouting over the wind and waves at Coney Island, only there we sat in my quiet turret room with our tea and our sand pudding. As usual she did not touch hers so, for the sake of tidiness, I ate it.

"But how did it happen? What made you remember all of this?"

"Simple. It was you-you may take the credit. So many electric shocks only made me more dim, but those words of yours-Wallenberg, Gerda, Majestic, Eichmann-yes, they were worth a million volts; they lit up the world. Back they came, the memories, pouring over me-slowly at first then getting thicker, just like a bath of hot chocolate. Now I am completely coated! I make a toast to you:" I held up my teacup, "the agent of my transformation!"

She looked embarrassed, tired. I thought, I must come quickly to the happy dénouement of my story.

"And now," I said, feeling a delicious glow of anticipation from what I was about to deliver, "there is something more I must tell you-the most important memory of all," and I could hardly wait to get it out. She bit on one of her fingers and I took another sliver of *torte* to give me courage.

"Your Swede," I said, rather thickly through my sponge, "he is not dead. No," I shook my head. "At least he did not die in 1947." I licked the back of my spoon. "How do I know? Because I was with him in a prison cell in the year 1955. How do you like that?"

I sat back and folded my hands into a Christmas braid over my stomach. So. She must be very pleased. But when I looked, her eyes were opened up so wide the brown discs were completely surrounded by white, like two *Ischl* tartlets-round, scalloped, cookie sandwiches with a hole through which dark jam appears; the ring of dough around the jam is brushed white with confectioner's sugar. She said nothing, only stared; the jam of her eyes grew moist. Happy? Sad? Perhaps she did not understand what I said?

"Are you not pleased to think he might still be alive?" I said, choosing my words as carefully as fresh cherries.

But she did not reply. She got up and ran away, knocking over her chair and slamming the door behind her. I was alone with my *Malakov Torte*; which, in its half-eaten condition, looked wounded and angry. Look what you have done now, it seemed to say, quivering slightly. I dropped my spoon, like a criminal caught in the act. Yet what crime? Was memory, after all, such a troublemaker?

Gerda

1

Ah, memories. We stew together into a thick *gulyas*. Mmmnn, I loved those dishes – Transylvanian stews, layered cabbage with sauerkraut, sausage and sour cream – I can smell them now. Who can make me such food? I will reward them. Memories. We pick and choose as we do our scenery. Here I have the famous river, the still-more-famous statue, the bridge with its squat towers like Buda Prison. These are picturesque; the tourists cannot get enough of them, their cameras are going snap snap all day long. For a change, let them point their apparatuses into the water, and what will they see? Garbage, bloated fish, canaries; men, women, children, babies, aborted foetuses. That is the *directissimo* route for disposing of our mistakes and our enemies. What kind of souvenir is a picture of a dead canary; or a butcher who loved to sing Italian arias? Yet I can still see them, floating in the shadow of the bridge, surrounded by garlands of flowers. May they rest in peace.

Mmmnn, I love rose-scented bubbles, they remind me of Budapest. Wherever I went there were roses, the Nazis were generous in that way. But we return to the question of choice – America thrives on it. Just around the corner you can have the cheap souvenirs and the bodies – or in here you can have *me*, floating in my rose-petal bath. Which will you have? Never mind the answer, I will choose for you. Today is my birthday; I am forty-two.

Happy birthday, gorgeous, they say. The window is open a slit, just enough for the interested to become more interested, to take in a freckle or two. I straighten one leg, point, wave it around; then the other. They certainly are an improvement on the skinny putters of Dietrich. Wait, I hear a whistle; what? Ah yes, I recognize it: Mona Lisa, Mona Lisa, men have made you. You're the something something something with the famous smile. I lift one shoulder and rub my cheek against it; those girlish freckles did it every time. Then I smile–ah, that would have brought Raoul running across the bridge, splash! But the whistler floats away like my thoughts. Never mind, even I am not immune from the ravages of time. Today I am a philosopher, it is my privilege. See here, how the flesh around the nipples has gone soft, spread like a loose dogpat. But come, let's be honest, what's a soggy nipple or two between friends?

Friends, admirers, lovers, customers–call them what you will–but oh, how they came, in droves, I couldn't keep them away. They would have gobbled me up alive. The little Italian butcher (just to take an example) would arrange my long limbs on the bed as if he were tucking into a three-course feast. He was a great muncher of parsley, that one. What did he want–blood? Oh no, he said I was bloodless, that was good. Blood reminded him of chickens and meat. "You are the perfect piece of flesh," he said, "no fat or gristle, all edible stuff." That was all right by me (they get their kicks where they can) but pretty soon he grew bored with admiring, stroking, munching, slapping, as if I were a piece of meat; it wasn't enough. What did he want? I'll tell you. He wanted to show off his choice cut in the market place. He wanted to flaunt me before other buyers and shake his head; no, she's mine, all mine, you can't buy her for love nor money. But that was going too far, that I would not have. I told him I was no lump of hamburger he could take out between two greasy buns and barter around. He spent his hour sitting with his head in his hands, broody as a chicken. "Get dressed," I said, "come back when it's in proper working order." That he didn't like. He started to talk about knives, the filleting knife in particular; how my flesh would make such perfect slices. The butterfly cut. Poor gentle Tony, what had got into him? What drove him to that sticky end? But the river washes everything clean. Cleaner and cleaner as you float out to sea. No blood, only music.

The trouble is they want too much. My body I can give, but my soul, never. Yet that's what they want, what excites them. Such is the nature of desire. They are used to obedience: tiny slippers to big boots. Big boot says: "Come out with me." Delicate slipper says: "At your service, Master." But not as far as I'm concerned, no boot has ever had its way with me. Don't forget, I'm a big girl, and I don't wear slippers, delicate or otherwise.

When they're in love they're boring, but when they want marriage, they're dangerous. They're like desperate squirrels hiding a particularly juicy nut for winter. No one else can lay eyes on me. They would like to bury me, they call it "rescue." But from what, I ask. From the big ugly dirty dangerous city, they reply, with hands busy inside my wrap. Let them have their little bit of fun, but they can't have *me*. No one can.

Let me tell you about one of them. He was a middle-aged bachelor with a round little mother who dispensed cocaine, sitting in a chair like Queen Victoria. His father was a tailor–a sweet, permanently bent man, who came to measure me for a suit and kissed the hem of my skirt. "Beautiful," he said, over and over, with tears in his eyes. But the son was annoyed and said, "What's the use of having such a suit–a work of art–if she won't go anywhere in it?" The father, a wise man, said, "Where should she go? She's like a statue already, a work of art in front of your eyes. Leave her." Ah, if only he'd been a little younger. I walked up and down in front of my full-length mirror, alone. Who else need admire me? I thought of the heroes who had had their fill, and the next time this son-of-a-tailor came to pester me, I told him where to get off. He begged and pleaded. Marry me, move out to the Island, give birth and raise our two-point-two children–they will be the most beautiful in the world, with blond hair and green eyes. I assured him my own green eyes were enough for me. At last he bowed his head and gave up. He ran and ran 'till he got to Texas and there suddenly he stopped. He's now president of an oil company. Every birthday he calls me, religiously. From time to time, when he's in New York on business, he arranges to see me. He's married with three daughters, all have green eyes, they live in an architect-designed box in the suburbs of Dallas, God bless 'em. But he has never stopped longing for me. He keeps my photograph locked in his office safe, when the going gets rough he takes it out to caress over a whiskey and soda. He cries over the 'phone, how I broke his heart and how all he's good for in this world is making money. My heart bleeds, Texas, but I don't complain. Love over the telephone and money orders in the bank, it's just how I like it.

That was how it was. Over and over they said: "I love you, I want you." But only the latter was honest. I fought them tooth and claw or they would have had me in their cages, their traps, their paddocks, their shacks, their suburban boxes, their Tudor mansions in Sweden. Oh no. Give me an absent lover over a constant husband any day. Best of all is a handsome hero, far far away, safely behind bars.

But come, it's my birthday, an evening for celebration. Soon the phone will ring. I put on my best perfume – there, can you smell it, Texas? But what's this coming through the door backwards? Surprise surprise – Rella carrying an enormous white cake. "A birthday cake for you, from Jack," she says, putting it down on a low table. Vitez buries his nose in the cream, I take a lick with my finger.

Well, well, it looks more like a wedding cake, I say. What are you trying to tell me, Jack? I have my suspicions about you, you know. Are you round and firm and fully packed, as they say, with your little legs planted on the ground; or are you as light and insubstantial as a bubble, liable to float away? Are you real, Nimble Jack? When do I get to grab hold of you? The cake slips easily between the teeth, the telephone rings, as predicted. "Coming, Texas, coming," I sing, floating along in a cloud of pale green chiffon and whipped cream.

2

Rella has a date with Jack-be-Nimble, I have a rendez-vous with *The Scarlet Pimpernel*.

I switch on the television set and arrange myself on the green chaise. Vitez guards. I dangle a piece of pastrami high above his nose and he jumps for it, snapping like a crocodile, his saliva watering the flowers. After six lunges, I drop the meat onto his muzzle; ah, the element of surprise!

Enter The Scarlet Pimpernel: Leslie Howard stars as the typical Englishman – ha! It makes me laugh. He's as English as I am, born in Pest. Without a trace of accent, also like me; all it takes is a good ear. But never mind ears – I like the eyes, not too soft, the lips drawn tight like rubber-bands. Come in, Leslie, make yourself at home. Sit down beside me on my chaise and allow me to pull off your boots.

Whose boots are getting pulled off up in the turret, I wonder. Rella and Jack-be-Nimble sit side by side, also watching *The Scarlet Pimpernel*. The lights are low. With his left hand he reaches for a cookie, with the other he strokes her hand; it feels like a lump of *gefilte* fish. He feels desperately for the palm – somewhere there must be a little warmth and padding. Ah yes, the soft folds excite him. He sneaks his left hand under his apron and after a few wiggles and bumps his stomach heaves like the white whale. Rella imagines he must be suffering from indigestion or a tight pair of pants. He wipes his fat little sausage with his apron and tucks himself away under his stomach. He reaches with his left hand for another cookie and pats her knee with his right one. He gives her a fatherly smile; she asks him what a pimpernel is.

So much for my peace. The door bangs open like the Arrowcross are coming. But I was always ready for them. "Be quiet, I'm watching a movie," I say. "Sit down, it's nearly over." She flings herself into the rocker. Who knows, maybe something more dramatic has happened after all: did Nimble Jack pounce on her, force her pimpernel open with the nicely-greased tip of his rolling pin?

"What happened up there?"

"He didn't die of a heart attack," she says. Rock rock.

"I should hope not, at his age. Stop rocking, you distract me."

"I'm talking about Raoul," she says. "He didn't die in 1947."

I look at her, raise a finely-plucked eyebrow. "How do you know this?"

"Jack told me."

"And how does he know, pray tell? I thought he has no memory."

"He got it back."

"Just like that – a miracle."

"I told him about you and Raoul and it made something snap in his mind. Now he remembers everything. He says he spent a night with him in a Russian prison cell, in 1955. So he couldn't have died in 1947."

"So these are the sweet nothings he whispers in your ear?"

"It means he could still be alive." Rock rock.

They lead Leslie Howard out to meet the firing squad. How do you do, gentlemen? Cool as a chilled hock, he is. A shot rings out but we do not see the body fall. The French fiend throws back his head and laughs like a hyena; his Adam's apple jerks up and down. That takes care of that.

"Why is he laughing?" she asks.

"He thinks they bumped off Leslie Howard. Now watch what happens. Watch." The door flies open. In strolls Pimpernel, picks up his hat and blows on it. Ha! The fiend's jaw drops open. "You look as if you've seen a ghost, my dear fellow," says Pimp. The fiend is apoplectic, soon to die by his own firing squad.

"How did you know they wouldn't shoot him?" she asks.

"I knew. The hero always survives in movies."

Next scene takes place on the prow of a very fake ship with close-ups of Pimp and his midget girlfriend (whom he has rescued from the clutches of the enemy). "Look, Marguerite – England," says the brave Pimp. She looks up into his face, like a wet kipper. The music swells and so do the wave machines. Any minute I'll vomit. Their capes flap in the wind. THE END – thank God. Wet kipper number two says, "He came back from the dead. Just like Raoul." Can those be real tears? God give me patience.

"Listen," I say, "I'm up to my eyeballs with this Wallenberg crap. Just because he was alive in 1955 doesn't mean he's *still* alive. Eleven years in a Russian prison is no holiday on the Riviera, so don't get your hopes up."

"But at least we know he didn't die in 1947. At least there's some chance. We can hope, can't we?"

"You can hope, my dear, but count me out. To me he's only a memory."

But what a memory. So he lays, year after year, on his hard pallet, thinking of me. He wears rough pajamas. There are terrible smells in his cell, insects, bare light bulbs overhead; it is deathly cold. He has sores on his graceful feet. He is physically weak but mind and heart are still ticking over. Of course it was ridiculous of the Russians to suggest such a thing as heart failure. When the imagination is exercised the heart does not fail, even in such an environment.

I am his sweet medicine. He lies on his back with a horse blanket covering him – yet to him it is salmon satin. His eyes are gravy boats. He sees mine as clearly as if I were there, over the years they have grown greener. The point of the exercise is to take as long as possible to unwrap the gift of memory. I am wearing a hundred kimonos which he peels away, one by one, as slowly as possible. He removes another scarf from my head and I shake out my honey-colored hair. Another button, another frog. At last he reaches bare skin, smoother than any satin, covered in freckles. He kisses them, one by one, starting at the neck and working his way down one side then up the other, as if around a laden dining-room table. It takes him hours to get to the center platter, but when he does ... ah, he is a man who knows how to use his tongue, who is not ashamed to lick his plate clean, every freckle nibbled, inside and out. The meal is over; he has feasted like a king. No wonder he survives, on such a diet.

* * *

What gift does my Nimble Jack send me tonight? Ah, candies, made with his own chubby hands, a work of pure devotion. I open the box – solid milk chocolate, each piece lovingly wrapped in foil. I choose the largest one. With a red fingernail I peel away the wrapper and lay bare the brown flesh. I brush my lips over the smooth cool back. The smell enters my nostrils. I slide the wedge in and out of my mouth until it begins to melt on my tongue. When only a sliver remains I bring my teeth together, breaking its back. It disappears down my throat; my teeth are washed in a chocolate bath.

So this is his delicious game. I get these secret messages via Rella, yet if I should wink or smile at him in the flesh, he scurries away as fast as his little legs will carry him. You'd think my name was Eichmann. Then – when the coast is clear – he communes with Vitez; they are in cahoots. Vitez would like to eat other men alive (one nearly lost an arm trying to hand me an envelope), but not him. At the sight of his comrade, he prostrates himself across the window sill, wagging his tail like Mary's little lamb. Cocks his head to one side, listening to the baker's silence as if it were a brilliant oration. His bad ear flops down; useless, impotent. Maybe that's the secret between then: dumb allegiance. My two faithful bodyguards. Good night to you too, Jack. Good night, Texas, good night, my Swedish Pimpernel. Good night, Vitez – yes you too. Sweet dreams to all my men.

3

Let me tell you about another one – this was in '46, about a year after I came to this country. He was the romantic type – square jaw, scarf around the neck, corduroy jacket. What I didn't see was a pair of eyes as grey and cold as the Danube. I was used to playing the game of cat and mouse, only this time it was different. I suppose I was a little hungry, so I nibbled on his piece of cheese – and boom, I fell into his trap. The tables were turned. I remember going to the window to smoke a cigarette, when I saw him across the street, just standing there with his camera equipment dangling from his neck. Mine was bare, I stretched it to get a better view of the river and sucked deeply on my cigarette. I knew he was watching me but I pretended not to notice. I was wearing no make-up – maybe some mascara, a little pale lipstick. I had bathed my skin in milk and plucked my eyebrows to the shape of two arches as graceful as the Margrit Bridge. I was ready for daylight – and there he was, ready for me.

Each day we played our little game. He stood across the street, watching, and I opened my window like a milkmaid on a farm. I inhaled deeply, turning my head sideways to reveal the shape of my cheekbones; it might have been true mountain air I breathed. Just so long as he kept to his post, everything was all right. It was as if we were chess pieces – he the white knight and I the black queen. I had him in check, dazzled so he couldn't move. But he had to go and spoil the game, silly boy. What did he do? I'll tell you: he waved. Just like that, the spell was broken. Then the sun came out in a great and glorious burst and I was blinded. Then I heard the click. Wham – down went the window and the shade after it. Enough. I felt as if he'd stolen something which didn't belong to him. How dare he? Why did he want my picture? What for? I was suspicious, and rightly so.

It was clear he wasn't interested in any polite game, no, he wanted to win. I ignored his tapping and hid myself away – a sacrifice of my only outlet from Rella's miserable, colicky screams. After a week I could bear it no longer, but there he was, ready for me. He jumped up from below my window where he'd been hiding like a Jack-in-the-Box, and grabbed my hand. (Lucky for him I didn't have Vitez then or he'd have lost a good left arm.) "Don't go," he begged, looking up at me with those melting ice cubes. The combination was lethal. "Look," he said, "I'm sorry I took your picture like that. I'm sorry, I'm sorry, I'm sorry. I didn't mean to offend you, or frighten you, or whatever it was I did. I had no right to take it without your permission. I humbly beg your pardon." And he bowed, right there, out in the street. How could I not laugh? He explained he wasn't normally in the habit of snapping strange women, but when he saw me stretching my neck – and then the sun co-operated so beautifully – he lost every ounce of self-control. How could I blame him? It had just happened, just like that – click.

"It's the most beautiful face I've ever seen," he said.

"But it's mine," I said. "You can't have it."

"I only wanted to borrow it. Here, you can have it back," and he produced the print he had made.

I studied it carefully. The window had been transformed into a picture frame. I seemed to glow from the inside like an icon. My hair in the sunshine was spun gold, my features were defined and soft at the same time, my teeth were pearls. It was a wonderful portrait. "Well?" he asked, waiting for my verdict. "It's quite nice," I said, ducking my head back in, smelling danger. But he was quicker than I. He caught the window with his long arm and propped it open. "Wait, please don't go away again. I've been waiting out here so long my knees are giving way. Come on, let me in, just for a little while." He let go of the window and I noticed his fingers – long and thick like Raoul's. "If you let me in, I'll apologize properly," he said. His timing – this time – was perfect. I closed the window and opened my door to him and the heavy equipment knocking against his thighs.

He started with my feet, a long way down from where I stood. "Get up, idiot," I laughed, but he was busy working his way up, kissing and complimenting as he went. He'd been watching me for so long – ankles. I reminded him of a delicate bird trapped in a cage – shins. He wanted to give me wings – knees. Make me sing – back of knees. He could do nothing but think about me – thighs. He had to have me or he would die – insides of thighs. By then I was ready to believe anything. Then he slid his hand under my kimono and raised himself to his knees. My own knees gave way and we collapsed together onto the new green carpet. It was like spring grass, the sky stretched overhead for miles and the sun came out again. "What's that strange smell?" I asked. "Photographic chemicals," he said, and we went tumbling wildly down the next hill.

I allowed him to come to me – to take my picture – once a week, but he became more possessive. Now he wanted me on his territory. I told him just because I let him take my picture it didn't mean he owned me, but he said darkly, "That's what you think." What I *think*? But he was shrewd, he switched tactics when he saw the look on my face. If I cared for him I would go away with him. How could he be sure he wasn't just another of my customers? Sure? I was giving no guarantees, he could take what he got and if he didn't like it ... "Listen," he said, "I know of a house in the country, an old wooden farmhouse in Connecticut, with a porch, snow drifts up to the windows, a log fire inside. It'll be nice and cosy, just the three of us." I said I had no intention of going anywhere. I had had my adventures in another world. It was enough. Now life came to me, I had no need to go out after it. As I explained, I had everything I wanted, where I wanted it, thank you very much, including a vivid imagination. Country – who needed it? It was his dream, not mine. He became belligerent. He insisted on rescuing me and my child from this terrible city; it was no place for a baby, she looked like a scrawny chicken. We belonged in the country with beauty all around us – open spaces, fields, flowers, trees, fresh air. He pictured me romping through a field of daffodils with Rella toddling after me; it would put roses in our cheeks. "Are you finished?" I said when he had come to the end of his speech. He nodded, crossed his arms over his chest. "Good," I said, "then I'll tell you something. First of all, I don't need rescuing; second of all, it isn't healthy for babies to be fat; and third of all, it's winter, there are no daffodils. It sounds to me like being buried alive. Forget it," I added.

About a week later he came to tell me one of "our" pictures had been accepted by a famous magazine. I said I was delighted; how much would they pay? "Nothing, unless you co-operate," he said. So, more threats.

"Look, what is it you want?" I asked.

"For you to come away with me."

"You want to play house, I'm not interested."

"They want a title for your picture, what shall I call it?"

"You can call it 'Greta Garbo' for all I care."

"What about 'Eichmann's Mistress in Budapest.' How do you like that?"

That stopped me in my tracks. I could feel one whole side

of my face droop, but I covered it with a crooked smile. How did he know? *What* did he know? I said I thought he should change it, I didn't much care for that one.

"What would you like instead?"

"Why not put 'Wallenberg's Mistress in Budapest' instead. I much prefer it. Can you do that?"

"I can do anything, if you'll come away with me."

"Then we go for a ride," I said.

Once we were out on the open highway I began to relax and enjoy myself. I opened all the windows and let the cold air blow in my face; how refreshing it was, after all, to be outside. I saw the leafless trees hold out their arms for me to dance and I ordered him to drive faster. Faster. At ninety miles an hour it was almost as exciting as the siege. Rella began to cry. I took her to my naked breast and my handsome friend nearly drove into the back of a Mac truck.

Then the world went silent. He had to dig out the drive. The house he had rented was old and rickety, the steps leading up to the porch creaked and sagged from the weight of snow on them. I wrapped myself and Rella in a blanket while he chopped wood, lit a fire and cooked dinner. It took forever. I drank Miller's High Life from a bottle and wiped the foam off my top lip with the back of my hand. By the time the food was cooked I didn't feel like eating. I brushed my hair back from my forehead and rubbed off my lipstick. It was impossible for me to look ugly, of course, but I tried. He beckoned me to the window to see a deer bounding along in the snow. "Who cares?" I said. I had agreed to come but I had not agreed to like it. The deer was smart and ran away; I was trapped.

Each day we got up from an old white-painted brass bed which had a sagging damp mattress, then he went out with his camera to take pictures of Mother Nature. One day he came back with a pair of boots for me. He stood me against a tree in the snow and snapped my picture. I wandered around, observing my feet, which seemed to me the most interesting objects in that desolate landscape. He snapped, again and again. I kept my hands in the pockets of the man's overcoat I wore. Once he tricked me by saying, "Look at that bird," and pointed to the sky. He got me looking up, with my mouth open – the oldest trick in the book. But he never got a smile.

One afternoon at dusk he shot a rabbit. He cleaned it on the porch and flipped the entrails out into the snow for the hungry deer. He cooked it in a cream and wine sauce – an old New England recipe, he said proudly, wiping his rabbity hands on his woman's apron. I drank my beer and refused his rabbit; I told him it reminded me of the horse *gulyas* we had to eat during the siege. He banged his fists on the table and dropped his head straight into the steaming plate; the howl could have woken the rabbit's guts and sent them hippity-hopping away into the snowy night. I laughed at the burn on his nose.

After supper I sat by the fire and nursed Rella. Snap snap went his camera. He swore I was even more beautiful than Mother Nature herself. "So what?" I said. He waited after each flash to see if I would come back to life, but I did not. I was there in body but not in spirit, with the snow coming half-way up the windows to bury me. What was in it for me? Nothing. I had had to cancel my life, to live here as his helpless victim in this cold, white prison. I sat staring straight ahead of me like a cigar store Indian, with my high cheekbones and my hair drawn back from my temples. Slowly I spread my legs. He began to snap faster and faster, leaping around the room like an excited, chattering monkey. When he threw down his camera and tried to kneel down before me to do his praying at the altar act, I snapped them shut; I too could play the game of blackmail. "Go stick it in a snowdrift," I said, and that was that. How literally he took my instructions, I don't know, but when he came back he looked as if he was melting; puddles formed around his boots in the warm room. The next morning he drove us back to the city.

I lay down on my green chaise, lit a cigarette and blew a family of smoke rings. He was still keeping a vigil out in his car but at about six in the morning I heard him start up his engine; he must have been frozen to death. Then he left, without waving goodbye. His photographs have become internationally famous, especially the series of me out in the snow, in my big boots. He sent me hundreds. Rella played with them the way other children play with cut-out dolls or playing cards. "Pretty Gerda" were her earliest words. The golden ones, of me throwing back my head and laughing, those were her favorites; she still looks at them. By the time she was four years old she could read the words "Wallenberg's Mistress in Budapest." Smart kid. That was before all the questions.

So you see, it was a lucky escape. I still get generous royalty cheques from him, with love notes attached. "You are the only woman I ever really loved," he writes. Absence, naturally, makes the heart grow fonder. What man loves a wife like this? He says he'd like us to meet again one day but he doesn't really mean it. He has my pictures, the way I have Raoul's. We never age, it's much better this way. Recently I received a picture of him standing against a palm tree in California. The sky is true blue. He's wearing a white suit and dark sunglasses. I can't see his eyes but I know what's there: an image of me walking away in the snow. It was Raoul's last shot, too. What keeps them alive.

4

Alive but something missing. Lacking some essential ingredient, like a stew without bones; thin and uninteresting. What she reads she repeats, what she sees she believes, what she hears she spews back. She lacks the ability to distinguish between fact and fiction, gossip and gospel, rumor and truth, not to mention the finer shades of meaning: she knows "alive or dead" but nothing in between. What does it mean to be alive? How? In what condition? There's alive and alive, I say, but she doesn't want to hear. She's like a puppet. Something or someone tugs on her strings and she responds: a crude library book says he died in the siege and she droops; I tell her he didn't, and she twitches with life. A suspect Russian document says he died of a heart attack – again droop; Jack-be-Nimble says he didn't – twitch twitch. I say so what, eleven years have passed since then, the goose may be well cooked by now – again droop, but only half-way. *Maybe* he's alive, she says. At least he hasn't been reported dead. Not known to be conclusively dead and buried. She manipulates the words to make it sound good. Not dead, but not alive either.

She flies around like a witch on her broomstick, going through her cleaning routines. Soon there will be no building left to clean. Day and night, scrub scrub scrub – halls, walls, ceilings, the sidewalk even – as if her life depended on it. Or his. She even toe dances down to meet the boiler – her old *bête noire* – with a spring in her step and her sleeves rolled up over her knobbly elbows. As she pours in the water, she pours out her heart: alive, alive, oh please God, let him be alive. How do I know? I can hear her through the pipes. So that's her god. Good luck to her.

She has written to the Wallenberg family – c/o the Swedish Embassy – asking for information. Do they know his whereabouts? Is he still alive? Any further details will be much appreciated, etc, etc. By way of reply she gets no personal communication from Mrs Wallenberg saying: "My son is alive! How kind of you to care, Miss Green." But now you see how it is, my little glutton for punishment, what it can mean to be alive. Not what you thought at all. She's like a dog who keeps coming back for more kicks. When will she learn? Never. Look, here is my bottom, kick me again. Harder.

She gets an official document. Here is the gist of the story. The year is 1961. A certain Doctor Nina Svartz – eminent physician and doctor to the Wallenberg family – attends a medical conference in Moscow. After one of the day's sessions she approaches one of her Russian colleagues – a certain Doctor Miashnikov – for a chat. They speak in German, just in case. She asks Miashnikov if he happens to know anything about the Wallenberg case. He replies yes, as a matter of fact he has personally examined Wallenberg who is at the moment in a mental hospital, in poor mental condition. He has spent years in solitary confinement and has been on hunger strike as a protest against imprisonment. These things take their toll, says Miashnikov. A pity, a sad case. Unfortunately, that is all Dr

M can tell Dr S; if she wants to go further on this matter, she will have to do it through diplomatic channels. Fine, Dr M doesn't want to get into hot water with the Russians, and who can blame him. When Dr S returns to Sweden she contacts the Prime Minister who obediently writes to Khrushchev asking for an explanation. Why are they keeping Wallenberg a prisoner? There is no reply to his letter. Surprise surprise.

Dr S goes again to Moscow and asks Dr M if she can have a look at Wallenberg for herself, in the mental hospital he happened to mention when last they spoke. Dr M is taken aback. What mental hospital? What Wallenberg? I know nothing about such a person. You must have misunderstood my poor German. Poor German my foot, says Dr S to herself, this Dr M is as fluent as Adolf Hitler. She returns to Sweden. The Swedish Prime Minister continues to write letters of protest to the Russians. Nothing doing. A further meeting is arranged between the two doctors, this time in Stockholm, on safe soil. Still Dr M sticks to his story: I know nothing about any Wallenberg, I said nothing, he says. Poor dumb Miashnikov; innocent Miashnikov. Finally the Swedish Foreign Ministry looks into the case and decides Dr M is afraid and covering up. They publish a book disclosing the whole affair (1965). Two months after publication, Dr M kicks the bucket. He had had an excellent health record – up until then. End of story.

Poor Miashnikov, it doesn't pay to tell cowardly lies, they get you in the end anyway. "Poor mental condition." What does this mean? Mad, deluded, sick, sick to death of being kept prisoner, insane with a desire to get out, talking to himself because there's no one else to talk to? To Rella this is the worst news yet, too terrible for words, worse than ... She sees him shuffling along the corridors of a filthy mental hospital surrounded by shivering, drooling, mumbling, exposed idiots, all whimpering into their *borscht*. He waves his arms in the air and screams. It's all a mistake, I was on your side against the Nazis, why are you keeping me here, I protest. Mad indeed. Madder than mad.

She is mad in sympathy. One day I'm looking out my window, watching the garbage men do their he-man ballet. They fling the empty barrels aside like discarded lovers.

Where is Rella to pick them up? One of the handsome Tarzans is about to dump one of the black plastic bags into the truck's grinding hole when he stops short. "Hey, wait a minute, what the ... Holy Christmas, I don't believe it. I seen people throw away all kindsa things in my time – dead bodies, okay – but never a live person. Holy shit." So she slipped herself into a garbage bag and waited to be hauled in and ground up with the rest of the rotting matter. An original departure, I have to hand it to her, I didn't think she had the imagination. The super comes out and wants to know what all the fuss is about. When he hears about her little trick he tries to fire her on the spot – he can't have a nutcase working around the building. Who knows, she might decide to set fire to herself and the whole building would go up in flames. "Just a minute," I say, calming him down, smoothing things over for her. Temporary insanity, I assure him; give her another chance. He can't deny she does a decent day's work. Meanwhile Miss Personality stands there looking from me to him, him to me, eyes like black holes, skin the color of fish belly. "That was a lucky escape," I tell her. "You might have been chewed up into a fine paté by now." But it doesn't register. Blank. Her spirit, if not her body, has gone to the great garbage dump in the sky.

To get her blood flowing, I send her on an errand of mercy to the butcher's shop for some veal scallops, but she brings me tripe. That can go into the garbage can too. Later that night, on duty, she chews the skin around her fingernails down to the bone so that blood is mingled with the filthy water in her pail. She has even more time to think, nothing but time on her hands. Towards morning she wakes me up to say she has decided he'd be better off dead than crazy. I say we'd all be better off if he were dead, and pull the covers over my head.

Part III

On the morning of 16 October 1976, a full-page advertisement appeared in the *New York Times* and the *New York Daily News* inviting information about Raoul Wallenberg. It read as follows:

RAOUL WALLENBERG – MISSING FOR 30 YEARS

The Swedish diplomat who saved thousands of Hungarian Jews during the last year of the Second World War is believed to be still alive in the Soviet Union. We would like to hear from anyone who may have information concerning his past and especially his recent whereabouts. All evidence will be treated in strict confidence.

The name, address and telephone number of the sponsoring committee followed, along with an impressive double-column list of supporters' names, drawn from the ranks of the rich, famous and talented. Some of them had been saved by Raoul Wallenberg, or had relatives who had.

This advertisement prompted both Jack and Gerda to write down something about their lives and how they had come to meet Raoul Wallenberg.

Jack

I was born with a silver *schlag* spoon in my mouth. My father owned one of Vienna's finest bakeshops, and my mother had a passion for his strudel, which she passed on to me. Most things in our house were fat: the Meissen dinner plates scalloped with gold, which we ate from on Sundays, the cherubs which leaned on their elbows, watching us from the heights of our drawing room ceiling, the Louis XVI chairs, very like my mother with their squat bow legs. If my schoolmates teased me for my rotundity, I responded by smacking my fingers to my lips in a careless gesture – thereby kissing away the culprits and enjoying the remains of a *Tascherl* or *Buchtel* which came every day, wrapped in silver paper, in my lunch basket. Small enemies are of no importance when one's father makes the finest pastries in all Vienna.

A special treat for me was watching Master Baker Baum, my father, in white apron and hat, arms white to the elbows in flour, make his famous strudel. I remember feeling my eyebrows covered in a fine white powder. The creation of the strudel was an occasion of high seriousness. I sat on my stool, knotted my chubby fingers together into a *krendl*, and watched in absolute silence.

A lecture on flour followed – the two distinctive types of flour used in Vienna: *glatt* and *griffig*. The first was slippery and smooth; the second rougher and grainier, like fine semolina. There were two schools of thought about Vienna's strudel makers: some preferred the one flour and some the other and some, my father regretted to say, mixed both kinds together. It was such minutiae that made it difficult to translate the inner meaning of a recipe, because elsewhere flour might be nothing more than flour.

So my father sifted his *griffig* flour onto the fresh white cloth which by habit covered his work table. Then he took a ball of dough the size of an orange and rolled it out to a thin circle. Walking round and round the table, he worked his hands mysteriously under the sheet of dough, up and down, and so went his eyebrows too. Around and around, he coaxed and stretched the dough until it looked to me like the ear of the elephant I had seen at the zoo. Next he sprinkled over the dough his fillings – brown bread crumbs, lemon rind grated into sugar, raisins, currants, finely sliced apples, almonds, a small pitcher of melted butter. Finally he tilted and nudged the cloth this way and that, causing the strudel to roll over and over like a happy dachshund until all the fillings were enclosed. I clapped in appreciation, but at the same time I was not easy.

"Come, come, what is it?" asked my father, patting me on the crown of my head with a floury hand so that I had a ghostly skullcap. "So. Speak, young man." I tried to explain. He had been so violent with the dough – pushing, pulling, pinching – how was it it did not cry out in pain and turn black and blue afterwards – as I had done when the class bully pinched me on my arm? My father's apron danced up and down; he thought this very funny indeed.

"How can a thing like dough feel pain? Only people feel pain," he said, giving me a little pinch on one of my apple cheeks, to demonstrate. "Not lifeless things like dough," and he stuck one of his big white fingers deep into a leftover dough ball. I felt as if my own stomach had been pierced. What would it feel like? I bit my lip, not daring to make a sound in front of my father, who then kicked the wooden leg of the table to make his point quite clear. "You see. It only hurts my foot, not the table." But I never felt pity for my father, only for the table.

In spite of his warnings, I decided that since I had feelings, then so must everything else in the world, including things they called inanimate.

"Why are you walking like that?" asked my mother.

"I do not want to hurt the earth," I confessed.

"Believe me," said my mother with her hand over her

heart, "the earth cannot feel you the same way you feel the earth."

Although it did not sit easy with me, I accepted her philosophy as it applied to the legs of tables or lumps of dough, or the ground under my feet. Life, I could see, would otherwise become quite impossible. But other things – growing things – I exempted from the rule. Never would I accept that the tree outside my window did not live and breathe. If it was alive ("Trees are living creatures," said my teacher) then it must have feelings. I can remember my first proof, when the tree stood before me groaning from the weight of new fat buds on the ends of its branches. I heard it, you see, clearer than my father's voice. What could I do for it? Only stroke and soothe it with human words. "It is only your growing pains," I said. "Nothing to worry about. Soon your leaves will open and then you will feel better."

Eventually I became my father's apprentice, although I already knew a great deal from watching and asking many questions. I will never forget again my first *Sachertorte* with its curiously dull glaze; I had forgotten to add cream. Yet it was from the mistakes that I learned.

There was something strange about the people who came into Baum's Bakeshop, and one day it became clear to me what it was. They were rich; as rich as any *Doboschtorte* with its eight egg yolks and its pound of butter. Of course it was a different kind of richness. These people wore furs, feathers, pearls, jewels; they drove up in chauffeur-driven cars. Never did I see an ordinary *hausfrau* come in, even to buy a simple *Gugelhupf*. It would have been an unusual event to see a hand without rings.

In my father's shop I heard people call Jews names: Capitalists, Socialists, Communists, Zionists, destroyers of German blood and members of an international conspiracy. Now I knew all of these things could not be true at once, but when I tried to argue, my father would silence me. Flapping his hands under a strudel leaf, he would say, "It is hopeless to struggle." Even when I pointed out to him that many of his best customers were Jewish – opera singers from the nearby opera house, great actors and actresses – he shrugged his shoulders and said, "We have a certain image to protect."

After work I took my bicycle and rode around some of the workers' districts. I leaned it against a railing or gently against a tree (begging its pardon) and overheard some of the conversations taking place at the cafés. People spoke mostly in whispers, or turned their backs. I might be a Gestapo spy. But eventually one of the groups at the Café Meteor lost their suspicion of me and let me sit amongst them. And so I listened freely. They gave me their newspaper, *Arbeiter Zeitung*, to read. After reading for a bit, and listening, I agreed Fascism was a very bad thing and Hitler should be stopped. As for their other discussions, they made my head spin. These people had a language of their own which I could not understand. They argued about conciliation, deals, lulling the workers, unpolitical thinking, and so on and on. Their party – the Revolutionary Socialist Party, or RS – seemed to me to be sliced into factions like a pie: first in half between the Conservatives and Militants; then in quarters between the Pessimists and Optimists. I never knew exactly where I stood in the pie, but somehow they accepted me into their ranks. When they discovered I was the son of Baker Baum, they said I could make myself useful; so long as I had the will.

Did I have such a thing? I was already so tired of their quarrels, and their smoky basement rooms gave me a headache. I could not bear the shouting over an issue which seemed to me as unimportant as a poppy seed. I turned to my friends the trees for comfort. Often I stopped after a meeting for some quiet meditation with a smooth-barked beech. How quiet, how handsome, how productive (leaves, flowers, fruit) I thought; such a perfect creature which never argues in a loud voice, never inflicts cruelty upon its fellows. Of course it was still winter and very cold and it came to me that the tree, naked without its leaves, might be feeling a sense of shame at such exposure. And so I whispered into a knotty bole in its trunk a private communication. "It is only natural," I explained, "a necessary period in the cycle of the seasons. You will grow your lovely leaves again quite soon, and all will be well with you."

* * *

How could I ever have forgotten such a weekend? Early in the morning (it was 12 March 1938) I heard bombers advancing to the airport outside Vienna. Our house shook for several hours. During that first Saturday, hundreds of thousands of police and SS divisions marched into the city and tanks and armored cars followed. Anti-aircraft guns were positioned along the Ringstrasse and aeroplanes circled overhead. Perhaps a quarter of a million people crowded into the Heldenplatz to hear Hitler's speech and another five or six hundred thousand lined the Ringstrasse to welcome him. It seemed to me there were more swastikas than people. I stayed long enough to hear Hitler say he was moved to tears by this joyous reception, and then I fought my way through the crowd with my bicycle and back to the shop. It was closed. I knew my father must be somewhere in the crowds. I opened the shop and sat amongst the *torten* and *krapfen*, and wept.

Soon the violence and desecrations began. Cars belonging to Jews were confiscated, shops were looted and apartments ransacked. They painted the word "Jud" in yellow on the windows of Jewish shopkeepers. And then came the arrests: unco-operative government leaders, Christian Socialists, Social Democrats, Revolutionary Socialists, Jews, Communists, workers, intellectuals, teachers. The risks of joining an underground resistance group became quite terrifying. Capture would mean torture, imprisonment in a concentration camp, or death. But I had become known to a small group of RS members, and they invited me to put away my baker's apron and join them in their brave struggle.

What could I do? That Saturday, instead of going to one of the newly formed friendship circles, I took my bicycle and rode out to the Wienerwald. I walked among the firs and birches until it was nearly dark, still asking myself that question. What could I, Hanno Baum, contribute to the resistance? The forest noises, once all the people had gone, were comforting. I had a contest of staring with a young deer, each of us listening to our own hearts beating, until I shifted my great weight and the spell became broken. The deer bounded away and I stumbled forward in my clumsy

105

way. An owl flapped, enormous and silent, from tree to tree, finally settling its claws around the end of a light birch branch which trembled under the bird's weight. Outlined against the sky, it reminded me of a big cat wearing a white napkin around its neck, preparing to eat dinner. Poor branch, I thought. And then my attention was caught by a terrible eerie noise. I walked further on and discovered a young fir had fallen down and was caught in the fork of an older tree. It lay there and moaned in pain. Together they swayed in the night wind, the tough old one cradling the dying young one in its arms like a *pietà*. I ran away with my hands over my ears.

Everywhere there were German soldiers; Vienna looked more like an army camp than a city of music and fine pastries. The ice-rink became a bad-smelling field kitchen. The fashionable hotels were turned over to high-ranking officers. Finally I made my decision: I would do my share; in my own small way I would "keep the wheels of resistance well-greased." I would distribute pastries from Baum's Bakeshop to as many anti-Nazi groups as I could manage of an evening. I knew I would not be very good at sneaking around on cat's feet, putting up propaganda stickers or painting slogans on walls, but I could perfectly well stay up at night baking, then drive my bike around the town with a big box strapped into my basket, delivering pastries to my hard-working comrades. It was a good decision. I was heartily welcomed, slapped on the back or punched playfully in the breadbasket, and then I was off again. I gave them my support, my freshly-baked pastries, but not my time, because there was always another delivery to be made.

One of the questions I came to ask myself was this. What would I do if an SS or a Gestapo officer should come into the shop; would I serve such a creature even a *krendl* ? What would I do? But I did not have long to entertain the question. They barged into the shop early one morning (it was April, the trees were blossoming) with a warrant for my arrest. My father had been piping cognac-flavored *schlagobers* around the top of a specially ordered creme caramel. Later, the two images became confused in my mind, so that my father's bald head appeared to me ringed round with whipped cream, while the creme caramel was topped by my father's white balloon hat.

My father was pointing at me and shouting, *"Nicht Juden, nicht Juden,"* but the stormtrooper leered at me, then at my father, then at the creme caramel. And then he spat, "Communist scum. Jew lover," and the caramel quivered in terror before collapsing on its handsome pewter tray. My father's cheeks jiggled and he cried, "That caramel was for my most important customer, a famous opera singer." A Jewess, he did not add. I could only guess that they had been watching me for some time, concluding that because I went from meeting place to meeting place, I was one of the ringleaders of the resistance. And there was I, only the boy who delivered levity.

Gerda

I was born feet first like a lady; I would not be pulled out by the head like a melon. No, I managed to turn myself right side up and slide out as far as my neck. Then there was a popping sound like a cork and it was all over – or should I say it was all about to begin? My mother fainted. I opened my eyes to see what was going on, and when I noticed blood on my belly I screamed for them to cut that hideous cord and clean me up; to warm me, hold me, feed me, admire me. They carried out these orders to my satisfaction. Even the doctors oohed and aahed. Perhaps the perfection of this child – they discussed the matter at some length – could be explained by the unusual method of birth, specifically the absence of manhandling of the head. While there are complications for the mother and so for the medical team, this method has produced a most beautiful baby. And so on. For me it was all quite simple.

I was the youngest of nine children, and the *filet mignon* of my father's eyes. My father, you see, was at that time a butcher. He owned a shop on the edge of the ghetto in Pest, and this fact was of some significance because my father was, you might say, on the edge of many things. He seemed to me then always to rise above the smallness of life. I can remember looking up at him in his blood-stained apron and thinking he was the tallest man in the world. He was only five feet nine inches in fact, but he created the illusion of a colossus; in his own way my father was a magician. He was not strictly kosher, but even the most orthodox came to his shop for their meat and poultry. Little did they know. The non-Jews also came to him because he had a reputation for pleasing the fussiest of ladies. He was, in a way, all things to all people. You see, my father was not only patient and charming, he was very very handsome. He had a smile that would melt chicken fat.

When I was small, my father took me with him to the shop. My mother dressed me up like a doll–in velvet dresses with ruffled petticoats or knee-high checked pantaloons to show off my shapely calves–so that all I could do was dance around in my patent leather shoes in the sawdust with my curls twirling around my head like fat sausages. I entertained the customers, but it was my father's eye I sought. By the time I was a little older (about four) I had already become bored with being a plaything; I wanted to make myself useful to him. But my mother would not co-operate; she continued to dress me up in those absurd clothes and I could do nothing without getting them stained in blood and gore. Perhaps she did this with some calculation in mind? Perhaps she thought, in her simple way, that when my father's green eyes flashed with pride at my appearance he would experience some vestige of feeling for her, at least some gratitude for creating this magical creature for his delight. This was horse trotters; his gratitude went exclusively to me. As he used to say, he could have eaten me up. And there were times when I feared he would–the way he would snort and nibble hungrily at my neck, my ears, my toes. He dismissed my efforts to help around the shop, saying it was enough for him to look up from whatever he was doing–stripping a thigh, breaking the back of a chicken–and see me dancing like a sunbeam before him.

My mother was dumpy and plain; an insignificant little woman. Her hair was frizzy and her nose and eyes were red. She made jokes about herself–how she could never wear red because it would clash with her nose. I suppose you could say she had a sense of humor, but I never found her jokes funny, and I did not laugh at them. To me she was pathetic. She wore long dark lumpy skirts and woolly cardigans over her fat arms and sloppy breasts. She sloped from the neck like a shoulder of veal. I could not imagine her as anything but a drudge; my father surely deserved better. Yes, to me she was already an old woman while my father–underneath his butcher's apron–was a Dapper

Dan. He would wash his hands six times and then put on a suit and tie, a diamond ring, a tie clip and a cat's eye pinky ring. He told me he loved things that sparkled; that was why he loved me. On special occasions he wore spats. To the shop he wore black and white shoes with little holes in them and tassels which flipped when he walked. Those were my favorites. I would watch them under the counter; sometimes I would sit on a low stool at his feet and play with his tassels. I do not know to this day how he managed not to drip blood on them.

I can remember seeing my mother crumpled up on the floor at home at my father's feet, pulling at his trouser leg like the chicken plucker. Soon I realized she was begging him to stay and he was trying to get away from her. She had nothing to offer a man like him. With one of his tasseled shoes he kicked her broad rump and she slid along the floor like a side of mutton. Then he gave his shoe a good brush with his elbow and marched out of the house. I vowed then never to beg a man for anything. Let them come to me, I said to myself, pirouetting after him out of the room. "Stay," wailed my broken mother, but I pretended not to hear.

My father presented me with a miniature apron. I was big now, bigger than all the other five-year-olds; a bean pole, my mother said, but of course she was jealous. I remember trying to yank my dresses down over my knees but it was no use. Knobbly as soup bones, my father said, pinching them and winking, so that I knew he was only teasing, that really he liked my knees. When I wore my new apron – which came down to my ankles in front – he sometimes tickled the backs of my legs. How soft the skin was there, he would purr. And then he would whistle like a bird and hack at a belly of pork. I held the scrap bucket.

And then misery came down on me like my father's meat cleaver and I thought I would die. How could they separate me from him? But they did – they summoned me to school. And when I refused to go, a truant officer came to the shop and eventually dragged me kicking and screaming away. My father, I knew, could have dealt with him – axed him in half, bribed him, thrown him out on his ear – but he chose

110

to do nothing. He stood there grinning from ear to ear. He betrayed me, he let them take me away from him; in fact, I saw enjoyment written across his face. That was another thing I learned from my father: that deep down men do not like their women to go like lambs to the slaughter. They like a good run for their money.

I dragged myself and my little satchel to school each day, but as soon as I caught sight of the school building and the other children milling around I began to feel sick. I took my place at the back of the queue of children waiting to go in and when the bell rang out it set off some reaction in my system and I vomited down the back of the child in front of me; this happened every morning. Eventually my mother got complaints from teachers and the parents of the children caught in my line of fire. She wrung her puffy hands and moaned, "What are we going to do with you?" but my father took me on his knee and held me firmly by the waist and looked into my eyes. "What is it?" he asked. "Do you want money?" I shook my head so hard I became dizzy. "Not money," I said, "you," and I tickled him under his chin and ran a finger lightly back and forth across his bottom lip. I told him if he would accompany me to school I would promise not to throw up anymore. He put me off his lap and said he had to think about it; I drove a hard bargain. I slept not a wink that night, but the next morning he was kneeling at my bedside, his warm hands under my night gown. "You win," he said, tickling me in all the right places, and I smiled sleepily up at him.

And so he accompanied me to school, dressed in his finest clothes, with his handsome curly mustache, and he held my hand and I did not once lose my breakfast. He sat beside me on a bench, to the admiration of all my little schoolmates, not to mention my teacher, who gave him the eye. But he was mine, all mine, and I tightened my grip on his meaty hand to remind him.

"Your teacher is a smart cookie, isn't she?" he said one day after school.

"Oh yes," I replied, "but she isn't very pretty, is she?"

He twirled his mustache and surprised me by saying, "Ah, not everyone can be as pretty as you, my little lamb chop, but there is more to a woman than looks, you know. A pretty woman with an empty head is no bargain."

"Yes, papa," I said, and from then on began to pay more attention to my lessons. Within a week I was so busy writing and waving my hand in the air, I failed to notice I no longer held his hand. And a week after that I gave him his marching orders. I had become a scholar; I didn't need him anymore. Now when he held me close and put his hands under my skirt I slapped it away. He grew angry. "Mind you don't get too smart, young lady."

But I continued to do well throughout my school years, ignoring his warning. How could anyone be *too* smart? It was nonsense. I was smarter than any of the others in my class; the teachers said I was brilliant – beautiful *and* brilliant. I skipped two years the way other girls skipped rope and still I was at the head of my class. It was not so much a matter of learning facts but of figuring out how to answer questions; it was not just right and wrong one was dealing with, but the issue of style. In the subjects I was poor at, I sat next to one of the class crammers. I knew they would never snitch on me; it was a thrill for them just to sit next to me, to have the privilege of letting me look over their skinny shoulders.

But just when I was doing so brilliantly, about a year before graduation, my father took me out of school. He said he needed my help around the hotel. "What hotel?" I asked. "You'll find out," he winked. And so, before we knew what was happening to us, he moved us out of our ghetto flat and up to the west wing of the Hotel Majestic on Schwab Hill. How had he done it? Somehow or other he had talked himself into the job of *maître d'hôtel*. As I said before, my father was a magician, and just as he was able to transform himself from a butcher into a high-class head waiter – practically overnight – so he also magicked us out of being Jewish. He got our papers changed and we moved up to the Majestic, high above everything. A smart move. I never looked back to school.

Jack

I overheard their argument at Gestapo headquarters. One of my captors hissed, "Here you have one of Vienna's most famous bakers and not even a Jew and you beat him to a schnitzel? What does it matter, you fool, if he is a Socialist?" I shouted from my bed, weak as I was, "See here, I am not Baker Baum, but his son Hanno, only an apprentice." It did not matter to me that I might save myself by keeping my mouth closed; I only knew it was not fair to usurp my father's place, nor did I wish to coat him with the same left-wing pastry brush as myself. But my denials were worth nothing. SS Krelle even quoted Shakespeare to me – I protested too much. But why would they not listen? Didn't they realize I was the wrong generation? The answer was no, they were not in a mood to make distinctions between father and son. After all, what is the difference between a *torte* and a *tortche*? All the ingredients are there; it is just a question of size.

I was given three heavy unappetizing meals a day, a private recovery room with clean sheets and blankets, where I must have slept for days – or weeks, I could not tell – dreaming of my father and the creme caramel and the moaning *pietà* in the Wienerwald. From time to time, uniformed men came in to check on me and to ask after my health. "And how are we doing today, Herr Baum? A bit stronger in the pins, yes?" But even if he and I were one, what was the point of all this solicitude? Were they fattening us up for the kill?

Too soon I got my answer. I was to be presented as a gift from Vienna headquarters to Kommandant Koch at Buchenwald, and so I had to be well enough to make the

113

long journey. Everyone knew about Koch and his baroque tastes – but what could he want with me? Did he wish to eat me alive? On the contrary, laughed my captors, I was to feed *him*. You see, I was to become the personal pastry chef to Kommandant Koch. A great honor, they said. Not that I had the chance to refuse.

Dachau was where most political prisoners were sent – Communists, Socialists, intellectuals, teachers, workers. That is where I belonged – head shaven, in striped pajamas with a red triangle on my chest. But instead I was sent far away to the place they called Buchenwald, which means beech forest. Why so far; why separated from my comrades? Because I was going as a "privileged" prisoner, to join the circus of Kommandant Koch. I would not wear striped pajamas or an identifying triangle, nor would my head be shaved. I felt like a dancing bear. But who was this Koch and why did he need a personal pastry chef? The trip to Buchenwald was long and I was entertained with stories about him and his wife Ilse which made my blood turn to curds like slow-heated soured cream. I tried at one point to jump from the train but they rescued me unharmed. The prize performing animal must be delivered in one piece.

Koch, who was already a millionaire from the belongings of thousands of Jews under his "care," was involved in a number of lucrative projects, such as hiring out concentration camp labor to civilian employers, racketeering in food supplies earmarked for prisoners, and so on. Ilse Koch, they said, spluttering and digging one another in the ribs like small boys, was "something else." I did not care to hear but they insisted. They said I would love to meet her, or she would love to meet me, ho ho. As a matter of fact, they confided, anything in trousers would do for Ilse, although really she preferred horses. She had had a special riding hall built for her amusement, which had cost 250,000 marks and thirty lives, where she performed *haute école* exercises to the accompaniment of the Buchenwald SS band. Just wait, they snickered, you will have the time of your life.

I was put in a separate compound, more like a quaint village cottage, with high ceilings and light coming in through leaded glass windows. I was bowed and scraped to by the "lower" kitchen staff who, along with most of the inmates, did not regard me as a prisoner. Only I knew what kind of prisoner I was. I was segregated behind a barbed wire fence, to prevent raids from starving inmates, and I was barred from organized camp activities. I was neither Jewish nor starving nor shaven, and what was worse, I felt like a collaborator, stuffing the already fat Koch and his gross wife with cream puffs–their favorites. I remember thinking perhaps if they ate enough rich cakes in one sitting, they would have heart attacks and roll off their chairs and die. And then I felt sick to my stomach to have wished for such a thing. Were they not still human beings?

My only consolation was the tree which I could see from my window–an old oak around which the camp had been built, and a favorite too of the poet Goethe. Its bark was gnarled and its boughs hung down like a house of prayer around it. Many times I stood at my window and prayed to it to turn me into a normal prisoner. I knew it would never happen because the Kochs were enjoying the fruits of my labor too much to get rid of me. But I drew comfort from the tree's strength and dignity; that it could stay standing in the midst of human swill and not crumble. I imagined its roots went lower than the blood which was spilled daily and its branches reached up beyond the bit of sky above us ringed with smoke from the gas ovens. There it stood in the center of that horrible universe just as I stood in the center of my kitchen in front of my black stove. My only comrade.

I was allowed to shave myself and was therefore able to save my used razor blades. No one seemed to take notice of how many I used. At first I did not know why I was collecting them, but the dangerous little piles grew like weeds under my mattress. Night after night I dreamed about razor blades: disguised as shaved almonds, as crystallized ginger, as slivers dipped in chocolate like *Schokoladen Streusel*. I had nightmares in which my collection was discovered and I was cut to ribbons with my own razor blades. One night I woke up screaming. I had been forced, in my dream, to eat one of my own *krapfen* which had been filled with razor blade parings; I was sure I had been shredded up inside like a macaroon. I lay awake, aware of the dangerous bright eyes snuggling under me, wondering how to make use of them, when the idea came to me. I would serve a special cake to Koch filled with finely slivered razor blades. I opened my window and silently told my idea to the oak which seemed, by a certain lowering of its branches, to give a signal of approval. I went back to sleep firmly resolved. By morning the plan seemed quite mad. At night it came back to me; next morning it seemed mad again. I did not know what to do.

One day a rich strange smell came from the kitchen compound adjoining my bakehouse. It must be the *soupe du jour*, I thought, but so foul was the stench I had to cover my face with a cloth. What could it be? I was soon informed it was *la soupe humaine* – the remains of a prisoner hungry, and unwise, enough to have killed and roasted one of the SS guard dogs. I watched from my pretty leaded window as a group of the man's comrades were forced at gunpoint to eat and drink every drop of their friend's flesh and vital juices, while Kommandant Koch stood by and laughed and ate – God help me – one of my cream puffs. The men vomited against the oak tree. "How do you survive?" I asked it later, as I swilled their vomit from the base of its trunk. I put both hands on its aged bark and felt a vibration which said to me: now he has given up his humanity. Yes, yes, you may do it. And as it was an old and wise tree, I decided to act on its advice.

The occasion presented itself – Ilse's birthday, for which there was to be a tremendous celebration in the riding hall, complete with band, horses (naturally), flowers and champagne. First there would be a special private dinner. Herr Baum was ordered to provide the *pièce de résistance*. He refused their offer of additional kitchen help, saying he always preferred the solo performance. He promised a dessert to end all desserts. So be it.

The thought of killing or even hurting anyone had always been repugnant to me; but this was like being in love. I imagined myself a bride-to-be, only instead of storing up lacy little undergarments, I collected razor blades. I imagined dipping my hands into light silky peignoirs, like beaten egg whites, when I was in reality sifting through the slivers I had made. My hands were red, cut in a million places. But what did it matter when soon enough the whole world would be red? I imagined my father, also, in his white baker's uniform, walking down the aisle beside me, carrying the wedding cake, innocent of my plot. But he would discover soon enough, when all the wedding guests lay in strips on the floor.

My difficulty was working with cut hands, so progress was slow and rather painful. I allowed no one into my kitchen; the artist, I announced, must be allowed to work in peace. I made six plain cake rounds out of flour and water–why waste good ingredients–into which I had mixed the razor *streusel*. On top of the cake rounds I piled stiff meringue and over that a layer of whipped cream. In the crest of the "mountain" I set an eggshell, like a crater, which I would fill with warmed cognac. I named my mountain Vesuvius; it would erupt as it was lit and set down on the white tablecloth.

The party was in full boil. Already they had devoured the main course–whole roast suckling pig. Kommandant Koch began telling a story about a Roumanian prince who was sent to Auschwitz to be cured of his sexual excesses. When they undressed him they discovered a pornographic picture show–his whole body tattooed "depicting every form of perversion the human brain could possibly invent." Pop went another champagne cork; roars of "Oh ho ho," from the assembled guests. The prince would do nothing all day but masturbate, continued Koch. The others banged their fists on the table and, I imagined, made obscene gestures under their loose belts. "What," demanded Koch dramatically, "were they to do with this freak of nature?" The answer was, put him to work hauling sand from the sand pits as therapy–except that he was too weak to lift a wheelbarrow, so depleted was he from his games of the flesh. It was all he could do to raise his hands to his own body. They tried tying his hands, but he broke his chains and crawled along the floor to look for another warm body, only he did not succeed but died on the floor masturbating alone. There came a brief silence, then a whoop like the war cries of Indians in Hollywood movies I have seen. "Oh poor prince, poor prince," moaned Ilse, tears of laughter streaming down her swollen face.

I sent a note to the Kommandant, via the cheese course, to say I would not be serving the dessert Vesuvius myself as I had a headache and would be going directly to my quarters to rest. I gave assurances that all was in readiness and that the waiters had been briefed on the correct serving of my sparkling creation. It remained only for the assembled guests to eat heartily therefrom. God forgive me.

I said goodbye to the oak, and assured it it would be standing long after all this was destroyed. Then I rummaged in the pocket of the Kommandant's jacket which was hanging from a hook in the ante-room of the dining hall and found his keys. I sidled up to his jeep, which was in the courtyard just outside my kitchen, and inserted myself into the driver's seat. Before I knew what was happening, I was stopped at one of the exits by a sentry. How was the party going, he wanted to know. Fine fine, a splendid affair, I assured him, only one thing was forgotten: there was not enough cream for Ilse's after-dinner party tricks. I reminded him what would happen if Ilse did not get her *schlagobers* for her horses – she would have *his* private parts for her roly-poly pudding. He laughed, as I intended he should, but still inquired where I meant to buy cream at that time of night. Oh, I said, I have connections with farmers in the district, and gave him a nod and a wink. And so the gates opened and I drove through – a pastry chef, not really a prisoner like the others, in search of a barrel of *schlag*.

I drove and drove, without thinking, hearing or seeing anything but the stretch of road before me. At some point I stopped the jeep on a steep dark track and let my body fall to the ground like a sack of camp potatoes. Thinking of the Roumanian prince, I crawled in the mud to the nearest tree, around whose solid trunk I wrapped my feeble arms and wept. My hope was to reach Budapest – by some miracle – without being stopped. Budapest, second only to Vienna in its passion for whipped cream.

Gerda

The Majestic lived up to its name and reputation. There was a handsome doorman in uniform outside to greet people as they emerged from their shiny cars, and a red carpet for them to walk on up the front steps. Inside it was like a palace to my fourteen-year-old's eyes. There were open tiers which seemed to go up to the sky. At regular intervals around each tier were classical pillars, giant rubber plants in archways, and chandeliers repeating the design of the great central chandelier. At the top, from the cupola, I was convinced one could step directly out among heavenly bodies. The walls were covered in velvet the color of dried blood. (My father must have felt quite at home!) From the lobby the main staircase curled upwards and divided at the first landing where there was a mirror so large it covered the entire wall; it had claws at the bottom and the wings of an eagle at the top. In it I could watch my progress up the stairs. Indeed, wherever I went in the Majestic I saw myself reflected.

For a time I became ugly. I was fed up with the fat men and their fat cigars who were always trying to take me on their laps and pinch me and tell me I was too skinny. To avoid them I spent more and more time in the kitchen. The cooks gave me things to taste, especially sweets, and in no time at all I grew fat and my skin became covered in red spots. At least then the men let me alone. I stuck my tongue out at the mirrors and ate more sweets. I watched my father as he flirted with the maids, the kitchen staff, the guests, the wives of guests; no woman was too high or too low for him, too young or too old; any skirt excited his interest. But he never had to wangle his way in; they always held open their doors to him. At dawn he would drag himself back to our apartment and I could hear all too clearly my mother's whining for him to prove his love to her; I stuffed cotton into my ears and cream puffs into my mouth.

One day I mounted the main staircase and looked up into the cruel mirror and there I saw a beautiful girl. Who was she? She was long and svelte, her skin was as clear as the moon. I approached the mirror with suspicion. The girl smiled, and her teeth flashed like the dewdrops of the seventeen chandeliers around me. She turned sideways, and I admired her boyish flatness. She hoisted her dress above her knees, and I saw her legs above her child's ankle socks were long, shapely and covered in attractive blond fuzz. Her hair, which had been pulled back behind her ears with a virginal pink ribbon, she shook loose and let frame her face like fluffy gilt – an inheritance from plain mama, but around this face a picture frame. Of course it was I. As quickly as the baby fat and pimples had come over me, so had they disappeared. Now I knew I could eat as many sweets as I liked and still be free of fat. I had grown up.

I went to my father and asked for a job. He looked me up and down: what could I do? No daughter of his would be a chambermaid. I told him I had no intention of being a chambermaid – or any other kind of maid – but my dream was to be a waiter. And then he had a real belly laugh on me; he told me I was insane to think of such a thing. Only men or boys could be waiters at the Majestic. To think of great buxom women with their clutter and fusses working here! Ah no, it must be males, wearing elegant evening suits or tuxedos, depending on their position. Quietly, discreetly they glided in and out between tables, giving subtle messages with their flat bottoms. Women were altogether too crude; their sprawling laps should be well hidden under a damask table covering or a bedspread. He snorted and patted me on the back, as if this pronouncement on womanhood had nothing whatever to do with me. I went away and cried; and then a brilliant idea came to me. I would teach him another lesson; I would show him I was not one of those embarrassing cow-like creatures. I too could glide and I too could deliver messages with my lean hips.

I went to the room of one of the young wine waiters who I guessed to be about my size and shape. Could he help me? He was more than willing. I outlined my plan: each night he would give me lessons about wine. I must learn everything: the classifications, the properties, the tastes and the vocabulary used to describe those tastes, the method of recommending, the method of pouring; nothing should escape me about the business of drinking and serving wine. And when I had mastered the subject and the techniques to perfection – then I would be his proxy for one night.

He was a handsome, agreeable young man and he appreciated my little scheme. He also did not much like my father, so jumped at the chance to trick him in this amusing way. He also appreciated me. I was an apt pupil so life was not difficult for him. He grew more confident in his role as initiator. "Do not forget," he would say, removing my clothes, "never undress the bottle in public." And I would stand there naked while he ran his hands over me as if I were a first-growth Margaux – a wine to lay down and treasure for the future. But alas, he could not wait. He sniffed and tasted and then, rolling my liquid around in his mouth, he said, "Ah, slightly sweet and full, but with that delicious cut of acidity in the finish."

When the time arrived for my debut, I was fully primed. I dressed in the uniform which I knew already to be a perfect fit. He straightened my white bow tie for me and I put on his patent leather shoes, thinking what a good thing it was God had given me such big feet. I wore a discreet amount of rouge, mascara and lipstick; my hair curled naturally into the short mop of a young boy. My collaborator swore I would confound them all. They would think I was an androgynous angel who had descended from the cupola.

My father, at first, was too busy to notice me, but soon it was impossible that he should not. Everyone else already had. Perhaps it was the sense of daring about me which excited their curiosity, the heightened suggestiveness of a young female underneath the male attire. Men and women alike were admiring me; they were ordering twice

as much wine just to entice me to their tables. I responded
to their enquiries with knowledge and discretion. I bowed
and flicked a long graceful wrist, and not a drop of wine did
I spill. I advised the correct color, type, and vintage to go
with every dish – fish or fowl or red meat – and I did not go
wrong once. I had learned my lessons well. I flashed a dry
Loire smile (white): fragrant, luscious but uncloying. That
night I collected in tips more than all of the other wine
waiters put together.

My father watched me from the sideboard. I could see
the emotions vying for attention on his face: fury and
pride, anger and amusement, disapproval and admiration.
When it was all over I had no idea if I would be congratu-
lated or beaten. In the event, he laughed his gambler's
laugh and said, "All right, you win. You can start the wine
shift tomorrow night." But he was suspicious: where had I
learnt so much about wines? Who taught me? Whose
uniform was I wearing? I told him I stole the uniform, that
I had learned what I knew from observing and asking
questions of the staff. Whether or not he believed me, I do
not know but he began watching me more closely.

My father had many friends – politicians, officials, book-
ies, celebrities; Jews and Anti-Semites alike – who came to
his tables at the Majestic, to eat and to play cards
afterwards. All it took was a special nod or wink to the
wine waiters and these people were served with extra
care – portions were heaped up, wine glasses filled more
regularly. One evening I saw the new Minister of Jewish
Affairs. He crooked his finger in my father's direction; my
father went instantly to his side. The man whispered
something in my father's ear as he bent over his table. He
eyed me as he spoke. My father looked nervous. He twirled
his mustache, then his thumbs behind his back; he rocked
on his heels. Finally he shook his head and strode away,
Burgundy red in the face. I knew the man must have
made some remark about me. "So the new Minister finds
me attractive, does he?" I said later, but he replied, "What
do you know about these things?" and then, "Never mind
about it." But when it happened again the following
week – this time, evidently, the Minister offered him a sum
he could not afford to refuse – his response changed

dramatically. After all, I was only to be introduced, nothing more. And was not Gerda a girl who could look after herself?

And so it began, the introductions, the private meeting rooms, the deals, the haggling over a price for his prize heifer. My father entertained offers only from those in the highest positions: his wares should not be cheapened. Sometimes I knew he experienced a pang of regret when he watched his cronies follow me to an appointed meeting room, but there was nothing to stop it now. My mother knew nothing.

As for me, I was never in a position to consider if it was something I wished to do with my life – it simply happened to me. Beauty is a responsibility, after all; one does not throw it away on the nobodies of this world. My father's customers paid through the nose.

Jack

When I was a child my mother gave me a book with the title *Rudolph the Bear Who Said No*. It was a timely gift as I was going through a period of saying no: to porridge, soup, even to puddings and favorite cakes I would shake my head and clamp my mouth shut. My mother warned I would shrivel up to a dried pea and die, but still I would not "Open Sesame." The book concerned a round bear named Rudolph who tried but could not say the simple word yes. No matter what anyone said to him he would reply automatically and quite helplessly: no no no no *no*, to even the nicest things. Eventually his mother threw him out of her house and he was forced to wander the roads of the countryside. He knocked at the doors of farmhouses seeking a bite to eat and was greeted by friendly farmers' wives who looked down at him and said, "Why hello little bear, would you like some fresh cream and honey?" as if they could read his mind. He was very hungry and opened his mouth to say yes, but a growly no came out in its place. One of the farmers' wives swept Rudolph off her doorstep with a broom and accused him of being ungrateful.

And that is what the proprietors of those small Pest bakeshops did to me as soon as my mouth was opened. Whether I said yes, no, please or thank you, they took notice only of my German accent. They either ducked behind their counters in fear or shooed me out of their doors like Rudolph. In the story, as it comes back to me, Rudolph the Bear sat down on a rock and cried until a fairy godmother flew down to him from the heavens and questioned him. Was he repentant and did he truly wish to say yes? He nodded his head very sincerely and she touched him with her magic wand on his furry forehead; a tear escaped down the side of his nose. Then he looked up and she was gone but when he opened his mouth a small yes noise escaped from his lips. "Yes, yes yes yes yes *yes*," cried Rudolph, bursting with joy, skipping down the road and off the edge of the last page of my book. "Will you now be good?" asked my mother. "Yes," I replied. "Yes yes yes," to whatever she put in front of me–so that I grew quite stout, not unlike Rudolph the Bear.

I felt there was nothing I could say to convince these people they should not be afraid of me; that they should give me a job instead of brushing me angrily out of their doors. What could I say, after all? That I had been in a camp myself, so I understood? But how could that be, if I was not a Jew? Oh, a political prisoner–so much the worse–a liability. And how did I escape from this camp? It was a highly unusual exit. By then the futility, even the absurdity, of my plot had dawned on me. My razor-stuffed Vesuvius had most likely succeeded in, at most, cutting a few pairs of greasy lips and precipitating a volley of bloody curses. But the intent was enough. No, they did not need a man like me working for them. They had enough with their yellow stars and armbands, without a murderous fugitive from the camps.

But if the Jewish bakers wanted proof of my Jewishness, the Gentiles wanted proof of my non-Jewishness, which I also could not, in good conscience, give them. "You are not by any chance Jewish, are you?" the owner of one shop asked, looking me in the nose. My nostrils quivered, partly from such close scrutiny, but also from the aroma rising from the warm bread inches away from this same nose. I rushed out of the shop without answering. You see, I had not eaten in a week.

I crossed the Franz-Joseph Bridge over the Danube into Buda. After walking for a time, I found myself in front of the Hotel Majestic, where prosperous-looking people were sitting at ornate white tables. A red scalloped awning protected them from the summer sun and window-boxes full of red geraniums dotted the face of the hotel. To look at this scene of lazy colorful summer ease, these people with their pipes and straw hats and white dresses, this white hotel glowing in the sunshine with its splashes of red at every window – to look at this, who could remember a Buchenwald? Perhaps I had been dreaming.

I dragged myself past a man in a white suit with a white goatee, the remains of a piece of white fish on his white plate, a glass of white wine next to his plate. My head ached from so much brightness, and from hunger too. I walked around the back of the hotel to the kitchen entrance, pushed open the white screen door with my belly. Who could have known how empty it was? A superior individual asked me if I knew how to bake and I replied in the affirmative: I had done my apprenticeship at Baum's Bakeshop in Vienna; perhaps he had heard of it? He raised an eyebrow. I said my name was Schmidt, just in case the Germans had followed me. "Is that so?" asked the *maître d'hôtel*. He looked me up and down but did not ask any further awkward questions. "Well then, let us see what you can do," he said, showing me to a cleared working space in the kitchen, and inviting me to create a typical Viennese dessert there and then. My brain began twirling like a cake stand. I asked, please might I rest for a few moments and perhaps have something to eat and drink.

I was brought a glass of beer and a bowl of *gulyás*. The spicy paprika made me feel rather ill, or perhaps food and drink of any sort would have been a shock to my starved system. However, the chance of work caused me to focus my attention. I asked the taskmaster if he wanted perhaps something simple – a *Gugelhupf*, or something a bit richer, say a *Linzertorte*. He pursed his lips. "What about ... a *Spanische Windtorte*?" he mewed, expecting, I felt sure, to confuse me. But I surprised him by saying, "Oh yes, the *Windtorte*, one of Demel's creations, considered rather vulgar at Baum's, but easily duplicated if you wish." He turned on his heels and left me there. I wondered if there really was a position or if he did this for his amusement. But as I worked one of the cooks informed me that they were indeed in need of a new pastry chef since the last one had disappeared. Disappeared? Oh yes, she said, disappeared; sent to a labor camp.

When I had finished piping *schlag*, adding rosettes and violets, the *maître d'hôtel* returned to inspect my work. First he twirled his mustache and then he twirled the *Windtorte* around on its silver cake stand, whose stem was a flower-shaped female, saying "hmmm" to himself, and then he cut into the cake which, if I may say so myself, was of a lovely texture and appearance; the aroma caused me to catch my breath. Finally, he took a piece on the end of his silver fork and munched it like a rather fastidious rabbit. He stood up, wiped his mouth with a damask napkin and put out his hand. "Very good," he said, as if admitting defeat, and introduced me in the kitchen as the Majestic's new pastry chef.

There came to be rumors concerning the mysterious Hanno Schmidt who appeared from out of the sky looking like a bloated camp victim, but who nevertheless produced a *Spanische Windtorte* at the manager's whim. "Come, come, you can tell us," said the cooks, becoming friendly. "Are you the one they say tried to slit the gizzard of the fiend Koch with razor blades and then drove out of the main gate as if you were going visiting?" "Of course not," I lied, beating more air into my egg whites. But at night I remembered the razor blades so clearly, they winked at me in my dreams, and I imagined Vesuvius erupting violently like a real volcano. I woke up in a terrible sweat. It was a comfort to me they did not ask too many questions at the Majestic; that they were above such things as whether a person was Jewish, or a Communist, or where he came from. For their money, they needed someone to do the job and that was all that mattered. Some day, I told myself, I would make strudel for the workers—and *Spanische Wind-torten*; why not? But until then I would suffer to practice my art for the patrons of the Majestic. A pity, but a temporary arrangement. "Who needs to go to Vienna with Herr Schmidt here?" said my customers, thumping me on the back or nudging me in the belly.

The Majestic's dining room was said to be filled with rich Jews and Fascists sitting table to table, elbow to elbow; but I knew nothing. I worked hard, practised a strudel dough which would surpass even that of Herr Baum of Vienna. Only one night a week did I leave the Majestic, and that was to attend Socialist Party meetings in a basement in the old quarter of Pest. Once my comrades discovered who I really was and what I had done, they welcomed me with much hearty enthusiasm. On many an occasion I smuggled pastries to them from the kitchen of the Majestic. Though the political situation in Budapest worsened during that year – it was 1944 – for me life was still rather uneventful. I kept my nose in my copper bowls.

Gerda

Most of the men I served at the Majestic knew nothing about wines. They gave the impression of knowing, with their pompous swilling and gargling, but they did not fool me. This one, however, was different. I had my eye on him from the moment he came into the dining room, wearing a raincoat and carrying a rucksack on his back. He removed these; underneath was a tasteful, expensive suit. He had full lips and eyes like braised meatballs, but his jaw and shoulders were square. Such contradictions were interesting to me. He was foreign, surely, but from where? He had come in for a late lunch – it was around two o'clock. He ordered a simple meal and a bottle of Pfalz to go with it, one of the only two Wachenheimer Mandelgarten Scheurebe Auslese we had left in the cellar. I brought it to him in an ice bucket, showed him the label, uncorked the bottle as deftly as ever, poured a small amount and stepped back while he tasted. He sipped. Only then did he look up at me and smile. "A fine wine," he said, to which I replied, "You do not find many customers who appreciate it. It is not expensive enough." He laughed, showing his teeth. And then I showed mine.

When I returned to refill his glass I took the opportunity to ask where he was from. Sweden, he said, but he had lived in the last ten years in many places: America, South Africa, Haifa. And what was his business in Budapest? He looked into his glass. "Import-export. Pickled cucumbers, goose breasts, that sort of thing," he said, and he looked quite unhappy; I guessed his heart was not sufficiently in the goose breast. But I was sure there must be something else, and I was right. When I returned for a third time he showed me a piece of paper and asked if I could direct him to the address written on it. It was the Jewish Community Office on Sip Street. Ah, so he is Jewish, I thought. This was getting more interesting by the minute. I told him I would personally show him the way. He protested but I assured him it was no trouble at all. I changed out of my waiter's uniform and joined him on the red carpet outside the hotel. I too wore an old raincoat.

I was not used to walking side by side with a man. The Swede remarked he had never before encountered a wine waitress; they did not exist in his country. "Nor in this one," I said. "I am an exception to the rule."

"Indeed," he said. For a time we said nothing; then, to break the awkward silence, I said, "So you are Jewish."

"Not exactly," he replied.

"Oh?" I raised a thin eyebrow. "Yes or no?"

"Actually, my great grandfather was a Hungarian Jew, but he converted to Lutheranism when he arrived in Sweden. So that makes me–let me see–precisely one-sixteenth Jewish. Does that count?"

"No, I don't think so," I said. "Not even Hitler would be interested in you."

"A pity, in some ways," he said. "And you?"

The question caught me totally by surprise. Of course I should have been prepared, but I wasn't. I shrugged and said no, but I was almost immediately sorry. There was something about him that made me want to tell him the truth–he seemed as equivocal as I was–but I was not used to the exercise and the moment was lost. "Of course I have sympathies," I said. He nodded. We were beginning to sniff each other out.

"Come," I said. "I will show you the tourist attractions along the way." I pointed out the Varos Ligit, Budapest's famous fake park. "It is entirely artificial, but rather pretty." From the park we walked down Andrassy Street past rows of grand villas where the rich were still living it up behind their swag curtains like there was no tomorrow. We came to the square with the statue of the Archangel Gabriel holding the double cross of Hungary aloft in his outstretched wings. It was covered in bird droppings. My Swedish friend told me the latest news: the SS and the

Hungarian Arrowcross together had slaughtered 20,000 Jews in Hungary's new territory. It didn't surprise me. More and more Jews were scurrying like mice into this one mousehole called Hungary, thinking they would be safe from the cat's claws.

I said, "They believe Hitler will be defeated before he gets here."

"And you doubt it?" he asked.

I hadn't really thought about such things but now I was thinking fast. "I see no signs of a Nazi defeat. With so many Jews coming here, it only makes their work easier. The Jews will be cornered, trapped, and cooked – a nice little snack for the Arrowcross and the Nazis. But, tell me, what makes you so interested in the fate of the Jews?"

"In Haifa I lived in a Jewish house, I met many wonderful people there who told me of the awful suffering in Germany, and the more I heard, the more restless I became. How could I just sit there in my little cage from morning until night – I was working in a bank – while such things went on? On one occasion, a friend of mine, a Jew with a Swedish wife, was detained in Berlin by the Gestapo. I was getting ready to go to Berlin to try to help them when the Swedish Embassy stepped in. It made me realize things can be done, but only if one is in the right position."

"And you are in the right position, as an exporter of pickled goose breasts?"

"Cucumbers," he corrected. "My partner is a Jewish refugee who lives in Sweden. He is very worried about his family, who are still living here."

"So he sent you as his bloodhound."

"I agreed to come. I wanted to do something myself."

"And what do you plan to do, an army of one?"

"I don't know. If nothing else, get as many Jews as possible out of here and to safety in Sweden."

We were crossing the Margrit Bridge over to Pest. I pointed out the Margrit Island with its mud baths. "You lie down on a waterproof sheet and hot mud is plastered over you. Then you are swathed in sheets so you cannot move hand or foot. You feel there is nothing left but to die a painless, rather warm pleasant death. But you do not actually die. Eventually you are allowed to get out and you are washed and stretched out to cool in the air like a wet noodle. Afterwards you sleep, for days and days, before you can face the world, and then finally you get up completely refreshed. Reborn. Your skin is glowing. There are people who swear by it."

"It sounds like being buried alive," he said.

"What did you do in America?" I asked, changing the subject.

"I was a student of architecture at the University of Michigan."

"Why did you choose America?"

"It was my grandfather's choice, he arranged everything in our family. He had been Ambassador to the United States, so he knew all about American universities. He thought the Eastern colleges were too exclusive, the Western ones too progressive, and the Southern ones too restrictive. The Midwest seemed just right to him and since the University of Michigan had an excellent reputation in architecture, that was his choice."

"You had no say in the matter?"

He laughed. "None at all. You would understand better if you knew Grandfather Gustav." I thought: How is a man who submits to the will of his grandfather and his boss going to save the Jews of Budapest? I noticed his hair was already quite thin on top.

"So what makes you think you can do something here?" I challenged.

"My company–the Central European Trading Company–is already helping the Red Cross to get food supplies into other European countries. But here, I don't know. I must think of something else, something much bigger. A rescue plan."

"Pity the Jews here don't all have Swedish wives like your friend in Berlin–then the Swedish Embassy could help them," I said.

His eyes lit up like the lights over the Varos. He told me I was not only the most beautiful woman he had ever met but the most brilliant. He would go back to Sweden and ask to be taken on at the Embassy. Just like that? I raised an eyebrow. A big talker, clearly. But he seemed very sure of himself. His family was filthy with diplomats, he said. He shared many of their talents. Among other things, he spoke five languages fluently. I said I liked a man who knew how to make deals.

We were outside the Jewish Community Center. I wished him luck. He said talking with me had inspired him, in more ways than one. He would discuss things with his partner and try to get backing from the Swedish Embassy. If he could secure a position in Budapest, would I work with him on a rescue effort? I shrugged my shoulders; who could promise anything these days? He could, he said.

"We'll see," I said, pulling down my hat and walking away.

Jack

How the unfortunate pattern of my life should so repeat itself, I cannot say, but having escaped from Koch and Buchenwald, I now found myself in the position of personal pastry chef to none other than Adolf Eichmann; out of the frying pan into the fire, as the expression goes. He had moved into the Majestic with his entire staff to supervise the "final solution." It was for me to satisfy the sweet tooth of this dried fish with his cold silver spectacles. Woe was me!

He was undiscriminating but pretentious, with a weakness, like Koch, for cream puffs. But he liked to make an impression, so when he entertained other high-ranking Arrowcross or SS officers, he asked for the most ostentatious concoctions, such as the Austrian *Rehrücken*-in German, "saddle of venison." The cake was baked in a special fluted mold with deep indentations to approximate the ribs of the animal, a decoration of almonds suggesting the larding of salt pork or bacon. Of course, it was a most ridiculous object, but it brought a round of applause from Eichmann and his cronies.

In general, when I knew an order was from him I religiously substituted margarine or even lard for butter and used half the required number of eggs, since I knew he would never know the difference. Why waste good ingredients on a Nazi? Sometimes I would use twice the amount of sugar, praying it would rot his teeth. But whatever I did I always received his frigid compliments, proving his palate was as numb as his heart. As my mother would have said, this was a man too skinny to be trusted.

One day I went to hear him speak in the Jewish ghetto. I

wanted to know what airs that flat sponge gave himself in public, how he disguised his poisoned words by folding honey into them. He strutted out of the kindergarten – now Gestapo headquarters – flanked on both sides by his SS guards like a double row of rosettes. The whole neighborhood fell silent – thousands had come to listen to him. Eichmann cleared his throat and smiled; he looked to me like a pale green *petit four*. "You do not need to be afraid of the Germans," he whispered in German. "It is true we are strict. We are efficient. But anyone who follows orders will do well. If the Hungarian Jews behave themselves, there will be no deportations. You will receive enough food. No one will starve. The accommodation of the Jews here is no worse than that of German soldiers during manoeuvres; it will do your health a world of good. You must remember the German people also suffer from hardships and lack of food. But we share, we are fair. Those who obey orders will have no complaints."

I was leaning against a plane tree for support, thinking that its roots probably reached to Eichmann's feet. How I wished that gentle tree could will its roots to rise up out of the ground and beat him to a pulp, as I did certain fruits and berries with my rolling pin to make his puddings. "Such a gentleman," said the lady standing next to me. "Maybe things are not so bad after all," another one said, and a third, "He doesn't sound like a liar to me, they're just trying to frighten us." I wanted to interrupt them and say, "Do not believe a word he says. He eats Jews with whipped cream for breakfast," but I did not. Instead, I walked back to the Majestic to prepare his *Rehrücken*, praying for the Russians to hurry up.

I went that night to my Party meeting, bringing with me a box of yesterday's poppy seed *kipfels*. There was an air of celebration among my young comrades. They said the Red Army had broken through German and Hungarian lines to the south of Budapest. We drank a toast to Marshal Malinovsky's Second Ukrainian Front. And another, and another. I reminded my comrades we were not yet liberated, but they assured me the Russians would soon be victorious. They would fight valiantly against the Nazi swine. I began wondering, with some apprehension, what sorts of desserts our future benefactors would enjoy. Perhaps I could begin trying out a few things on Eichmann: *Pryanichki* instead of *Indianerkrapfen*, *Blinchiki* instead of *Kaiserschmarren*. It would be my small, but sweet, revenge.

My comrades were getting quite carried away with themselves, suggesting I resurrect my razor blade trick for Eichmann and his henchmen – or on second thought, perhaps arsenic would be more effective. But I reasoned with them. Who did they think would get a bayonet in the stomach as Eichmann fell face forward into his creme caramel? Hanno Baum of the pseudonym Schmidt, a plump cherry on the tip of a spear. No thank you, I said. They found this quite hilarious and fell to stroking my tummy in its white apron as if to make the imagined wound better. "There, there," they crooned drunkenly, as to a child.

But I had had enough of them for one evening; it was time to go "home" to sleep off what I had drunk. Soon we will be drinking vodka, I thought, and everything will be wonderful again. Again? When were things wonderful before? "No," I criticized myself, "that is a reactionary position, Herr Schmidt, whatever-your-name-is, we cannot have that." Oh I was as tipsy as a *Baba*. I stopped in front of my favorite weeping willow which had not yet lost its foliage though its long fronds were quite yellow and dry. I sneaked under its boughs and wrapped my arms around its middle, told it the story of my sad life in a close whisper. I said, "My name used to be Hanno Baum. Formerly I was a guest at the Hotel Buchenwald where I baked for Kommandant Koch and his lovely wife Ilse. Now my name is Hanno Schmidt and I bake for Obersturmbannführer Eichmann at the Hotel Majestic, who is not so much a cream puff as Koch, more of a lemon tart, although he too is partial to cream puffs. Two of a kind: one fat, one skinny. But I, what am I, I asked the tree, thumping my chest as if it were a bread board. I am a coward, I whispered. And then I laughed and laughed, and then I hid my face, which had sprouted sudden tears, in the willow's long crinkly hair.

I crawled up the back stairway to my small room under the eaves, still giggling and making rude noises from all the beer I had drunk, but when I opened my door and saw Eichmann sitting there in my cane chair, I became instantly sober. His white stick and metal spectacles flashed in the moonlight which shone through the window. I switched on the light and blinked. He did not. Perhaps he is a lizard, I thought, and a half-giggle escaped me. He gestured for me to shut the door behind me. Then his lips stretched sideways into a smile and he put his white gloved hand up to his ear, like a policeman directing traffic. He said he had enjoyed my creme caramel that evening so much he wanted to present his compliments to me in person. "So, let me congratulate you, Herr *Baum*," he said, emphasizing my real name. Baum? I jumped backwards, bumping my *derrière* on the doorknob. I thought, it will be blue and black tomorrow. But I had bigger worries than my bottom. Eichmann had me trapped under that roof with not a mousehole to escape into.

"There is no reason to panic," he said, taking off his gloves, finger by finger, and smoothing them in his lap. "We do not plan to remove you from the kitchen of the Majestic since you are such an important person there. I simply wished you to know that we know who you are and that we are watching you. Do you follow me, Baum? You are doing an excellent job; if you were to disappear too suddenly, many people would be quite upset. No, you must continue as you are. Only a small warning, Baum, no funny business with razor blades. And I would suggest not attending any more of your Communist meetings." He flexed his chicken-bone fingers. The glove fell to the floor and he pushed it towards me with the tip of his stick, indicating that I should pick it up. However, I miscalculated and stepped forward directly onto the glove, depositing on it a large black footmark. As I bent down to pick it up at last, he rapped me smartly on the back and called me a clumsy oaf. "See to it the glove is spotless before you return it to me," he said. And he clicked his heels and said, "Good night, Herr *Schmidt*." His eyes, behind his glasses, looked like the bitten-off ends of thin chocolate mints.

Gerda

A year later Adolf Eichmann came to see for himself what was what in Budapest. He commandeered the Majestic—offices, rooms, suites, kitchen—for his Kommando unit. He made himself at home. Everyone on the staff hated him and tried to keep out of his way. I was no exception but it was my job to be of service; my father saw to it I did not shirk my duties. One unfortunate move and we could find ourselves across the river. The downtown branch of Eichmann's Kommando was in the back wing of Pest County Hall on the eastern bank of the Danube, disguised as the International Warehouse and Transport Ltd, but known more accurately as the Hungarian Jew-Liquidating Company. It was only a hop, skip and jump from our safe Schwab Hill.

When the deportations began, Eichmann threw the first of his infamous parties at the Majestic, at which I presided as wine waiter. He invited Ferenczy, Endre, Baky and others of his Hungarian collaborators. They drank champagne flown in from France; they fondled women, also flown in from France. Eichmann sat in the corner, with his silver spectacles and his forehead glistening, and watched his performing imports. From time to time he would crack his whip and make the women crawl on all fours with their skirts hitched up—he called them sows and bitches—and he ordered his Arrowcross underlings to crawl behind, lapping at them like dogs. It took no superior intelligence to see how they disgusted him. Yes, he hated women, but it didn't stop him from being in love with me. He couldn't take his eyes from me in my wine waiter's uniform with the precise white bow tie and the three little white buttons down my waistcoat. Compared with me his fat French whores could crawl straight into Jew-ovens. I was his Venus and Adonis rolled into one.

I went to my father. I asked to be relieved of my duties to this master of perversion. I asked for his protection. I reminded him of our Jewishness; surely he must draw the line somewhere? He pulled nervously at his lapels, then at his mustache and drew himself up; what was I saying? No, Eichmann was our most important guest; he must be treated like a prince. Prince, hah! I laughed and spat. Nazi runt, queer, sadist, freak; that, I said, was what I thought of him. My father slapped me hard across the face; how dare I say such things? He pointed out of the window to the Jew-Liquidating Company; did I prefer to live out my days there? I shook my head. He reached out to touch my red cheek but I turned away from him. I thought: no man who crawls up Adolf Eichmann's backside can call himself my father.

Not long after that, Wallenberg reappeared on the red carpet. It had been over a year since he first came to the hotel to drink his Pfalz. I was just peering out from the velvet curtains when I saw him standing there with his old rucksack. He wore a long leather coat and an Anthony Eden hat. I was so happy to see him I ran out the door and down the steps and only just restrained myself from throwing myself into his arms. I shook his hand. Perhaps he would save me from Eichmann and his obscene parties and from my bullying and cowardly father. But it was I who had to protect him. I told him he must leave at once unless he fancied sharing a room with Adolf Eichmann. He laughed. No, he would go to the Embassy, but first he wanted to make sure I knew he had kept his promise; better late than never.

I lit a cigarette and said, "I knew you would come eventually."

I took him to a private room where we could talk. "What is Eichmann doing here?" he asked.

"Overseeing the deportations. Already seventy percent of the Jewish population have gone."

He showed me his gun. "Not that I will ever use it—it's just to give me courage." I was happy to see him.

But what had taken him so long? He explained it had proved much more difficult to get support than he had imagined. He had run into disapproval from the Swedish diplomatic officials and from Stockholm's Chief Rabbi, who found his approach to diplomacy too hot-headed. I laughed; and what did that mean? He said, "It means I asked for complete authority to save lives, even if it should involve pay-offs." In the end the Americans had intervened. Herschel Johnson, the American Minister in Stockholm, took him to the Bellmansro, Stockholm's Majestic. "So you're the gutsy young man who has volunteered to go to Budapest, the hyenas' lair," he twanged, and by five in the morning he had clapped Raoul on the shoulder and sent him off with diplomatic *carte blanche* and bags of money. Swedish approval followed, though reluctantly, and he was appointed First Secretary to the Swedish Legation. Now even the Chief Rabbi relented and blessed him. "Those who are on a mission for good deeds are protected from harm," he intoned. He had forced their hand, but he was here.

But what about me – what was I doing serving the German Kommando? I explained my position, how my father kept me there. Of course I didn't let on how far my duties went. He said it was an outrage; he offered me a position working with him. It was a great effort, but I knew I had to say no. As private wine waiter to Eichmann, I was in a unique position to get information; I was there but not really there. Words, as he must know, were often spoken in front of servants quite openly, so that I was privy to secret conversations. For example, Endre, the Under-Secretary of State at the Interior Ministry, had been on a recent inspection tour of the camps and I had heard him say gaily, "The camps are like sanitaria; at last the Jews are getting some fresh air instead of living like animals." And they had drunk to Eichmann's good health. I had also heard Otto Hunsche, one of Eichmann's henchmen, in a conversation with a Jewish leader who had come to protest against conditions on the transports. "Stop bothering me with horror stories," he snapped. "In any single transport there are no more than fifty or sixty dying on the way." So, I concluded, I would be most useful to him staying right where I was. Who else would know when the early morning transports were to leave, the secret round-ups begin? Only I would be in a position to get this information from Eichmann. He looked very unhappy. I could see he was struggling between allegiance to me and to his rescue mission, but I never had any doubt who would win. It was not a fair contest.

By the end of his first week in Budapest he had re-designed and issued five thousand new protective passports. "Look at these, would you," snarled Eichmann, producing a batch from his files. The new passports were quite enormous, printed on heavy paper with the yellow and blue Swedish flag on one side and the triple crown of Sweden on the other. Each document was numbered with an official ministerial seal impressed in red wax and with the Royal signature – which I suspected was Raoul's. It stated the holder was under the protection of the Swedish legation. "These are all over Budapest," said Eichmann, waving one of them in the air. I snatched it from him and put it in my pocket. "What are you doing?" he snarled, like a dog whose dinner has been taken away from him. "A souvenir," I said sweetly, biting his cold waxy ear. Now, especially, I had to keep him amused with my tricks.

Raoul published a report describing in detail the horrors of the deportations; and this, in turn, inspired the Jewish executive committee in Budapest to issue an underground leaflet appealing to the Hungarian people to put a stop to them. To our surprise, Regent Horthy agreed and gave his support. He allowed all five thousand of the *Schutzpasses* to be distributed, he sacked Endre and Baky, he put a stop to the deportations, and he signed an early armistice with the Russians. It seemed as if the war would soon be over in Hungary, that Eichmann would be out of business and Raoul would be free to return to his family in Sweden by Christmas. Next morning, indeed, we discovered the Majestic had been abandoned by the Germans; Eichmann, we heard, had been recalled by Himmler, awarded an Iron Cross and sent on vacation to Endre's castle near the Austro-Hungarian border. I met Raoul at the Arizona Club for a celebration. Afterwards we took a walk together, quite openly, and there were people ripping off their armbands and dancing in the streets. Already he had proved himself a magician, with powers far greater than my father's.

But our celebrations were premature; we should have known it was too easy a victory. Within a week German music was being broadcast on the radio and then voices began announcing the names of well-known Arrowcross mobsters. These were Hungarian Fascist Party members – the most extreme of all right-wing groups. They were seizing power, propped up by the Germans. In fact, the Germans were taking over. They re-occupied the radio station with a few rifle shots and that was that. Horthy's son was taken hostage. Horthy caved in, abandoning his country to the Fascist dogs and allowing himself to be spirited away across the border. The Germans installed Ferencz Szalasi as "Leader of the Nation," and by the end of the following week Eichmann himself was back at the Majestic. "You see," he told a group of Jewish leaders who were quickly summoned to the Majestic, "I am back. Our arm is still long enough to reach you."

"Welcome back, Adolf," I crooned, holding out my long arms to him.

Jack

When an orthodox Jew went by on the stairway at Party
headquarters, one of my comrades pointed and said, "Look,
there goes another Swede." That was the big joke around
Pest. I thought it was quite funny, myself. Of course it was
not funny what the Arrowcross were doing to these
innocent people – pulling them out of their apartments by
their long sidewhiskers, leading them through the streets
with guns pressing into their backs to St Stephen's Square
or the brick factory at Obuda. From there, we knew they
would be deported to the camps, either labor or exter-
mination; which would depend on whether their muscles
were stringy and resilient, or soft and sticky.

As I worked at my hot oven, I tried to convince myself
that a particularly delicious pastry for breakfast would put
Obersturmbannführer Eichmann in a good mood and
therefore incline him against a deportation that day. I was
fooling myself. More likely the reverse was true; when I
served him hot coffee with milk, fresh *Semmeln* with plum
jam and stewed prunes, then the transport ran more
efficiently and brutally. Oh dear. I knew I should have left
the hotel, refused to work for such a man; but where was I,
a German, to go? The Majestic kitchen was a hot prison in
which we regarded one another with mutual disrespect.
Which of us would have the courage to serve Eichmann a
cup of poison and then walk away down the red carpet,
wondering on which step the bullet would come for us? It
was our only dream of bravery, but it meant suicide and so
it remained in our dreams. Only this Swede, Wallenberg,
whom everyone had heard about, carried out his dreams.
He seemed to have no fear and because of this, there were

no consequences. He went around Budapest with his protective passports bringing people back from the dead. Everyone knew the stories; perhaps they were only stories, I do not know. But we needed them to be true, we needed to believe someone would rise out of his own fear like a soufflé out of its basin. We heard how he followed the deportations – how he knew when they were going was also a mystery – and before the trains had a chance to leave he set up his tables right there on the tracks between trains and made an announcement: anyone with a Swedish passport should step down from the transport. The people watched him from behind their tiny barred windows. And then the doors of the train would open. Some came forward, others stayed behind – because it took too much effort to find a piece of paper; or they did not understand; or were too old; or they were looking forward to the ride; who knows the reasons? But the ones who stepped down were eager to live and they found papers of all kinds – scraps, notes, newspapers, pieces of books, checks, anything – and they took their places in the queue and held their breath and prayed. And if the officer in charge was not looking too carefully, Wallenberg would say, "Yes, yes, okay, let's not waste time. Next!" and another would be saved. At the end of each of these sessions the saved ones would follow him down the track like baby ducks and he would lead them back to Budapest. They would not look back to the cattle cars making screeching noises, preparing to leave in the other direction. One of our cooks had a relative who had twice been brought back by Wallenberg in this manner.

Szalasi, the new Arrowcross leader, had ordered an international ghetto to be set up. All Jews protected by neutral legations were to be herded together into one area of Pest, in buildings marked by yellow stars and the flags of their hosts. These were the Safe Houses. But not far away was the other ghetto, where the majority of Budapest's Jews still lived. Here the Arrowcross roamed the streets stealing, beating, raping; leaving the bodies of their victims naked and bleeding in the gutters. By now there were already rumors of a Russian approach, but this only made the Arrowcross more desperate to do away with every Jew they could find, using more and more violent and horrible methods. Late at night I would go for a walk to the river, using my uniform as protection, and I would hear the machine guns at the wharves on the other side. How long, I asked myself, would it take a body to turn into a block of ice after it had been thrown into the Danube? It was very very cold.

But Wallenberg was as busy as a baker transferring as many Jews as he could from the ghetto into the Safe Houses. When there were no more houses available he bought more. By now there were seven thousand Jews under his protection.

But then the worst thing happened. Trains could no longer be used to transport Jews; they were needed to bring food and military supplies for the German army. Eichmann brooded for two days – he ate nothing, not even his cream puffs – and then he rose from his chair in the dining room and I could see the evil light of inspiration in those colorless eyes behind those cold silver spectacles. He was like a mad chef, concocting a dish so foul the hardest stomach would regurgitate it. His new scheme was the *Vernichtung*, or Final Solution, and it meant the remaining Jews of Pest would be forced to walk to the Austrian border. These became known as the death marches.

Gerda

Szalasi's first act was to make all protective passports invalid; defunct, *kaput*. He sent Raoul a personal message to this effect. Raoul called it "a love note from Szalasi" and tore it up. That is what I call style. But he would be impotent without them; what to do? He flouted the ban and behaved as if nothing whatever had happened. He continued to send out volunteer crews to record the names and ID numbers of Jews; signed passports with a bigger and bigger flourish of his pen—such was the Royal signature. He said the ban would not last, and they couldn't stop him anyway. Sure enough, the next day, Count Kemeny himself made a live radio broadcast: protective passports issued by and authorized by neutral legations were once again legal and valid. How did he know? How did he wangle this one?

The answer came from Eichmann. He was furious. He said, in confidence, the Swede was behind it—the Swede and the wife of the foreign minister.

"Oh? What has she got to do with it?" I asked innocently.

"She's a Jew, and pregnant. Wallenberg has been seeing her," he said. "He spent six hours at her house yesterday. And now this." He cracked his knuckles. She had accompanied her husband to the radio station to make certain he delivered his message. Someone had persuaded her to take a keen interest in the reinstatement of the protective passport order.

She was quite a pretty little thing, with hair like a brillo pad and the personality of a chicken liver. I imagined Raoul taking her chubby hand in his, looking into her frightened wet eyes. Did she realize the Germans were losing the war; soon it would be over and the Russians would be in power? And then – how would she like to see her child's father hanging from a rope? Or face a firing squad? Oh no, she would not. Pause for effect. If Kemeny could be persuaded to rescind the passport ban, then he might be treated more leniently. He, Wallenberg, would do what he could. "You will?" she asks, looking up into his eyes like a Madonna with indigestion. "Of course," he whispers, brushing away those fat little tears with those sensitive lips of his. Such are the trials of a hero.

Meanwhile Eichmann produced his master plan for the Final Solution – the *Vernichtung*. The very idea of it seemed to make him grow; or perhaps it was his new pair of elevator jackboots. He went personally to oversee the death marches – that is how they became known – to make sure everything went smoothly; that the weak and wizened creatures who could hardly stand up straight should be kept going at a good clip; that if they were unable to do so, they should be allowed to "rest" on the frost-thick ground of a field or a market square. After all, why waste bullets on them?

Only Wallenberg was in his way now, he said, grinding his teeth and fiddling in his pockets, as if those shriveled sausages of his were hand grenades he would lob across the Danube into Raoul's headquarters. Somehow or other the Swede always seemed to know when the marchers were leaving: how did he know, who was informing him, he stormed – as if I should know the answer. He described how the now familiar crocodile of black Swedish embassy cars always caught up with the marchers, how his arch enemy emerged from the front car and jumped into the middle of the nearest crowd and announced, very loudly, in German, how he had orders to take three hundred people with him; or five or eight hundred. He would read from a list of almost certainly made-up names and gesture for people to follow him. No one was able to stop him. "I'm Raoul Wallenberg," he would say, and they would follow him like he was Moses.

Jack

Eichmann ordered me to produce a *Sachertorte* for the next night's dinner. Very good, I said, a classic choice. But to whom would the *Sachertorte* be served? You see, it mattered so much, for I could always contrive to make my cakes look nice by cosmetic effect, when even just beneath the surface the ingredients were quite rotten. As I have said before, why waste a fresh egg on a Nazi? But when Eichmann informed me "the Jew-dog Wallenberg" and the lovely daughter of the *maître d'hôtel* were coming as his guests, naturally the picture changed. Not only would I use the freshest possible ingredients, but I would make the surface of the cake glow for them. I could see and smell the smooth span of chocolate, as beautiful to me as a polished leather boot to a shoemaker. I turned to leave, my nostrils already working, but Eichmann caught me by the collar. He explained how this was not to be an ordinary *Sachertorte*. This made me quite angry: my *Sachertortes* were never ordinary. But he waved his hand in front of my face and told me to shut up and listen. What he meant, he said, spitting out his words like nutshells, was this: the cake he envisaged was not to be round or square like an ordinary cake; rather it would have four branches. In short, it was to be made in the configuration of a swastika. "How you accomplish this is your business," he said. "Only make sure it is the correct shape and the chocolate is hard and shiny," he added, jiggling one hand up and down in his pocket, as was his curious custom. "Is that clear?" he shouted. Unfortunately so. Hard shiny chocolate, you see, is incorrect; the proper icing is lusciously firm and with a deep rich glow. I nodded my agreement to be rid of him, but

I thought to myself that while there were many things I might be forced to do, this, *this* I would not. Such an abomination cannot be, I said to myself. It would be a torture to my eggs, a corruption of my finest bitter chocolate, and a crime against the memory of my father and Franz Sacher. No, not on this piece of earth. Not by these hands.

I would not make a cake in the shape of a swastika. I was prepared to disobey his order and suffer the consequences. But I must make something else instead; what? I stirred my brain all morning, left it to rise during the afternoon, punched it down and left it to rise again. By night-time an idea rose, light and inspired, to the surface. I saw what it was to be; a creation which would substitute the sparkle of life for Eichmann's perverted *Tod-torte*.

Yes. I would make the *Croquembouche,* most exquisite of all baked things, more of a fairy tale than a sweet. And what would be my punishment? Death to the disobedient *Croquembouche* maker? I shrugged my shoulders. Let death come; at least my last supper would be crowned with the glory of the white mountain wrapped in its silver threads. And to be honest, I was not so afraid because I calculated Eichmann would not kill me, for he was by that time running for his own life; the Russians were so close, the war was so nearly over. He would be thinking of other things; much would depend on how the dinner went with the Swede. He might even forget the swastika-*torte* when presented with the noble *Croquembouche*. Perhaps, I thought to myself, I should make a Star-of-David-*torte* or a Hammer-and-Sickle-*torte*, but I did not feel brave enough for that. Besides, they would be quite difficult to execute well. No, the *Croquembouche* it would be: non-religious and non-partisan; less a slap in the face for Eichmann, more a celebration for the Swede.

I went early in the morning to my kitchen to begin preparations. First I made eight sponges which were to form the body of the mountain; rich but light with the addition of many beaten egg whites. While these sponges were baking I made a filling using twenty egg yolks, eight cups of milk, a cup of cognac, four cups of sugar. I divided the filling between two bowls, added grated orange rind to one, lemon to the other. Then I cut the cakes into descending sizes, from ten to three inches, to form the cone shape, base to summit. Next I cut each sponge in half horizontally. With these preparations complete, I set up the wooden cake stand, which had a center spindle rising about two feet out of the base – this would form the spine of the mountain. Then I carefully lowered one of the largest cake rounds over the spindle, having first cut a hole in the center with the point of my knife. I sprinkled it with a mixture of cognac and water, controlling the flow with my thumb over the opening of the bottle so that the cake should be well saturated but not mushy. Then I spread this first layer with the lemon filling. The next sponge layer I centered on top of the first and spread with orange filling. This procedure I repeated with each layer, first sprinkling with cognac, then spreading with alternate fillings of lemon and orange, until I reached the top of the spindle with the sponge round of three inches. I had climbed to the top and still the mountain stood secure on its base; I was pleased. Next I covered the whole with whipped cream and smoothed it with my palette knife. Then I decorated it with liqueur-flavored meringues, beginning with the largest ones at the base and ending with the smallest at the top. I placed here and there sugared almonds, to symbolize good luck. And for the final stage I made a caramel syrup which, as it cooled, formed into threads with which I spun a shimmery web around the cake. It was like a snow mountain wrapped in moonlight.

It was time. I heard the voice of the Swede raised above the others and in the distance the booming of Russian guns. It was an hour at least since they had finished their main course and so I must certainly make my appearance soon. Eichmann would be waiting, perhaps chuckling to himself, anticipating the effect of his miserable surprise. Little did he know his dark plottings were transformed into such a tasty morsel of innocence. I stood in the passage waiting for an appropriate moment to enter. Someone had blown out the candles; there were red flares on the horizon out of the east window. Suddenly Wallenberg held up his glass and said, "Ladies and Gentlemen, let us drink to the end of Nazism." Eichmann and Schmidthuber did not drink, of course, but the beautiful Gerda, who sat on his right, turned and clinked glasses with him in quite a familiar way, smiling her perfect smile. It was as if the sun had come out over one side of the table and a thunder cloud sat over the other. I did not understand why she was touching glasses with the Swede when she had come as Eichmann's guest; perhaps she had decided to change sides at the last minute? I did not know, but as I stood behind them, they seemed to me like two beautiful and precious dolls who might at any moment be broken, and I had an urge to pick them up and secrete them away in my apron pocket. She was wearing a red dress whose straps were as thin as the sugar piping on honeycake valentines and her back was bare and covered with star-shaped freckles. I should have liked to sleep under such a blanket of stars.

I placed the *Croquembouche* in front of them on the white tablecloth. Someone relit the candles and Eichmann pounded the table so hard a few of the meringues jumped off; but the mountain itself stood firm. I was afraid but I forced myself to look at the cause of the earthquake. In spite of his anger, I saw that Eichmann's face was like a thin eggshell, ready to crack. I saw I would get away with my crime. He would not shoot me; he would shoot no one. He would go away with his tail between his legs. I drew out from under my apron an exceedingly sharp curved carving knife and with it I slit the *Croquembouche* quickly from summit to base. I am quite sure it felt no pain. And then with a silver spoon I served Gerda and the Swede.

Gerda

"I have been to the Arizona Club to meet the Swede," said Eichmann.

"Oh? What did he want?"

"To invite me to dinner."

"How kind of him. Will you go?"

"No, the Jew-dog will come to me, here at the Majestic. I succeeded in turning the tables on him."

"How clever. And what is his interest in such a soirée?"

"I am certain he wants to make a deal with me over his Jews."

"Will you co-operate?"

"We shall see. You will come as my guest. With you at my side I cannot lose."

By then I had his number, from his hammer toes to his pointy skull; his claim to aristocratic parentage was a lie, his fluent Hebrew was a sham – one Biblical quotation on the creation of the universe was the extent of his mastery. He shielded his face when a camera approached; the sweat dropped off the end of his nose when he was forced to fly. He was afraid of his own shadow. No surprise, if the shadow was as hideous as the man.

Two weeks before, he had summoned Raoul to the Majestic to accuse him of being an enemy of Nazism. "Correct," replied Raoul and sent Wilmos, his chauffeur, down to his car to get a bottle of Scotch. I fetched two glasses. A few shots under his belt and Eichmann was a new man. "You know, Wallenberg," he said, slipping an arm around Raoul's shoulder, "I have nothing against you personally; actually, I rather like you. Let me do you a favor. If you want, and of course if the price is right – say seven hundred and fifty thousand Swiss francs – I would be happy to put a train at your disposal. You could take all your protected Jews to Sweden. What do you say?" What did he say? Something to the effect that he could insert his choo-choo up his protected rear passage. Oh, do not misunderstand me, Raoul was not above a deal, with Eichmann or anyone else, but he was not ready to abandon the majority of Jews in the ghetto for the sake of his minority of so-called protected Jews – the more privileged ones, the ones with connections, with money, with clout. No, he would not make a deal with Eichmann to abandon the others.

Eichmann was left quietly foaming at the mouth. I know, it was my job to calm him down. He said through his teeth, "I'm going to kill that Jew-dog Wallenberg if it's the last thing I do." As soon as I could get away I sent a message to Raoul to watch his step. Next morning his car was found demolished – run into by an SS truck, but there was no body found in the wreck.

I wore a backless red velvet dress with thin spaghetti straps edged in gold lamé. My hair was pulled up and hidden under a matching cloche so that the lines of my neck and shoulders were nicely exposed. The gold around the hat framed my face and shimmered like the halo around an icon. I wore ruby ear-rings, so large they brushed my shoulders, in the shape of two crosses.

Eichmann wore his uniform. He was marching back and forth, swearing to himself. Raoul was already forty-five minutes late for dinner. At last Eichmann stopped still in the middle of the room and stamped with his boot like a Rumpelstiltskin and hissed, "Where *iss* he?" I had to suck deeply on my cigarette to avoid giggling. You forget, perhaps because of my appearance and sophisticated behavior, I was still only a girl of eighteen. He was beginning to look like a fish out of water. His mouth twitched at the corners. And then he became depressed; perhaps the Swede would not turn up after all? It made me wonder what he had planned for the evening – perhaps some childish party trick, like an exploding cake? It might be just as well if he didn't come.

But he did, finally, turn up; he offered not one word of apology for his extreme lateness but said in an offhand way that he had been rather busy, what with the typhoid outbreak in the ghetto. "Typhoid?" Eichmann shouted as if we were all deaf. The Swede ignored him and I sniggered into my hand. I knew, of course, it wasn't true, but a rumor put out to discourage the Arrowcross from going into the ghetto. I knew – because it was my idea. How handsome he looked in his dinner jacket.

Soon we were settled in the dining room, Eichmann and his sidekick Schmidthuber on one side of the table, Raoul and I on the other. As we drank Fino sherry and sipped at our soup – a brown purée of calf's brains served with parsley and lemon wedges – Raoul dropped this remark like a hot *knedlicky* (he was warming up nicely): "Nazism is not really a bona fide ideology, you know." Then he paused, his soup spoon in mid-air. "How can it last?" Schmidthuber slurped his soup and Eichmann swore at him. I flashed the Swede my most brilliant smile. Eichmann slapped his napkin on the table and called for the next course. I suggested a Sancerre with our fish – a ten-pound baked stuffed yellow pike. *Csuka* in Hungarian. It filled the table, stared back at us. Raoul calmly poked it with an elegant index finger and said, "Perfectly done; just firm when pressed lightly." We ate until all that was left was a tail, an empty head and a clean skeleton in between. Schmidthuber picked his teeth. Raoul said conversationally, "Your SS are pathologically uncouth, your deportation policy is immoral and indefensible, your leader is schizophrenic and impotent," here he paused to suck a bone, "and your people are tired of clicking their heels and making those obscene parrot noises." He patted his mouth with his napkin and sat back in his chair. Eichmann snapped for another bottle of wine. I dug my heels into Raoul's ankle; maybe he was going too far. Schmidthuber was drooling and clenching his fists at the same time.

But he had no intention of stopping now. He leaped out of his chair, snapped off the lights and pulled back the curtains from the east windows. The horizon was red with Soviet artillery fire; we could hear thumps from the big guns. It was like a stage play with Raoul standing next to the window commenting on the action: "Look how close the Russians are. Your war is almost over, Eichmann. Nazism is doomed, finished, and so are those who cling to this hatred to the last minute. It is the end of Nazism, the end of Hitler, the end of you, Adolf. Ladies and gentlemen, let us drink to the end of Nazism." He raised his glass above his head and I felt myself drawn towards him –how could I help it? I touched my glass to his and said, "Hear, hear," not caring if Eichmann shot me right then and there. Just at that moment the pastry chef arrived carrying our dessert – a white mountain of a cake which looked more like an altarpiece than a dessert. It had a sort of magical, anaesthetizing effect. We took our places at the table as if nothing whatever had happened, and the little fat chef set his masterpiece down where the fish had been. Were we to eat it or pray to it? Eichmann broke the spell by banging his fist and swearing, about what I never knew; he seemed not to approve of the chef's choice. But before he could do anything else, this chef drew out a huge knife from under his apron and slit the cake from top to bottom, and then he gave each of us an elegant serving with a silver spoon. He said it was a French wedding cake, and he bravely announced it was to celebrate our victory.

We ate our *Croquembouche* –that is what it was called –in silence and then went through to the private drawing room for coffee and liqueurs. I crossed my legs and swiveled my ankle. Schmidthuber stared. Eichmann flung himself into an overstuffed chair and bounced like a raisin. "All right, Wallenberg," he croaked. "I agree with you. I will admit it. I never believed in Hitler's ideology. You are right –soon, very soon, this comfortable life will end. No more aeroplanes bringing women and wine from France. The Russians will take my horses, my dogs, all of this." His voice trailed away.

Raoul leaned forward –this was his chance to make a deal with Eichmann. He smiled and lowered his voice. "But why? Why lose it all now? You agree it's the end, so why bother with any more of these senseless deportations? Why not leave now and save yourself?" I closed my eyes. It was clear from Eichmann's face it had not worked; in fact, it had accomplished the reverse. He stood up and whacked the floor with his stick. All the evil life seemed to flow back into him; he was reconstituted, more determined than ever to destroy what was left. He said in a calm voice, "For me there is no escape, no liberation. There are, however, some consolations. If I continue to eliminate our enemies, the Jews, until the end it may delay, if only for a few days, our defeat. And then, when I finally do walk to the gallows, at least I will know I have completed my mission." I took a large gulp of brandy. And then he added for good measure, "Don't try to stop me, Wallenberg. I shall do my very utmost to defeat you, even at this late stage. And your Embassy status will not help you if I consider it necessary to do away with you. Even a neutral diplomat might meet with accidents; your luck may not hold forever."

He stood up; the party was over. Raoul had failed to make his deal and now Eichmann smiled the victor's smile. It said to me: That will teach you to betray me in front of my enemy. And he put a hand around my wrist—his prize possession who would soon pay for her little lapse in discretion. But I would not; there was little left to lose by this time. I pulled my arm away from him and took hold of Raoul's arm. "Good night, Adolf," I said sweetly; "lovely dinner," and waved goodbye.

Jack

It began as the best Christmas of my life, with a basket full of *Faschingskrapfen* –filled doughnuts made with rum, cream, egg yolks, orange juice and apricot jam. They were poems. I had baked them for the traditional holy anniversary, but I believe our real celebration that year was for the sudden departure –in the middle of the night –of Adolf Eichmann. Instead of our dear St Nikolas having come, he had gone –a much better gift. We danced in the kitchen of the Majestic to the music of the accordion and the clanking and clattering of pots and pans. Only the *maître d'hôtel* was unhappy because his beautiful daughter had run away with the Swede.

But the day turned quickly sour. We heard, on that day of peace and goodwill, that the Arrowcross had raided the Jewish orphanage –lined up the younger children and shot them, then led the older ones through the snow and across the Danube to Buda and into the Radetzky barracks. God knows what happened to them there. Heavy tears like olive oil dropped one by one into my mixing bowl; I might have been making mayonnaise.

In spite of this latest atrocity there was to be, that night, a special Christmas dinner to include people from the International Red Cross and the Jewish Council. I made for them plum puddings, well soaked in brandy, and hoped they might be joined by the Swede, and perhaps even by the beautiful wine waitress. But we heard he had gone to the Swedish hospital to stop the Arrowcross from taking the sick away. I asked myself: Do they never stop, these beasts, not even for Christmas dinner? The answer was no. Just as I was weaving my way through the tables, serving my brandy puddings and setting them alight, with my guests admiring the spectacle of the blue flames dancing in the darkened dining room and the highlights of polished mahogany and silver reflected in the great mirrors and chandeliers; just as we were enjoying the warmth and beauty of this glowing atmosphere and trying our best to forget the horrors of the day – there came the clatter of boots; quite close, then very close. It was the Arrowcross. They pushed me out of the way and took away my guests before even one mouthful of plum pudding could be enjoyed. I begged to be taken also, but they were not interested in me. Soon I was alone in the dark dining room and all the flames had burnt away. A few moments later I heard the roar of a car engine outside the hotel and when I looked up the Swede had materialized. "You are too late," I said and he sank down into a chair. "Please," I said, and offered him one of the abandoned puddings to eat because I could think of nothing else to say or do. But he shook his head and said, "Perhaps another time," and smiled at me. So polite.

I had dreamt for so long of the Russians that when they came I did not recognize them. They would be kind – weary from their battles, but kind. They would have a penchant for sour cream and buttermilk and for all things being shared equally. Perhaps the Majestic would become the People's Hotel; indeed, people would come from the ghetto and the work places as well as from the fine districts to eat strudel, elbow to elbow, fork to fork. And the Russians would wave their arms like big branches and sweep people in; no one would be turned away.

I was quite wrong; they were only human, and soldiers could not be expected to behave very well. Even so, I was shocked when they forced their way into the hotel and broke things, stole the silver, drank the liquor and did violence to the female staff. It was a terrible disappointment. Still, I thought, give them a chance. Once the Nazis have capitulated and there is some agreement with the new Hungarian government, things will be different. That is what I told myself. And meanwhile I practised making Moscow doughnuts, sweet *Pirozhki* and curd pie, things which might please them; but they made the same grunting sounds no matter what. Also I baked vast quantities of poppy seed rolls and Hungarian white bread which I delivered to the Swede's headquarters in Pest. By this time he was living in the ghetto amongst the Jews, people said, like a shepherd amongst his flock. Then the street fighting started. I remember once I had to duck behind my truck using my tray as a shield until the crossfire stopped. It was terrible. The streets were like the inside of an oven; one could bake a *linzer* cake in such a heat.

When the fighting stopped it was very cold and the streets were layered with ice. I delivered some bread to the Swede's headquarters that day and right away knew something was wrong. They said he was gone. Gone? Dead? I sat down. No, not dead, just gone to the Russian headquarters in Debrecen. Well then, I said, he will be back. Soon we will all be working hand-in-hand with the Russians and everything will be better. They shook their heads. The way he left, they said, it looked like he might never come back. He said himself he was not sure whether he was going as a guest or a prisoner. He went in his own car part of the way but was guarded by Russian motorcycle police. "But what reason would they have for arresting him—he is friend not foe?" I said. But I might have been a piece of inconsequential puff pastry; nobody replied to my question.

By February the siege was over. All German and Hungarian Nazis had been either shot or sent to prison camps in Russia. A Hungarian Communist government was being set up in Budapest. This was the liberation. One day two Russian officers came into the Majestic and I greeted them with a lovely warm *Gugelhopf*; this, I thought, they will surely appreciate. But no, they swept the coffee cake out of my hands and dragged me out of the hotel still in my hat and apron, and without a coat in that freezing weather. They threw me into their filthy military van and took me to army headquarters. Why? Perhaps they wanted to question me about Eichmann; I might, after all, know where he was hiding. Perhaps they have discovered about my Buchenwald escape and wish to congratulate me, honor me, for my small valor. And then the thought washed over me like a warm milk glaze that what they wanted was to make me *their* official pastry chef. I relaxed on my bench, leaned back and smiled at the officer opposite me. Oh gladly, gladly; I thought that my life had come full circle like a wreath. But the officer did not smile back.

The commanding officer at headquarters questioned me in German. "You were Eichmann's private pastry chef, correct?" he accused. "Yes, but ..." "And Koch's also at Buchenwald, between 1940 and 1943, correct?" "Yes, but I was a prisoner, I had no choice," I said. And I told them about my razor blade plot and my escape and then I showed them my draft card from Vienna with the notation *Wahlumwurdig*, which meant "not suitable for military service" on account of being politically radical. And then I showed them my recent Hungarian Socialist Party membership card, with dues payed through June 1945. I spread these things out on the table but he laughed at me; his face was sinister. He called me "the Fascist baker" and pronounced me an enemy of the Soviet people. I tried to explain – Me, Hanno Baum, an enemy of the people? – but he hit me across the jaw and I must have passed out. The next thing I knew I was in a train watching the trees go by, bare cold trees, I shivered for them. We travelled for weeks, I lost track of time, but at the end of it I was put into a prison with hundreds of other foreigners – Poles, Germans, Americans, Finns, even Turks and Greeks. They seemed to have grouped themselves roughly according to politics and it turned out there were nearly as many Communists or Communist-sympathizers as there were Nazis and Nazi-sympathizers. Why had they put us together – fruit and liver dumplings? We did not mix. Inside we went on fighting, while the war outside was over. It was a terrible time. When would they let the faithful out to enjoy the sweet fruits of victory?

On the day when they threw me into a cell with Wallenberg, I understood. I thought to myself, if they can arrest such a man, then there is no more hope. After all, I myself was a German and had baked for Eichmann and Koch and was therefore in their terms guilty by association; but what point of international law could be so stretched out of shape as to convict the heroic Swede? In my mind I thought of the law as an enormous expanse of strudel dough getting thinner and thinner until small transparent bubbles formed, and finally, holes. And then the whole thing came to pieces.

The next day they plucked him out of my cell, put me in solitary confinement and warned me never to speak about him to anyone. Who did they think I would tell – the bedbugs, the lice? I was in solitary for a year, maybe more, I lost track. For a time I practised reciting recipes, trying to keep the ingredients and amounts clear in my mind. I conjured up visions of the coffee table and the bakeshop from my youth in Vienna until the smell was so strong that the saliva bubbled to my lips. Years later – in fact it was ten years – I saw Wallenberg again in the Corpus II hospital block. He had lost almost all of his hair, but mentally he was still alert. He whispered quickly that I was to tell people on the outside he was still alive. He seemed to know an Austrian exchange was on the cards and that quite soon I would be released. He was right.

Over and over I prayed his name; it came easily to my lips. But even as I made my way to America, a sort of hard shiny darkness like cheap chocolate closed in around my memory and for a long while I forgot the Swede and everything else that had ever happened to me.

Gerda

The little beast crept away during the night leaving a trail of *eau d'Adolf* behind which would take decades to disinfect. His threat to deal with Raoul was merely posturing – the response of a threatened goose. There was only one way he would have liked to "get" his "admirable adversary". It would explain certain things. Ugh.

I installed myself in Raoul's beautiful eighteenth-century house on Gellert Hill, not far from the Majestic. He had hardly used it since going to live in the ghetto; most of the time he slept on or in an office chair – if he slept at all. But this night was an exception. We stood together in the moonlit bedroom looking out across the Danube. The Russian firing had died down for the night and the city was quiet. I removed my gold-trimmed velvet skullcap and let my hair loose onto my shoulders; then I removed my dress and lay on top of the salmon satin bedspread. He caught his breath as if the stars had just come out in a shower across the sky. "Freckles," I said. "I was born with them."

The next morning Raoul left early for the ghetto. I was safe in his house meanwhile, but bored. What was I to do – twiddle my thumbs and wait for him to visit me between rescue missions? No, I had a scheme or two of my own. There were rumors of a plot to destroy the ghetto Jews before the Russians arrived, but now that Eichmann was gone it was difficult to get information. I decided I would get it out of Schmidthuber, who was under orders from Eichmann to stay and see the job through. I sent him an invitation to come and see me on Gellert Hill. It was risky, but I knew he would come. He was so stupid he was not likely even to put two-and-two together about my connection with Raoul. Anyway, he could be flattered into informing.

I petted him, said how much I adored his big belly, his chins – so comforting in a man! I waited for the right moment and then I asked about the new plan to deal with the ghetto problem. He replied, "Oh, you know too – yes, everyone knows already. Imagine, seventy thousand Jews blown up all at once. Yes, it will be our grand finale. You can watch the fireworks from here."

I sent an urgent message to Sip Street to alert Raoul. The next morning he went to see Schmidthuber and whisper a few sweet nothings in his hairy ear. What? Schmidthuber, listen to me, if you carry out your horrible scheme you will be strung up like a crow and shot by the Russians, your guts will be flung to the fish in the Danube. Schmidthuber, I will personally see to it that you are flayed alive and turned inside out and stuffed like a *derma*. It warmed my heart to think of him saying such things and Schmidthuber standing there like a tub of lard. And it worked. The pogrom was called off. Schmidthuber slipped away from Budapest like a greasy *wurst* in the night.

The most desperate thugs remained, however; gangsters like Rettmann and Dannecker who were out to get Raoul. They sent him death threats and hunted him in the streets at night. He played down these dangers. He said, "It is not my intention to worry about myself or about my safety. I care only about getting the remaining Jews to safety; I must keep giving out safe passes, no matter what." But in the quiet of the night he admitted he was afraid; he felt very close to death. I did what I could to comfort him.

Then the Arrowcross invaded one of his safe houses. By the time we got there (I went along to give him moral support) they were rounding people up. He made Wilmos, his chauffeur, drive the car straight through to the courtyard, then he leapt out and shouted at the officers in charge: "This is Swedish territory. You have no business here. Get out." They replied, "We have orders to take the able-bodied away from here." Raoul countered, "Nobody will leave. If you try to take anybody from here you will get into trouble with me. As long as I am alive, nobody will be taken. You will have to shoot me first." And then he added, "But think about it. If you obey me I promise you safety after the Russian victory." They could have shot him right then and there, but they did not. They looked at each other. They were in a weak position and they knew it. The war was virtually over; if they played their cards right they might have a chance of surviving under the Russians; if not, not. This Swede might put in a good word for them. They lowered their rifles and left. All safe.

At last the great moment came and the Russians rolled through our streets. They were big handsome bears who looked like they would know how to hug a woman. Little did I know. Not hugs but the crushing of bones; not love but rape and plunder was their game. And there was no quick liberation as we had imagined. The more hardened of the Germans and Arrowcross did not lay down their arms immediately, so the battles went on. I watched from my perch on Gellert Hill. Only the Jews had reason for hope; in the clash between Nazis and Communists, they might be overlooked.

Raoul abandoned his intention to return home for the new year. By this time he was already planning for the future. Soon the siege would be over, Nazis and Fascists and collaborators would be taken prisoner and Budapest would become peaceful again, presided over by these kindly Russian teddy bears. There was so much to do, he said, and he would recite lists to me of his recovery plans: restore Jewish assets, reunite families, care for war victims, distribute food, fight epidemics, re-establish businesses, create jobs, provide housing – and so on. It made me tired to hear of them. And who did he think would be interested in his fancy plans – did he think the Russians would want him sharing in their glory? No, he should go home to mama before it is too late, I said.

He was stubborn and would not listen to me. He began making contingency plans. If the Hungarian authorities were cool to his ideas, he would form his own company or foundation with outside funding; he had done this before. But what of the Russians? Malinovsky – on seeing so many Swedish flags flying over the safe houses – had asked sarcastically if he was in Stockholm or Budapest; and yet

Raoul completely failed to appreciate the implications of this remark. He was so naive. He believed the Russians would approve of his reconstruction plans and invite joint co-operation. He believed in his own powers of persuasion. Just as he had talked Schmidthuber out of the pogrom, so would he talk Malinovsky into a great Jewish rehabilitation program. Idiot. Why should this handsome Swede with his filthy capitalist lucre interfere with their own liberation schemes?

He insisted on going to the Russian headquarters in Debrecen, 140 miles outside Budapest. He claimed it was partly to escape the Arrowcross mobs who were still trying to murder him. He said when the fighting was over he would return; the Russians, meanwhile, would protect him. I thought he was going soft in the head, like an old cheese; but I would not beg him to stay. He saw to his valuables, distributed money to be used for the rescue operations in his absence, gave me his passbook and safe deposit box key; he said there were diamonds and other jewels kept there. He told me if he did not return by spring I should take the diamonds and go to his family in Sweden; they would help me start a new life. Who needed help starting a new life? I considered telling him about the new life already well started inside me: what would he do if he knew? He would not go, I was sure; he would stay to protect me; he would want to marry me, take me back to Stockholm as his prize. I would not tell him.

The high Russian military command escorted him; I rode with him part of the way. At the last minute he seemed rather confused; he said, "There is no certainty when I will return. Make sure they continue my work." And then, as if it had only just occurred to him, he said, "You know, I am not entirely sure if I am going as a guest or as a prisoner." He said he would come back for me, if he could. I got out of the car and walked away; another car was waiting to drive me back to Budapest. The roads were coated with ice; in my condition I had to watch my step.

The Russians picked me up soon after and took me to their Budapest headquarters for questioning. Now I knew the answer to Raoul's conundrum: he was unquestionably a prisoner. Anyone who had had anything whatever to do with him was under suspicion. It was clear they wanted him–his entire operation–out of the way. The only question was how to dispose of us. As for me, I had several possible escape routes, but basically I had to use my wits. First I told them I had information about the head waiter at the Majestic, an individual they would be most interested in. I said he was a Jew, a pimp, and a Nazi collaborator. But that was not enough for them. They wanted to know about Wallenberg. Who was he working for? I said I did not know. They said if I told them, I could go free; otherwise . . . What could I do? I had to protect myself. So I said the American Herschel Johnson had hired him; his rescue mission had been financed by the U.S. War Refugee Board; President Roosevelt had given him his blessing–that was all I knew. It was exactly what they wanted to know. I was a free woman.

Part IV

1976

Jack

The message from the Wallenberg Committee, to whom I had sent my testimony, came as a shock. They informed me of certain investigative procedures to be followed: could I meet with the Committee in two days' time to clarify a few things? Also – if I did not object – they should like to make a tape recording of my testimony. No, no; no objection whatsoever, I fibbed. But oh, it made me so hungry remembering those cells washed with thin *borscht* and thick blood, exercise pens not bigger than those of animals. And the thought of the Swede still there after all this time made me shrivel in the middle like a sponge baked too quickly. Had I not already done my duty by staying up half the night, laboriously reviving and composing my memories on paper? And now there was to be an inquisition; a swearing on bibles, cross-questioning; God knows what else. The woman on the telephone had sounded to me suspicious, although she had said another piece of first-hand evidence would be very welcome indeed. She said she looked forward to meeting me. I replied rather weakly that I too looked forward to meeting her; and hung my receiver back to rest in its white plastic cradle.

I ate a piece of Christmas *Streizl*, golden and fat as the criss-crossed legs of a roasted turkey, to feed my failing holiday spirit. Two days! But perhaps it would be a day of release, of rising? If others such as myself came forward with information about Wallenberg, perhaps the Russians would relent – admit he was alive and release him?

Rella was to accompany me. We would go somewhere rather special, as a reward, for lunch. I dressed for the

169

occasion in a grey suit. My hair had been cut so that my ears and nose stood out quite dramatically from my head. My hair was grey and in my grey suit even my skin looked to me grey. Perhaps I should pinch my cheeks? But compared with Rella I looked as ruddy-complexioned as a redcurrant tart. She herself had made not a single concession to the occasion; she might have been *en route* to scrub halls. The legs of her jeans hung down in pale blue and white strings, covering the tops of her feet like the fringed legs of a starving cart horse. She wore a sort of duffle coat the color of our Austrian *loden* coats, with wooden pegs for buttons and a hood which was far too big for her head. With her toothless mouth, her transparent skin and her sunken eyes, she looked out from deep in her hood–God forgive me–like the skeleton of death. I thought: One cannot live on peanut butter sandwiches alone. I said, "You realize we are going to take lunch out?" and she looked pained. "Can't I go like this? Are we going somewhere fancy?" I had not meant to sound censorious; therefore, to correct the impression, I said, "Oh, perhaps not fancy but ... Still, they must take you as you are or we will not be interested. It is the mark of a tasteful establishment not to judge its patrons by appearances. Agreed?" She smiled and then, remembering her teeth, covered her mouth. She said, "Besides, you look so elegant, it won't matter about me; they'll think you're my father." She took my arm and I felt the color coming to my cheeks and spreading like pink cream cheese icing. I felt inside my breast pocket to make sure my testimony was still resting in its brown envelope.

"You know," I said after we were settled in our subway car seats, "soon people will become interested in the connection between you and your family and Wallenberg. You must be prepared for this."

"Me? My family? What do you mean?" She sounded quite alarmed.

"Well, I mean Gerda, actually. Your mother. It is inevitable that the public should be curious. Journalists have a talent for sniffing out such a thing, as a baker can a batch of cinnamon cookies; they will undoubtedly find the ingredients too succulent to resist. Gossip always surrounds such a hero; that is one of the unfortunate consequences of fame. But you – and Gerda – must be prepared. Sooner or later she must speak up concerning her ... shall we say relationship, with Wallenberg." Rella said nothing. "Does that surprise you?" I asked. She merely turned her head and wriggled out of her coat. The train was very hot, our feet particularly were being steamed inside our shoes like puddings. I stared: the color and texture of her blouse made everything else evaporate from my mind. We chugged slowly through the tunnel, then the train stopped quite suddenly and came to a screeching halt and Rella fell against me, and the red satin material of her blouse brushed my bare hand and made me shiver. Back went my memory, back back through its own dark tunnel; to where? Oh yes, the Vienna Botanical Garden. I was a small boy. My mother had taken me there one Sunday in May and I had fallen in love with a scarlet rhododendron from Yunnan Province. I began to caress the waxy blossoms with my hands and face but my mother threatened to call a caretaker. I can still feel them. But then there was something else, also red, though not so far back in my memory. Oh yes, the red dress – Gerda's dress with the thin straps – but I have already told of that.

So Rella had after all made an attempt to decorate herself for the occasion. I was so pleased; and although the cheap red material against her skin caused it to look like a dry sage leaf, I said, "I think your blouse is splendid. It reminds me of a rhododendron."

"What's that?"

"A beautiful flower from China. I saw such a great bush when I was a child in Vienna. Perhaps they have them here also, in the Brooklyn Botanical Gardens. I will take you there one day." She did not reply but put her coat back on. I suppose she did not like to think of herself as an exotic flower, or perhaps she thought I was making fun of her. Was I? Oh dear.

By the time we had made our way out of the subway station at 42nd Street, it was pouring with rain; I was pleased with myself for bringing an umbrella. We walked fast, with our heads down, holding onto hat and hood, trying to protect ourselves against the rain making pastry with our faces, cutting like knives. We danced around vast puddles, slippery grates and crowds of rather warlike people holding their umbrellas cocked at dangerous angles. The iron railings of the Library flew past in a melting blur. I checked my breast pocket again to make sure the brown envelope had not jumped out. Rella looked sideways at me and said, "You look like you have a TV aerial growing out of your head," and she giggled; her face was wet in spite of her protective hood. I looked up to see that she was quite correct: the wind had stripped my poor umbrella naked, though my arm still held it open to ridicule. Quickly I folded the sad skeleton away and threw it into one of the Keep New York Clean garbage cans at the end of the street. We had eight more blocks to walk still, and so we grew rather bold and carefree. We would get wet in any case, so we carried on, laughing and flapping in our wet clothes, wading bravely through puddles which were now rivers. We arrived well soaked, like two fingers in a *pavé au cognac*, only this was rain, cold rain. I licked my lips; there was nothing good to taste.

When we reached the building of our destination, the outer lobby was crowded with people taking shelter from the weather, but a guard was stopping them from going further in. One man was trying to make jokes – "I'm not in the mood for swimming today, I think I'll just ride up and down in the elevator" – but the guard was not in the mood for levity and barred the man's way. It was a high-security building, that was clear. Gently we pushed through the crowd and I offered my name and gave that of the person I had come to see. "The lady too?" he asked suspiciously, and I nodded. He checked my name in his book, then gave each of us a visitor's pass to wear; then he held open the glass door for us to pass through. We must be privileged, I thought. We both pressed the elevator button.

The receptionist, who was talking on the telephone, pointed with a long red fingernail to a closet in which to hang our dripping coats, and a couch on which to sit. I hesitated since we were so wet, but she winked at us and made a motion with her hands as if closing a suitcase (she held the telephone tucked between her neck and shoulder). We sat down; a pool quickly formed around our feet. I looked up and saw a short round man in a pin-striped suit standing on one leg, tilting himself sideways around a corner to observe us. I stood up, "My name is Jack Baum," I announced. He gestured with both his hands for me to come closer, and I began to wonder, do people not speak here? Then he said in a most agreeable way, "Come in, come in, we were expecting you."

"I am sorry we are late, the rain ..."

"Don't worry in the least, I only just got here myself. The weather is atrocious. If your daughter would like to come in too, she's perfectly welcome," he said, indicating Rella. "No, no, that is quite all right; I think my friend would prefer to wait for me out here," I said, and looked at Rella for confirmation. She nodded. The little man – who introduced himself as Jerry Cohen – arranged for one of his assistants to show Rella some materials from the files while she waited. We might be some time, he said. Rella said she didn't mind. Mr Cohen ushered me into his office and shut the door.

He was there, he told me, "to get the ball rolling," and so after a few jolly introductory remarks to prepare me, he turned me over to his rather formidable colleague, Mrs Kornblatt. "Come with me," she said, leading the way into a further office. She pointed. Already I could feel myself being squeezed and kneaded by those strong hands. "Sit," she commanded and I fell like a large lump of dough into the appointed chair. She sat behind a large desk and put her fingertips together. Now we must be serious, I thought.

"You understand we are after the truth," she said without any running around the bush. "We appealed to the Russian-speaking community as a source of information, and now we are faced with a problem: there is hardly a soul in New York City who has not seen Raoul Wallenberg; suddenly he is the long-lost friend of everyone. One lady saw him in Bergdorf Goodman's last week trying on hats. Another saw him squeezing grapefruits at a supermarket in Queens. Such people are time-consuming and annoying. More difficult was the Russian woman who called with great excitement – she had the very proof we needed – photographs of Wallenberg in a Russian prison camp from the fifties. Photographs! When she arrived with them I saw a tall thin man who did indeed look very much like him. Only something was wrong; what? Finally I realized the man in the picture had thick curly black hair. As you know, Raoul was practically bald, even at thirty-two. Information like this we do not need.

"That is not the worst of it. I could tell you stories. There were, for example, several attempts to exchange so-called information for money. We had one offering to go to the Soviet Union to look into Wallenberg's case if we would promise, in return, to have certain things published in the Western press. And so on. I won't bore you with the problems and annoyances we have had. Nevertheless, I must impress upon you the seriousness of our mission and the need for utter truthfulness; I do not have much time to waste. Now, do you mind if I tape record this interview?"

For a moment everything disappeared again; I saw only the familiar blessed whiteness, and no words came to my lips. Meanwhile I longed for something solid and reassuring into which I might sink my teeth to stop my cheeks and chins shaking like a blancmange. "Come, come, Mr Baum, I'm not going to eat you," she said. I closed my eyes and took a few deep breaths and then remembered the brown envelope nuzzling in my breast pocket. "Do you have any objection if I refer to my written story?" I asked. "Of course not," she said, consulting her watch. And so I told my story.

When it was over, the fierce lady came around from behind her desk and embraced me. I was quite surprised. "You can relax now," she said, her whole face different, like an unmolded mousse. "I have no doubt whatever that what you say is true." And then she patted my arm and told me to wait there a moment. She returned with two cups of coffee and a small dry biscuit for each of us. The disappointment was almost enough to make me weep; I had hoped at least for a Danish pastry.

But I was not to be allowed to leave yet; the interrogation was just starting. Why had I waited so long to come forward with my story? I explained how, since coming to America, I had suffered from total amnesia. I confessed to having spent ten years in a hospital after an unfortunate mental breakdown. "Can you tell me something about that?" she asked. I looked into my coffee cup and saw myself floating round and round in the milk, a swastika wrapped round my arm. I took a bite of my lip. Now I would sink to the bottom, my testimony would be worth no more than a few grounds of coffee.

"I'm sorry," she said, "but I must ask these things. I realize it isn't easy for you."

"Yes," I said gulping. "It was the year 1956, Hallowe'en night. I impersonated Adolf Hitler. To this day I cannot explain my actions."

She looked so fierce I thought for a moment she would strike me. But she closed her eyes and said softly, "I didn't hear that. Now tell me under what circumstances you were able to regain your memory."

I felt like a Viennese jam pocket which had been sucked dry; there was nothing left inside. I said it had been a gradual process, over the last ten years; certain things had jarred my memory. But I did not say what they were. I realized some things were better left unsaid.

"Well, well," Mrs Kornblatt said, "never mind. The point is you have remembered. As it happens, your timing is good; very good. Other people have waited too, simply because there has been no appropriate organization to hear their stories. So." She stood up, leaned forward across her desk. "I must say that was, on the whole, a most satisfying interview. So much of the time, you know, I am frustrated. So many people need to talk, they think we want to know how a second cousin by marriage was saved by Wallenberg, or an uncle or grandmother. We even have women in here claiming – of all the absurdities – to have been his mistress. Already we have had half a dozen. As if he had time to nibble on earlobes between rescue missions. Of course, these things are human interest stories, but that is not our function, Mr Baum; you understand? I cannot sit here talking to people who come forward to say they went to bed with him or were in love with him; who wouldn't be in love with such a man? But it is not my job to listen to gossip. My business is to assemble the evidence for the case that he is still alive – now, today. We know he was alive in Budapest in '44. Now we know he was still alive in '55 – thanks to you. But what about today, Mr

Baum, what about right now; where is he *now*? Remember, one can live a long time in prison."

I asked, with some hesitation, about the disturbing evidence of Professor Svartz; this meant bringing up the whole unpleasant question of his mental condition. I saw him shivering in a corner, mumbling mad plans for the reconstruction of Budapest. I closed my eyes because I did not wish to see such things. I thought to myself: if not dead, perhaps better dead, as Rella had said, and I almost regretted having come. Mrs Kornblatt said, "Ah, that is another question. In a way, we cannot afford to ask it, you understand? Our purpose is to demonstrate through a mass of evidence that he is alive and a prisoner in the Soviet Union. Our aim is both political and humanitarian; we wish to force the Soviets into retracting their statement that he died in 1947 and, eventually, to secure his release through world pressure. In a sense, his mental or physical condition – so long as he is still alive – is not of the utmost importance. Although naturally we are all concerned for his wellbeing.

"So, Mr Baum, we have some puzzling statements and some disturbing ones, but on the whole, we have enormous optimism – and I hope you will share in it. You know, of course, about the international tribunal which is to take place in Stockholm in 1981 – the anniversary of Raoul's seventieth birthday. It will be a review of the documents and evidence from all over the world, and we hope it will prove our thesis conclusively. Of course it is still five years away; a massive effort, as you will appreciate, I am sure. But we will see. I have hope." She held out her hand. "And now I must say goodbye, Mr Baum. We are most grateful for your contribution to our cause. Perhaps we will see you again in Stockholm in '81?"

I had remembered everything, had delivered my story honorably. Afterwards other people at the Committee had shaken me by the hands and shoulders and said they were honored to make my acquaintance. I was flattered, but above all greatly relieved to have done my duty. I was free. And I was very hungry.

We emerged to find the streets basted in clarified butter

which was dripping off buildings and running away down gutters. The city smiled down on me with its fourteen-carat skyscraper teeth, as if to say: congratulations, Jack.

As I looked out of the window of our uptown bus, I grew nervous at the sight of so many broken and abandoned umbrellas, like oil-slicked blackbirds washed up and splayed out on this concrete beach. Did I notice a few still twitch with life? But come, I told myself, now is not the time for such gloomy thoughts. The squall was over; already garbage trucks were chewing up the tattered corpses. The sun dropped lower in the sky, baking the city to golden perfection, and Rella looked at me and smiled. I could have eaten an umbrella.

We got off the bus at 86th Street. I noticed there were fewer people than at 42nd Street, and of a different kind – rather elongated and expensively groomed. The architecture was older and more noteworthy, cars were smooth and silvery, doormen gestured for taxicabs. The smell of greasy, salty nuts gave way to the subtle perfume of smoked salmon. Going west, we passed a row of fine brownstone houses with etched glass and mahogany doors wearing Christmas wreaths. Then we reached the splendor of Fifth Avenue and the Metropolitan Museum with its enormous banners. Advertising what? The Venetian paintings of Turner. Golden sunsets over the canals; how appropriate. The pools flanking the grand staircase bubbled and hissed like pans of baking gold. Statues on the tops and corners of buildings flung out their wing-tips to catch the sun. Where was I? For a moment I thought I must be back in Budapest or even Vienna; had I come home? A chauffeur in a braided hat – which also caught a sunbeam – opened the door for a teenager. No, I was not home, but it was a different world from 42nd Street or Brooklyn Heights; of that I was sure. I feared the stone angels would soon take flight.

"Where are we going?" asked Rella.

"To a restaurant for lunch. Are you hungry?"

"Yes," she said, to my surprise. "But it doesn't look like there are any places along here, only buildings and the park."

"Eventually we must come to something. Don't worry," I said.

"Have you ever been to Central Park?"

"Oh yes, it is quite lovely in the spring when all the trees are in leaf."

"Gerda says it's the most dangerous place in the city; she says they steal bicycles out from under their riders."

"In that case we are quite safe since we are not riding bicycles." She looked offended. Was I laughing at Gerda? Where were the bicycle thiefs, the muggers, murderers, rapists, handbag slicers, perverts? Rella had her purse strapped diagonally across her chest, like a schoolgirl, just in case of trouble, and she looked suspiciously this way and that at the women in fur coats and men in camel-hair coats and the poodles in red plaid coats. It was not what her mother had prepared her for. Had Gerda got it wrong? And if so, could she have gotten the other things wrong too?

The Café Pierre was decorated in white and gold Empire style – a simple classic bar with a few side tables. It looked quite nice but as we walked in every head turned to observe us, so we quickly fled back onto the street and hurried on. Were we such an odd couple? At the end of the block was the Sherry Netherland; we looked through the window. Each table of black marble had pink embossed napkins. No. Across the street, just at the lower edge of dangerous Central Park, was the Plaza, picked out in gold swags. It was in the center of an island; in front waited horse-drawn carriages and drivers in grey uniforms. A red carpet and gas lamps decorated its front entrance. "That is where we shall have our lunch," I announced, leading Rella across Fifth Avenue.

"There? You must be kidding," she said.

"No, I am perfectly serious and extremely hungry. Why not, in your beautiful red blouse?"

She ate more than I had ever before witnessed: a portion of shrimp salad and a taste of chocolate mousse. I had the same thing with the addition of a cream of sorrel soup. We shared a bottle of white wine, and found ourselves growing quite cheerful. The world was not as it had seemed – hopeless, fixed, dangerous. Rella's eyes, which were so often dull like coated stale chocolate, grew wide and dark and rich as the mousse she ate. We discussed possibilities. The world was expanding before those eyes. That she should be eating lunch in the Plaza; that she should have walked along Central Park and still be alive; that there was every indication that Wallenberg was still alive – these things were making her feel alive; and hungry.

"What did the young woman say to you?" I asked.

"Oh, she was very enthusiastic. She called him Moses of the North and the Swedish Pimpernel. It makes him sound like a cartoon character; you know, like Casper the Friendly Ghost or something." She giggled, licked her spoon.

"The other woman, the receptionist, called him 'a gorgeous hunk of a man' and said 'I sure hope they get him out in one piece.'" We both giggled.

"So they think he is still alive?"

"Yes, definitely," she said. Her cheeks were flushed with the wine; I saw how pretty she would be if she had teeth, some healthy color to her face. "There's so much evidence now, it can't be denied by anyone – except the Russians, of course. Why, don't *you* believe it?"

"I don't know," I said.

She leaned towards me. "Listen. A Russian Jew named Kaplan telephoned his daughter in Israel recently and told her he had met a Swede who had been in prison for thirty years and was doing well. Several other people have spotted him very recently in various Russian prisons. They all say he is in good health." The girl had shown her a mass of articles, newspaper clippings.

"Have you forgotten about Svartz? What about his mental health?" The light went out from her eyes; in sympathy the sun went behind a cloud. "Now, come, forget I said that, I was only being gloomy. I too believe he is alive, and well." I patted her hand. "Come, let us drink a toast to him."

I ordered another half carafe of wine. Together we grew more and more forgetful of sadness. I finished Rella's mousse and ordered a cheese board to go with the wine. Rella tasted a sparrow's mouthful of each – camembert, blue stilton, chèvre. The sun came through the window

179

again and into our eyes, but I implored the waiter not to pull down the blinds. For a time in the middle of that floating afternoon, everything was golden again, anything was possible. We blinked.

I said, "There is to be a great world-wide tribunal in Sweden in 1981. All the evidence will be brought together and presented to the Russians. Then they are certain to acknowledge their mistake and release him."

"Maybe he will come and live in New York City," said Rella, "at the Plaza. Maybe Gerda will come and live here too. They can go jogging together in red velvet jog suits." And she sprayed me with her wine giggles.

"Perhaps," I said, doubtfully, and ordered two strong black coffees.

The sun had set and it was now freezing. Quickly we walked the two long blocks to the subway station. I held Rella under the arm. At every street corner there was a Santa Claus ringing a bell like a warning gong. How easily a great hero can be ill-used, said the bells to me; how easy to claim false association, to exaggerate a connection, to imagine having known him, if only in a dream. "He is fast becoming a celebrated figure," Mrs Kornblatt had said. "A public figure, a cause and a symbol for which people will fight. But also, and this is the problem, one which can all too easily be exploited, aggrandized, trivialized, romanticized. That we must guard against at all costs. He could so easily become our victim, don't you see? Now it is up to us not only to get him released but to protect him while he is still imprisoned. Do you understand how careful we must be?" Her words rang in my ears.

We put our tokens in their slots and pushed through the stiles. What about Gerda and Rella? The whole story was itself too much like a fiction. I tried to put myself in the shoes of the Committee. How do these people suddenly jump out of the woodwork? Why do they wait until now to announce themselves? What proof has this Gerda of her "association" with Wallenberg? How is she different from the other six women claiming mistress status? Ah, but that is where I am her witness, am I not? I could have said: I know, I saw her leave that night with Wallenberg. She was wearing a red dress. I served them a *Croquembouche*. But I did not tell about that. Why not? Because Mrs Kornblatt had made it quite clear she would close her ears to such stories. I myself had felt in the head like the batter of a hazelnut *torte*-egg yolks, ground nuts, bread crumbs-one can hardly turn the spoon to stir such a mixture. So I said nothing. But suppose I had told her about Gerda and Rella-*His* daughter sitting in their waiting room!-and suppose she had believed me? Soon people would be banging on Gerda's door seeking entry with their cameras and recording equipment and bright lights. Give us a statement, they would say, and the flashbulbs would be going pop in her weak green eyes. They would have a million questions about her relationship with Wallenberg, also with Eichmann. And they would not rest there: Why don't you go out of the house? Are you doing penance? What do you do for a living? We understand you used to be a great beauty? Is it true your daughter is a super's helper? No, I thought, now it is up to me. I pictured Gerda stretched out on an elegant silver serving tray with her arms at her sides; as slim as a lady's finger. Over her I pour a mixture of sweetened cognac and water and when she is well drenched but not disintegrating I preserve her in chocolate; the richest, thickest coat she will ever wear. Over this I place a glass dome; to protect her, to keep her young and innocent.

We took our seats on the subway. Rella's head fell against my shoulder and I thought: Mr Wallenberg, we rest our case. It is too early to say *finis*. Therefore, we pronounce you alive and well; and we adopt you; we embrace you. Now you are ours, you too will be safe with us.

Gerda

At fifty most women are old bags, used up and wrinkled, ready for the garbage can. But as I have been kind to the years, the years have been kind to me; I too know how to make a deal. I don't claim prettiness. Mine is a mature face, a face which tells a story. Many stories. It is a face which survives to tell. Within this country of a face there have been shifting sands, erosions of earth, cracks and rivulets – I do not deceive myself – but the high cheekbones, the straight nose, the square chin, these landmarks still stand firm. And there is always Madame Rubinstein to magic away the odd pouch or wrinkle. Ask Rella, she will tell you. She still watches me do my face. But what about the body, hidden behind the window ledge? I do not deny it, I have grown stout. So? Rubens, Rembrandt, Giorgione; they all loved a woman with flesh on her bones. Ask Raoul, when they release him; he will tell you how thin I was once: too thin. Nothing to sink your teeth into. Like Rella. One day she will disappear.

Jack-be-Nimble is to blame, of course, for feeding me sweets like goodnight kisses. Still, I would rather be fat than shriveled up like an Eichmann. Yes, I am full within my skin; it doesn't hang on me like an old nightgown. I fill the window frame like a portrait of Woman. The world looks in at me and knows I am somebody. They cannot ignore me or look through me or around me. They know I am still beautiful.

So Jack-be-Nimble has crawled to the Committee to give evidence; what evidence? That he shared a cell with Raoul on one, maybe two, occasions? What does it tell them? Nothing, except that he may still be a prisoner, which was already established. What does it tell them about the years before? Does it constitute familiarity? Oh no, not like mine. What I have to tell will make them dance a polka in the streets.

"Well, what did he say about me?" I ask.

She shrugs. "Why should he tell them anything about you? He had his own story to tell. Besides, what does he know about you?"

"He worked at the Majestic; therefore, he knew how ... instrumental I was to the rescue operation. He might have felt it his duty to reveal such an important connection. You have, I presume, told him who you are? Do you think they are likely to ignore such a revelation – the daughter of Raoul Wallenberg? Don't be a fool."

"I don't think you understand," she says. "They really aren't concerned about his personal life. They're trying to find out if he's still alive, that's all."

I laugh. Not concerned about his personal life, ha! "What's the difference?"

So Jack-be-Nimble is telling nothing. He is covering, protecting; or perhaps he really didn't know what went on at the Majestic. It's possible he's innocent, and just as well. What could he have told them? She was a beautiful wine waitress; she knew more about wines than any man. She knew nothing of politics. She did her job and everyone admired her. She was very friendly but virtuous. She spat on the Arrowcross bigshots; even Eichmann she told to, well, go to hell. Her father, you see, was the *maître d'hôtel*; she was under his protection. It was only when the heroic, handsome Wallenberg came along that she was swept off her feet. She left with him the night of the dinner. Eichmann was very angry ... In his dreams I am as slim as a bread stick in my waiter's uniform. Or in my red dress. I remember his desserts – the *pavé au chocolat* – lady's fingers drenched in cognac. I remember drinking up the leftover cognac at the bottom of the dish, late at night in the kitchen. And I remember the *Croquembouche*; but I have already told of that.

Yes, it is better that he doesn't remember, or makes it his business to keep silent. Perhaps *he* is the real hero, the man who practises discretion. Certain things, you understand, are repeatable; indeed, they are worthy of much attention; the more the better. But other things merely hurt and confuse; that Rella, for example, should know more about Eichmann than she already knows. No, certain things should be preserved, as a cake under glass. Jack-be-Nimble may know what he knows, but he is no informer.

I have decided: I will tell my own version; why not? If Jack can give evidence, then so can I. I have written to invite the Wallenberg Committee to come and see me. No, I tell them, I will not go to their office; I do not go out for anyone or anything. But they will travel further than Brooklyn Heights for such a hot story. I am sure they cannot wait to hear it; it could be the key to everything.

I pull down the shades, draw the curtains and light the lamps; artificial light is best. I lock Vitez in Rella's room, as he will try to eat a strange man. I wear my black jersey wrap-around trimmed with black fur, a black turban to match and my largest gold hoop ear-rings. I wear gold sandals, with straps as narrow as vermicelli between the toes – a small sacrifice to the occasion.

The bell rings; before me is a young woman, a ballet dancer, perhaps, or a social worker. It must be a mistake. I tell her she has come to the wrong place and close the door in her face. She rings again. "Raoul Wallenberg," she whispers before I can react. So this is who they have sent me; this girl, this child. "Come in," I say, sniffing. What can she presume to understand about life, about anything? So this is the value they place on my story. Well, I will show them. I blow smoke in her face. I will tell her nothing, she can beg. "Please, Mrs Green, I know it's difficult, talking about these things. I do understand. But we need to know for *his* sake. We want to know the truth so we can get him released." Truth, huh; what can she know about truth?

But come, I will tell her things to make her pointy little ears burn. She is wearing a full skirt and ballet slippers. She is light and graceful; I feel heavy and old. Never mind, I will recline on my green chaise and she can sit on the rocker. Another nothing of a girl, like Rella.

"What makes you so interested in him?" I ask.

She replies, "I'm doing a thesis on him. It's for a degree in peace studies at a college in London. I'm here collecting data."

"Ah, so I am a piece of data, like a piece of cake."

"Well, I wouldn't quite put it like that, Mrs Green."

"Gerda. Call me Gerda."

"All right, Gerda. My name is Sarah. Pleased to meet you. Now would you like to tell me about when you last saw Raoul?"

And so I tell her about our first meeting in '43 and then how he came back as he promised. I tell her how we worked together; without me his rescue operation would have collapsed like a circus tent. It was I who knew the times of the transports, I who knew which blocks of the ghetto were to be rounded up.

"Yes," she interrupts. "You said you worked at the Majestic. Wasn't that the place Eichmann lived while he was supervising the death marches?"

"How clever you are, my dear. We despised him, of course, but it was from him I got the most precise information; from the horse's mouth, as they say."

"How were you in a position to get such information, if I may ask?"

"You may ask. As a wine waiter, one is always present at sensitive interviews. There the wine flowed like water, I was always fetching and carrying. I worked my poor fingers to the bone."

"I'm sorry you had such a hard life, Gerda. But tell me more about Wallenberg. We understand he disappeared after the siege; is that correct?"

"Disappeared?" I laugh. "Oh yes, into the jaws of the great Soviet beast. He was arrested, as you know, and never seen again."

"Well, that isn't quite true. Some people have seen him pretty recently. Tell me, you were close to him, as you say? Did the Russians ever question you about his activities?"

"No. Why should they want to talk to me? They didn't know about me."

"I thought you drove part of the way with him to Debrecen the day they took him away? That's what you said."

Smartass. "Ah yes, as a friend, I went with him. But why

should the Russians be interested in an innocent wine waitress?"

"I don't know, I just wondered." She smiles like a wet dishrag. "Well, I'd really like to move on now. It's his recent whereabouts we're really interested in. Can you tell us anything about that?"

"Everyone knows his 'recent whereabouts' as you so charmingly put it. I do not have anything to add to that information."

"Well, we believe he's still in a Soviet prison, but recent sightings are very important to prove our case. He *has* been seen in various prisons and psychiatric hospitals over the last twenty years. It's that kind of information we're most excited about. Don't misunderstand me, Gerda, I don't mean to put down the importance of your ... association with him; it's just not so relevant to what we're doing, the Committee that is. As for my thesis, that's about political prisoners, so what happened in Budapest–or might have happened–in Raoul's personal life, is really a kind of side issue. If you see what I mean." Oh I see; the impertinent jealous little prune. I waltz her to the door. Such a waste of an afternoon.

For two days I smolder; how dare they send this young idiot to me! Finally I telephone to complain. I speak to a certain Mrs Kornblatt. I tell her, woman to woman, I am disappointed with her little messenger girl; perhaps she had not quite understood what it was I had to tell. I say, "So many are known to have shared a cell with him, but how many a bed?" She clears her throat in my ear. "I am a busy woman, Mrs Green, and Raoul Wallenberg is not getting any younger. You are the seventh woman claiming to have been his mistress; does that answer your question? To be frank with you, I simply do not believe he had the time to canoodle between rescue operations. As far as I am concerned, you can take your so-called testimony and send it to Hollywood. Here we are running a serious organization. We do not have time for such gossip. Goodbye, Mrs Green." And she hangs up on me; me, Gerda. She will not get away with it.

Part V

1981

Jack

1

From the dark cupboard I brought her out into the white light. I lifted her wax-wings and sniffed: mmmnn, delicious. I caressed her dark satin rump and then I perfumed her with a third dousing of cognac. She winked at me with her currant eyes, my plump companion, and I put her to rest and absorb until Christmas eve. Then she would be mine.

I mourned for the trees being sold like trinkets on street-corners. I thought of woods outside the city populated with surprised amputees wondering what could have happened to their limbs; for these were merely the branches or tips of trees. Oh you must not worry, I whispered, your spare limbs have been taken to the big city to earn their fortunes. If they are lucky they will be taken into warm homes, where they will be cherished for their fine aromatic oils and decorated, and if the children are careful to obey instructions on the care and maintenance of Christmas trees sent to all families by the New York Fire Department, they will not go up in flames. Meanwhile, your offshoots must be patient: lean against the brick walls of subway stations, one on top of the other, hardly breathing, stumps inches deep in dirty slush, weeping needles, bald as ... Yes, these too made me think of Wallenberg. Perhaps if he walked amongst us today we would throw tinsel over his poor bald patch to make him more presentable for the holiday season.

I hardened my heart and pushed my stomach through the subway turnstile, and the rest of me followed. The train took me under the wide grey river and brought me to the borough of Manhattan. There I got out of the train and, blinking, rose from under the earth into the daylight of West 4th Street. There were the smells of damp fur collars to sniff; sour pickles, hot chestnuts, more Christmas trees, and of course bakeshops. I poked my nose into the 8th Street Bakeshop to look at the croissants but I was sadly disappointed. A drop dripped off the end of my nose. The croissants in question were lined up like so many pale sea creatures turned inside out. No, they should have been smaller, and crisper on the outside (Where were their protective shells?). It was quite wrong to let their soft insides show, and how embarrassing. They did not smell sweetly, as they should, of butter. Next, my nose led me to a Viennese pastry shop on Christopher Street, called Schlagobers, which was supposedly in the business of selling more serious confections to the connoisseur. I sat down and ordered a piece of strudel and a cup of coffee. *Mit schlag? Oh, ja.* Ah, you are German, sir. Yes, originally, though I have been in this country now for many years. In that case you will appreciate a real piece of strudel when you are tasting it.

I thought of coming to work in such a place instead of my sad bialy factory where variety, imagination and good taste were forever frustrated. It could mean a return to my profession. I would receive a salary worthy of my abilities, live in a building with a doorman who would salute me (Good evening, Mr Baum.) and hold open the door for me to pass through. I would become a distinguished gentleman, my hair would be cut in silvery layers, close to the scalp like a *Bischofsbrot*. My suits would be cut and tailored to flatter the figure; no longer a starchy white loaf would I be, but a solid, pin-striped pumpernickel. And in such a place there would be people to appreciate my strudel (not a cardboard pouch like this one)—Europeans, intellectuals, poets, artists. I would be summoned from my kitchen to receive congratulations. I would be famous.

But I would be alone, even more alone than I already was; bereft of the only people in my small world: Rella and Gerda. Perhaps that seems strange to you. But to me we were the ingredients of a world like a magical fruitcake. I was the plump white raisin, Rella was the snip of green angelica, Gerda the luscious red cherry. All those years she ate my offerings, but we refrained from common intercourse. And yet I felt we were baked together in a mold. Wallenberg was the essential ingredient; he bound us together and added a taste of ginger. No, I would not defect to Manhattan.

I visited a fruit and vegetable market where knobbly and twisted, bright sleek creatures were on display. Such color, such curiosities! I felt like a child in a toyshop; which would be my playmates? The beautiful peppers displaying themselves like parrots, or the large but shy and retiring uglis? My eye went with admiration to the peppers but my heart went naturally to the uglis. I wanted to take them home with me and protect them from scorn. *Look*, people were saying, *uglis*. *Ugh*. And pointing as if to a bushel of freaks. I chose two of the ugliest – though to me they were beautiful. But how difficult it was to leave the others behind; how they accused. I cradled in my arms six baby eggplants because there was no more room in my small basket.

On the way home I planned my Christmas menu: first, a soup of puréed celery root served in orange halves, followed by peeled broccoli stems in a lemon butter sauce. After that the different colored peppers (red, yellow, green and black) and the roasted baby eggplants. Yes, that should be enough for Rella, I thought. And the bird? How can one eat Christmas dinner without a bird? Consider a flavorful Muscovy duck, I told myself. But no, it was bad enough plucking innocent vegetables out of the earth; I would not have the blood of a bird on my hands. For dessert would come the queen of plum puddings, not unwelcome after a light meal.

Everything was ready. I awaited my tired asparagus but she arrived transformed, in her red blouse with a red velvet skirt (which, however, did not quite match), and her bird's legs encased in nylon stockings. On her feet she wore long brown shoes which she swiveled from side to side. They reminded me of the commercial product called "Devil Dogs" and I feared at any moment they might attack me. Her hair was cut very short, exposing ears and neck. Her head resembled a brioche without its topknot, narrow at the base, wide at the crown. It was the first time she had been to a beauty parlor; they had cut and blown her dry.

191

She patted the smooth loaf of her head proudly. Her lips were painted red, her eyelids black. Gold hoops pierced her earlobes; I had to look away. She made me think of one of the Christmas branches weighted down with ornaments. I wanted to undress her, return her to her familiar jeans and sneakers, hair dropping down her back. The only familiar – and therefore comforting – features were her blackened teeth and her arms which hung at her sides like the vegetables I had seen at the market; my mother, I remember, called them "dead men's fingers."

But the real miracle was to come. On the center of my white table stood a poinsettia and two red candles. I held out a chair for her and she sat, bending her poor shaved neck forward. The skin looked rare. I lit the candles, served the celery purée and poured us a glass of wine each; it was a Châteauneuf du Pape, 1975. I proposed a toast to Gerda; she to Wallenberg. She said, yes, Gerda would appreciate such a wine; she herself knew nothing about it. Eventually she raised her head and lowered her spoon into the purée. I held my breath. The spoon was now up to its neck in hot creamy soup; the little dollop of cream, the sprig of parsley, were disturbed. At last she put the spoon before her lips. She gulped and I could trace the travels of the liquid down her throat. She took another mouthful and then another. I was so absorbed I nearly forgot to eat myself. Soon the orange shell was quite empty. She patted her lips with her white napkin – they were bluish and caked in the corners: food, I realized, was what she needed. She covered her mouth again with her napkin and smiled behind it. "That was delicious," she said, with much self-consciousness, for she was unaccustomed to such rituals of pleasure. I put my nose into my glass and sniffed; my eyes were rather tearful. After the plum pudding she licked her lips (which were now quite bare of paint) and asked for some more cream. She closed her eyes. The candle flame made shadows on her thin lids. Of what – or whom – was she dreaming? Wallenberg, perhaps; alive and well, released from his prison cell. I knew she was more convinced than ever this would happen, and I worried. But what does it matter – I asked myself – if this is what hope can do?

We took our coffees into the living room to watch the

English BBC Special, *Missing Hero* – about Wallenberg of course. I cannot say exactly why but we were both quite nervous. I offered Rella a chocolate mint, which she accepted. We watched. A tree is being planted for him in Israel; he becomes another Righteous Gentile. We ate more mints. An announcer's voice said, "In the continuing efforts to obtain certainty, one must presume Wallenberg is still alive, otherwise it would be pointless to pursue the matter. Yes, it is very likely he is alive." Rella chewed and nodded. Suddenly she stiffened like a wafer. The suggestion is being made that Wallenberg might have had a lover in Budapest whom he was protecting. Would they mention Gerda? Or the other six mistresses spoken of by Mrs Kornblatt? No. They conclude there is no other explanation for his deeds than his courage and humanity. Rella crossed her legs and lit a cigarette; her hands were trembling. They flash pictures of him on the screen: a little boy with chocolate-covered almond eyes; a handsome young man resting his foot on the bumper of a pre-war car on the Golden Gate Bridge in San Francisco; a diplomat with thinning hair sitting at a desk in Budapest. And then it was I realized for whom Rella had made herself so beautiful. I nibbled the last mint.

We exchanged Christmas gifts. I gave Rella the book which had just been published, called *Righteous Gentile*, by the same man who had produced the television program; also a silver medal to be worn around her neck. The Jewish Heritage Society had offered the image of Wallenberg engraved in a choice of metals: fourteen carat gold (£900), solid sterling silver (£75), silver plate (£35), and bronze (£15). Hers was silver plate, the most I could afford. She hugged the book to her red bosom and I clasped the medal around her poor neck. She said she would never take it off.

She presented to me a large square box wrapped in red and brown striped paper with a red curled paper ribbon. Carefully I removed these, then I lifted the deep lid from its box, parted the layers of tissue paper and beheld a copper mixing bowl. I lifted it out, using the hem of my apron to protect it. The bowl was perfectly round with a small rim around the top and a ring on one side for hanging. It was well balanced; although it had no base it stood upright without wobbling from side to side. It was the most beautiful copper bowl I had seen in my life. A little booklet came with it, telling its many uses: for beating eggs, cream – but I did not need to be told such things. There was a note on the care of my new copperware. Oh I would care for it, cradle its cold smooth bottom in my arms, warm it with the heat of my own body. I would protect it and keep it safe and it would last forever.

2

I opened maps of Europe in my head; I wrote imaginary letters of excuse. I strutted up and down my kitchen like a fat Hamlet, saying to myself: To go or not to go? However, my indecisive journey only took me around in a circle. At last I managed a small action: I entered the office of a travel agency to inquire the price of an airline ticket to Stockholm. When the woman behind the counter told me, I said, "That is quite expensive," to which she replied, "You get nothing for nothing these days." Then she asked if there was any special reason why I should want to go to Sweden in the winter, and before I could answer, she said, "What's wrong with Florida? It's gorgeous this time of year; sunny and cheap, why bother with Europe? Especially Scandinavia; the polar bears can have it, if you ask me." But I do not ask you, I said to myself, and left the shop before she could entice me into buying a ticket to Miami Beach.

It was to be such an occasion; the making of history. How could I not go? Mrs Kornblatt would be so disappointed. But in truth I did not wish to go. It was so far away, there would be so many strange people, all shaking hands and drinking cocktails. There would be so many self-congratulations; and for what? My testimony – for what it was worth – could easily be read by Mrs Kornblatt; what could my own personal bulk add to the weight of my written statement? Furthermore, I concluded, my testimony was by now out of date and relatively unimportant;

only more recent "sightings" would have significance. If Wallenberg had been seen alive within the last, let us say, half year, one could hope; otherwise, what was the point? No, I would not go, but I would follow the proceedings on my new radio.

It was very early in the morning of 16 January 1981, the day of the long-awaited Stockholm Hearings. I sat in my kitchen adjusting the dials of my new machine, a short-wave radio purchased from The Radio Shack. Rella was with me, drinking a cup of coffee, half dozing in her chair. In Sweden, I thought, it would be lunchtime; people would be mopping raw herrings from their plates. At first my twiddlings produced only intercontinental static, but soon we could hear a noise like the testing of microphones, then coughing. And then we heard, in three languages, the news that the first afternoon session of the Wallenberg Hearings was due to begin.

I mixed a quantity of rich yeast dough, with eggs and spices. I began kneading the dough, pulling it into an oblong shape, folding it end to end, then pressing it down and pushing it forward with the heels of my hands. For ten minutes I continued this process until the dough was quite smooth and elastic. *The hero may live. One day he may be released* (rise, like my *Wienerbrod*). I sprinkled the dough with flour, wrapped it in plastic wrap and put it to rise slowly in the refrigerator. *Let us pray. The panel will now hear the evidence.*

Witness A: An American professor of biophysics. "In 1960 I spent time in cell number 33 of Vladimir prison with a Ukrainian, who told me of a Swedish prisoner who had been in that cell before me. In 1962 I was transferred to cell number 31 with a Latvian, who also spoke of a Swede called 'van den Berg.'"

Question: How did you first become a prisoner in the Soviet Union, Professor M?

Question: Why do you assume "van den Berg" is the same as Wallenberg?

Question: Do all prisoners in Vladimir have shaved heads? *   *   *

195

Cocks' combs, snails, envelopes, bears' claws, who could eat things with such shapes, such names? Of course these Danish or Swedish pastries (as they are also known) are really corruptions of the noble Vienna Bread. Nevertheless, a Swedish confection was appropriate to the occasion. I tested the butter; it should hold the impression of a finger. I put the sticks on a sheet of waxed paper lightly dusted with flour and, with a rolling pin, flattened them into a rectangle. I did so also with the other two sticks of butter. Then I covered both sheets with waxed paper and put them, one on top of the other, back into the refrigerator to chill.

Witness B: Informant unnamed. "I met with a Soviet general who had been jailed between 1948 and 1956, who says he spent time with a Mr Wallenberg on three occasions, during transports from one prison to another; in 1953, 1955, and again in 1956."

Question: How can the evidence be admissible when the informant does not submit his real name?

Panel Reply: One cannot expect people to reveal their true identities for fear of reprisals to relatives still living in the Soviet Union.

Question: Can you compare diets in Soviet prisons and labor camps?

Witness B: In both the diet consists of fish soup, potatoes, sometimes a small piece of meat, dry black bread.

I rolled the dough out to a large thin rectangle, then placed one of the sheets of chilled butter across the center of the dough and brought the end of the dough over the butter and sealed it along the sides. I placed the other sheet of butter on top and brought the other half of dough over that, again sealing the butter in at the sides. I dusted the whole with flour, wrapped it up and again put it into the refrigerator to chill. My hands were nicely oiled, fragrant with sweet butter.

Witness C: Informant now lives in Paris but was

imprisoned in the Soviet Union from 1930 until 1957. He will be questioned in Russian. "During my twenty-seven years in various prisons I saw the Swede on several occasions, I cannot remember exactly the dates, between 1945 and 1957."

Question: How did he appear to you on these occasions?
Witness C: Healthy at first but a little frightened.
Question: Frightened?
Translator: Perhaps depressed is a better word for that.
Witness C: His situation was most uncertain, you see, and this made him rather anxious.

I rolled the dough into a skinny strip. Then I folded the narrow ends so they would meet in the middle, and then I folded it in half, which gave me four layers. Again I chilled it for twenty minutes. *Frightened, depressed.*

Witness D: Ex-British spy G. W., released in 1964 in exchange for a Soviet spy. "One day in early 1963, I was up on the roof when I heard a voice call out 'Taxi.' Given the filthy conditions of the lifts, this struck me as a piece of defiant humour, which I greatly appreciated. About five days after that the same thing happened – the cage came up and the same voice called out 'Taxi' and this time I heard some conversation between the prisoner and his guard. I could tell from the accent that this was another foreigner, so I called out, 'Are you American?' The voice answered 'No, Swedish.'"

Such a pity the pastry was not already baked; I could imagine its perfume mingling with that of the toasted almonds on top. A wreath. For now perhaps just a small piece of carrot cake; not fresh, but something to chew on. Rella? Yes, she would have a small piece with her coffee. The change was already dramatic, there were not so many bones stretching her skin. She smiled; the stumps of her teeth were covered in cream cheese icing. So lovely she would be with new teeth. She repeated the word

197

"Taxi" and took a mouthful of coffee to wash it down.

Witness E: Not present. Testimony to be presented
                by Mrs Kornblatt of the New York Wal-
                lenberg Committee. An Austrian, now
                living in America, formerly at Buchenwald
                Camp and then arrested in Budapest by
                the Soviets and sent to Vladimir prison
                until his release in 1955. "On two occas-
                ions, Mr B shared a cell with Wallenberg,
                first in December 1947 (five months after
                he had been reported dead by the Soviets),
                then later, in 1955, before Mr B's release."

Question: How can your witness be so sure this was
                in fact Raoul Wallenberg?

Mrs Kornblatt: He had met Wallenberg on several occa-
                sions while in Budapest. Mr B was a pastry
                chef at the Hotel Majestic. He encountered
                Mr Wallenberg there at a Christmas din-
                ner party and later he delivered bread to
                the Swedish Safe Houses.

I brushed away the carrot cake crumbs which had gathered
themselves in scattered colonies on the mound of my
stomach. I smothered myself, patted myself. My testimony
would be recorded for posterity.

Question: But what were Mr B's reasons for not
                coming forward sooner?

Mrs Kornblatt: Mr B was in a mental institution until
                the time he came forth with his testimony.
                During that time he had no memory what-
                soever of past events.

Question: A mental institution?

Mrs Kornblatt: Yes. But this fact, in my opinion, should
                in no way prejudice his testimony. Mr B is
                today as sane as anyone in this room.

The dry cake caught in my throat. I thought, I must
remember in future to wrap baked goods more carefully so
that air cannot spoil them. "There," said Rella, "it's all over,
your testimony has been accepted into the record."

For the last time, I took the dough from the refrigerator and pounded it down with the rolling pin. I whispered apologies to the battered dough, and counselled patience. You will rise up, I said, full of air and richness, the color of sunshine. You will see. You will suffer no lasting bruises. I divided the dough into three long pieces and braided them. I brought the braided ends together to form a circle. The perfect circle, representing all things: luck for the future, as in a wedding ring; luck for death, as in the funeral wreath. I sprinkled shaved toasted almonds over the top, drizzled an abstract pattern with a mixture of confectioner's sugar and sour cream, and over that I painted a clear varnish of thinned apricot preserve. I dedicated this wreath to Raoul Wallenberg: 16 January 1945, the last day he was seen alive in Budapest.

Witness F: Not present, since re-arrested by the Soviets. A reported telephone conversation between Soviet Citizen K and his daughter in Israel: "When I was in Buyturka prison hospital in 1975, I met a Swede who told me he had been in Soviet prisons for thirty years, and he seemed reasonably healthy to me."

Witness G: Also not present. The reported conversation between an ex-Russian lawyer and the Director-General of a Soviet prison camp, dated 1972. "I came prepared with a bottle of vodka. After a while the Director became quite loose in the tongue, talking about how he was responsible for a certain prisoner of state. Among others, he told me, there was a Swede who had been in camps for more than twenty or thirty years. He was apparently ill and refused to transfer to a hospital because he was afraid of getting poisoned."

Witness H: Not present. Statement quoted from an informant who in turn was quoting a prison guard at Spets Korpus in the Gorky prison region. "In 1980 Wallenberg had a tooth extracted in the prison but he did not return to

> his cell after the operation. Unfortunately,
> this guard was transferred to Kirov so I had no
> indication about whether Raoul Wallenberg
> was still in Spets Korpus."

A bad taste came to my mouth. What did they mean, these tantalizing crumbs; this fear of prison, this toothache? Was he still wandering the corridors of Spets Korpus holding an ice pack to his swollen cheek? I held my stomach, forced myself to listen to the summation which followed:

> A vast array of witnesses have individually produced
> evidence and statements of having seen Raoul Wallen-
> berg on many different occasions since 1947, when he
> is said, by the Soviets, to have died. Individually the
> statements might be wanting; each strand of evidence
> may be weak; but when put together, it becomes a
> massive substance.

Like the carrot cake. I considered how the strands of shredded carrot come out of the grinder and collapse into the mixing bowl with weak knees. But add flour, eggs, honey, baking powder, sugar, set the ingredients in a medium oven for an hour and you have solidity. Over the top you put a sweet white substance. Just so, it was sitting in my stomach, rumbling.

Rella left to give the oil burner his morning drink of water. I thought, observing her leave, she will match him with her glow. Not an evil glow like his, but a gentle glow, like a candle. She has no suspicions. She burns. She is a believer, a convert to the faith. She is learning to eat but still she is as light as a candied violet, a chocolate curl. And I thought of this "mass of evidence"; what was it? Blind testimony, hearsay, speculation; the words of drunks, spies, lunatics, those who have since mysteriously died or disappeared. As light as a packaged pre-cooked pudding. But where, where is the proof?

3

I put the *Wienerbrod* into the oven. Then I made my way
downstairs to get the morning newspaper and to clear my
head, which was thick enough to coat the back of a spoon. I
felt quite ill, my legs were so weak. Shreds, crumbs, slivers;
oh, it all came back to me as from a dream. My tired *derrière*
dropped onto a revolving red stool at the coffee shop
counter. Perhaps one more cup of coffee to wake me up
while I read the report of the Hearings. I folded the *Times*
into a long strip, like a businessman. On page sixteen was a
picture of Wallenberg and the headline: SWEDISH HERO
IS IN SOVIET UNION, PANEL SAYS. The young man in
the photograph was not as I remembered the Swede, not as
he was in prison. I stared into my coffee cup to try to see
him more clearly but all I could see were small globes of fat
floating in a pale brown ocean. The printing of page sixteen
was also unclear, so black and smeared was the ink I could
hardly distinguish one word from another. Perhaps it was
just my eyes playing tricks? However, this much I could
read: "There is a great weight of evidence ... that he did
not die." And then: "Therefore we cling to the idea that he
is still alive." I finished my coffee and left, with my
newspaper tucked under my arm. It was time to rescue my
Wienerbrod.

We cling to the idea that he is alive. As I walked I pictured
rows of specially imported cling-peaches such as in the
Village market. The flesh clings to the stone; it is a
tenacious fruit. But surely it is time to let go, I thought, and
as I did I seemed to let go of myself. I tripped over the tree
root outside Gerda's window and found myself sitting on
the sidewalk, just like one of my neighbors, Mr Bovino,
who had broken his ankle the week before Christmas.
Such a fool I felt. But what damage was done? No, the root
was not hurt. I looked up and saw Gerda watching me from
her window, smiling her brilliant smile. Like a bruised fruit
I smiled back. After all these years, I thought, not a word
has been spoken between us. I knew all about her, of
course, but what did she know about me? The red dress

appeared before my eyes. Did she think I was inebriated? I hoped not. I crawled on my knees over to the tree and put my arms around its waist. It felt familiar and comforting. I apologized to it for having fallen down on one of its private parts, but I assured it no damage had been done. I felt Gerda watching me; what did she see? A clumsy white bear indulging himself in hugs and one-sided conversations? No no no; I remembered Rudolph the Bear, my childhood story, and I thought it would be only right if one of the neighboring *hausfraus* were to come out and sweep me away with her broom; or telephone to the mental hospital to come and take me away again. But Gerda beamed down on me; I knew she would not break our pact of silence; she would protect me from harm.

I removed my apron and covered the exposed root. It seemed to me the only gentlemanly thing to do. This, after all, was no Eden. I remembered the Wienerwald where I had walked as a boy. There the trees had no shame; roots were not forced to hide themselves under concrete or to push hopelessly against brick, or tunnel down, down, into empty sewers, waving their fine root ends in the blinding darkness. No, in the Black Forest the whole world was having picnics, roots abandoned themselves to earth and sky alike; they wrapped themselves lovingly around other trees, grew audaciously across a path to greet one's feet, wiggled and danced along the forest floor like happy snakes. But not here; here, trees do not have right of way. First come the cars and buildings, then the people, and only then the animals and trees. But you must not worry, I told it, soon the sidewalk will be fixed, they will push your essential part back into its safe hole; you will be quite all right, you will not die of exposure or shame. You must live like other city trees, try to contain your enthusiasms. I thought of a prisoner at Buchenwald who had been kicked so hard in the stomach he split open like a melon; only he pushed his seeds and strings back in and tied a belt around his middle and went on as before (he died later of an infection). But that will not happen to you, I said; you, my friend, will find a new route – trees always do, they are so strong. Indeed, you will probably break through again in some other inconvenient place. So you had better watch what path you take underground. You will be under suspicion as a troublemaker, the way you trip people up as they are walking past, minding their own business. Yes, I said, lifting myself up (using the tree for support), you had better be careful; trees are expendable and streets are not.

And then I remembered my *Wienerbrod*. It would be overcooked – dry, cracked like the sidewalk. Such a crime, I moaned to myself, running up to my apartment as fast as my short legs would carry me. Perhaps it was not hopeless; perhaps I would rescue it in time. And all the way up the stairs the smile of Gerda followed me, hanging in the air like the Cheshire Cat in another of my childhood books. It was almost as if she had enjoyed watching my foolish performance.

Gerda

1

Life is a hole, that's my philosophy. One step forward and boom, up to the armpits. You grab onto a tree, somebody stretches out a helping hand, a ladder, a rope – somehow you find a way out. But you begin to notice they're all around, these curious holes, you can't dance around them forever. Eventually you drop your guard and fall in again, and then see how easy it is to climb out! You are older now, your legs are not so strong; your insurance policy doesn't cover such-and-such a natural or unnatural disaster. So you decide to stay until you recover your strength; you realize you are quite safe, there are no further holes into which you can fall. Ah, soon your hole is your castle! Welcome home.

Consider, for example, the sidewalk outside my window. Cracks suddenly appear; something is forcing its way up, but what? Some monster lurking underneath? And then the concrete splits open and what do I behold but this tree trying to wiggle its toes in the fresh air. And why shouldn't it want to escape from its underground dungeon into the light of day?

Somebody is bound to fall in – but who? Maybe the white Russian princess who resembles a bullfrog, so fat she can't see the ground under her feet; they'd need a crane to lift her out. Or Jack-be-Nimble, or Rella herself – late one night on her way down to the cellar. Not watching where she's going, in a fog, trailing her big feet – oops, straight in, her chicken's bones shattering to a heap of splinters. It will be many months before the sidewalk is fixed; between now and then, anything could happen.

I observe my neighbors. They are like so many chess

pieces: step, clack, jog, clump, they manoeuvre themselves around the hole. I offer a wave and a greeting which I adjust, like a Hallmark greeting card, to suit any occasion: *Merry Christmas, Happy Hannukah, Watch Your Step*; Buddha-face, clown-face, poker-face, vamp-face – the flesh is infinitely mobile. I am sorry for them. Only the tree and I are out of danger; we do not shuffle our feet on this treadmill. Only when we're dead will they cart us away.

But who is this coming to say Merry Christmas? Mr and Mrs Bovino from the second floor. They have each deposited a neat brown bag of garbage into the barrels like gifts from the Magi. As they stroll towards me, I picture them together in bed. (An inexcusable habit, but I cannot help myself.) What do I see? Deep lines under two sagging bellies, his member at half mast waving at her simpering triangle. The amused smile on my face conveys goodwill; so be it. Mrs Bovino waves and Mr Bovino – distracted by my wink – fails to look where he's going, misses his footing and trips over a piece of the broken sidewalk. Mrs B reaches out but fails to save him. Down he goes – plop. And that strange noise as from someone who has sat down on a cucumber. What can it be? Ah, poor Mrs B – she screams. And there they huddle together in their hole, waiting.

Life inside is not without its own pitfalls. Business is not, I may say, what it once was. Naturally I am older and the flesh begins to spread. Many of my most faithful customers have disappeared; died or moved to California. Quite a few still come around for a wag of the head, a swiss cheese on rye and a glass of beer, a game of chess – but the pleasures of the flesh, alas, are few and far between. The younger men are into, as they say, other things. Such are the ups and downs in the business of love.

However, one must find solutions; that, after all, is the meaning of survival. One day I get a visit from my old friend The Butler. As a young man he worked the coast of Maine as a real butler (that's how he came by his name). He served the aristocrats in their white houses with dove-gray shutters, surrounded by family portraits, monogrammed silver in mahogany boxes, libraries of leather-bound books, oriental rugs. He became a man of culture, with his shiny black hair, shoes, and Mercedes Benz. There were times he reminded me of my father. He too is known as something of a slippery customer. But how could I turn down the gift of love from such an old admirer?

However, he has come for more important business. We are neither of us getting any younger, he says, smacking his knee with his white pigskin gloves just like Adolf used to do. Such wisdom. We are both silver under our blue-black rinse. "What's on your mind, Butler?" I ask, getting a little impatient. He says, "A little deal. You may be interested, you may not. It's up to you." So I say I'm listening and make myself comfortable on my green chaise. How many proposals have I had in my day? I lose count. This one could not have come at a better time; I might even consider it, seeing as I am without a means of support for the first time in my life. Something usually turns up, but you never know; there are so many holes to fall into. "What would you say to a little babysitting job, Gerda?" Babysitting, me? A job for a teenager? I smell a rat.

"What is this, Butler? What are you talking about?"

"A very small baby, but precious. Never cries and it makes you feel good all over. It comes wrapped in a plain brown diaper and it's pure white inside."

That kind of baby. "So you're a dealer now, Butler. This is news to me."

"Mostly I run high-class diet salons up on Park Avenue," he says, "but this is a little sideline. Much more profitable than diet pills. One brick is worth a couple of million."

"You want me to take care of it for you."

"Until the heat's off."

"When will that be, Butler?"

"That I can't say."

"And what's in it for me? I'm not crazy about babies. Too old, I might not have the patience."

"A thousand in advance, another two thousand on delivery, and a final payment of ten thousand on pick-up, whenever that may be. You want to think about it, Gerda?"

"No, Mr Butler, you have yourself a deal. I love this baby already. What's the name?"

"Gold Dust. Dusty for short."

"When do I expect Dusty?"

"We'll let you know. Soon."

"Merry Christmas to you too, Butler."

So, I am to become a woman of substance. Pure white. Who would have thought it, a baby, at my age? But I must make preparations; Dusty must have somewhere to sleep. Somewhere nice and dark and secret. I clear out my bottom drawer. This will be his cradle. Every night I will rock him to sleep and sing him a lullaby: Come to me my melancholy baby.

2

Tonight my daughter makes her debut as a Vogue Christmas tree. She presents herself in all her shining glory: cheap red satin blouse with matching pom-poms dangling from her ears; hair sprinkled with tinsel that has fallen from the tree she has been decorating in the lobby. I wave a hand to brush the tinsel from her hair, but she ducks away from me; the new cut-and-blow job must not be disturbed. So smooth and neatly parted down the center, it reminds me of the head of a circumcised dingdong. Unkind, I know, but what else can I say? It isn't the first time I've wondered how she could be mine. I had thought there might be room for a little improvement on nature, but tonight I see the folly of my thinking. Before me is the reality of a Rella coiffured and frocked and rouged – and what is my judgment? An eyesore, a gangly gargoyle, a human icicle. Whose can she be? Only one man's, and it isn't who she thinks.

She has another date with Jack-be-Nimble. First they have dinner and then they watch a special TV program about you-know-who. Could be they dare to hold hands after all these years. As for me, I won't be watching; why waste a holiday evening watching television? Spoil the appetite following the movements of green and yellow ghosts? Out of the question. My customers – hypocrites that they are – are all at home with their charming families. No, Gerda's entertainment is an evening of another kind of succulent flesh – a kosher butterball. Even now I can smell her, those fat thighs sizzling, that broad breast turning a Miami tan, stuffed to the hilt with Pepperidge Farm Dressing Mix, sewn up with double duty black thread. Now all I do is wait until her drumsticks wiggle freely and her juices run clear. Then she'll be mine.

The telephone rings. Which will it be – California or Texas? They never forget me, those tough old Toms. Ah, Texas, hello. And why is he 'phoning this Christmas? His wife has finally kicked the bucket, may she rest in peace, and would I reconsider his proposal of marriage – two old birds flapping together? Ha! I should say not – not on his pipeline. Having resisted for so long, why should I give up now? The game isn't over yet. It isn't for himself he's concerned, he says. Oh no. "You have no security, Gerda; no pension, no nothing. And you aren't getting any younger, don't forget." Oh I do not, Texas. "How can you live not knowing where the next meal is coming from, Gerda?" he asks. But I do, Texas, I do, she's in the oven right now, waiting for me. "Oh, I manage, I live each day as God delivers it to me," I say, heaving a sigh. "Much more interesting this way, Texas." But all the time I'm thinking, if not for The Butler, who knows? A yoke for Gerda might have been on the cards; a tragic ending. He confesses to a paunch and false teeth. Ugh! A lucky escape. But what about mine, he'd like to know – just out of curiosity. Oh, mine are just the same as when he last laid eyes on them; a perfect set, I tell him, the famous smile never fades. How do I manage it? "The protected environment in which I live," I say, "is the secret of eternal youth." I describe a few more attractions – how I'm sitting with one leg up, no bloomers. Can this be heavy breathing I hear? Come, come, Texas, I'm surprised at you. He sighs, says he's going away to lick his wounds; Bermuda, maybe. And I'm going away to lick my fat hen. Bye bye, Texas, talk to you again soon. Dirty old man.

What next? I'm just getting my teeth into a nice juicy thigh, when the 'phone rings again. This time it's my photographer friend calling to say he finds himself in New

York on business; could he possibly see me? *See* me – after all these years? It's out of the question. I say no, I'm much too busy, another time maybe. He insists; I say very sorry, California. "Tell you what," he says, "how 'bout just a peek, that's all I ask for. How can you refuse me?" In that case, California, maybe we can do business.

"All right, a look I can arrange," I say. This is what I tell him: "Drive past my window at such-and-such a time and I'll be there. You can look as hard as you like, but you will not stop the car or get out. If you like, you can drive twice around the block. After that you'll find me gone, the window closed and the curtains drawn. Well, that's my deal – take it or leave it."

"What about a picture?"

"Not on your life."

"Do I have any choice in the matter?"

"No."

"Then I guess it's a deal," he says, and we share a laugh on both of us. We agree on a time for our little performance, a little later that day, just as it's getting dark. He pretends I'm cruel, but he knows how kind I am really.

Rella returns from her orgy with Nimble Jack. "You look like the snake that swallowed the pig," I say, pointing to the pimple of stomach she seems to be sprouting. She'll get fat if she isn't careful. But what's this? Another gift from my most humble and obedient servant – ah, cognac, a plum pudding; mmmnn, heaven. And a precious pot of *schlag* to decorate it like Marie Antoinette's wig. He has poetry in his soul, my little baroque friend. Merry Christmas to you too, Jack – and I wave my fork in his direction. And her? She plops herself down and rocks; something must be on her mind. "How was the TV program?" I ask politely. She doesn't reply. Uh oh, more bad news. "If you want to tell me, tell me; if you don't, don't." I'm not really too anxious to hear, but it looks like I'm not going to get let off the hook.

She clears her throat, lights a cigarette. "Well, there were all these people being interviewed – you know, people he saved, people he worked with, his family, even old girl-friends from Sweden. But it seems odd for them not to

209

mention you. At first I thought they might be going to–somebody said he might have had a lover in Budapest he was trying to protect. But that was brushed aside. They said the only reason he did the things he did was his bravery and humanity. That's what they said. It was as if you didn't exist."

"Why should they mention me–they don't know about me."

"I thought you told the Committee–you had somebody visiting here–about your relationship with him. So how come they're ignoring you like this?"

I laugh. "Simple. Because they don't want to know. Not about me."

"But they mentioned the other women–Viveca Lindfors and Jeanette von Somebody or other. Do you know who they were?"

I'm busy with my plum pudding. Why should I answer her riddles? I ignore her, but she keeps talking.

"Viveca Lindfors was one of his girlfriends in Sweden before he went to Budapest. In the interview she said she thought he was trying to seduce her by telling her about the plight of the Jews in Germany. As for Jeanette von Somebody, he proposed to her in a park outside Stockholm, near a lake. She turned him down because she was more interested in her career, and anyway she wasn't in love with him. She says he went on the Budapest mission because he had a broken heart."

End of speech. "In that case he found the right glue to mend it," I say.

"How come you didn't know about these other women?" she accuses.

"How come? What kind of question is that? Why should I? Do you imagine we had time for confessions, autobiographies? Do you think he knew about my amours? We lived from day to day, forgetting the past; it was behind us. Besides, you shouldn't believe everything you hear on television. These old actresses will say anything for a little free publicity."

She's still doubtful, suspicious. "Listen," I say, "use your head. Those women were flotsam and jetsam from his early life. Background material. As a young man he was so-

and-so: naughty, rich, a playboy, a flirt; they can make up any cock-and-bull story they like. But then he goes off to Budapest on a mission for Uncle Sam. No more fun and games, this is serious stuff, he's got to pull up his socks and get on with the job. No more girlfriend nonsense. He saved Jews, remember, he didn't make love to them. Oh no. Women are a distraction to a man, a destroyer of true purpose. No, they don't want to know about this peccadillo of his. The great hero having an affair with a wine waitress – impossible. Anyway, what does it matter what they say; we know what we know. Here take this."

I hand her a small box, her Christmas present. I don't bother with wrapping paper, I like to get down to business. She'll never guess, Swedish heroes don't come in jewelry boxes. Ah, but this one does: a solid gold Wallenberg on a chain. Next best thing to the man himself; an improvement, in some ways. Lighter to wear around the neck.

"Oh," she says and puts her hand to her throat. It's the enthusiasm I love.

"Real gold," I say. "It cost me nine hundred – you can thank The Butler next time you see him."

"The Butler? Who's he?"

"Ah, The Butler is the bringer of miracles," I say. "Come, I'll show you a secret." And in a moment of weakness, I take her by her skinny hand to show her the babe who has been providentially born, white as snow. I look proudly down at the white bundle in its brown wrapper. Ah, lovely, I could kiss its bottom. But what's this? My little puritan doesn't approve, she says it's wrong, it can kill. Thank you, I say, but I don't need a sermon at my time of life, it's against my religion. If you don't like it, you can get lost. I slide the drawer closed, smoothly so as not to disturb the babe. We drop the subject like a hot *wurst*.

She disappears, reappears with a big box behind her back. A Christmas present, for me? Of course I forgive you, my sensitive slice of baloney. All is forgotten. Come, what have you brought me? Please God, I pray, no Wallenberg trinket. Ah, but she knows my taste; that much at least, bless her lean heart. What have we here? A gown from Lord & Taylor – pale green with floating leaf-shaped sleeves made of green silk veined with beads and a turban to match, with seed pearls and iridescent paillettes.

"It's perfect, perfect, my love. How did you know I needed something exactly like this?"

She smiles, covers her mouth. "Can I see you in it?" she asks.

"Even better. You can watch me model it."

I'm all set up, sitting in the window, looking out towards Liberty. This way he'll get a good half-profile view. Make-up just so, turban in place, one green silk sleeve draped over the window sill. New iridescent eyeshadow matching my eyes and the gown. I blink, my lashes are giving me trouble. I lick my lips. Rella is across the street, making sure the lighting is right. She gives me the sign. I hear a car coming up the block, suspiciously slow. Yes, he's here, just as arranged, exactly on time. So slow he's getting a line of cars behind him, honking their horns. "Hey, Mac, c'mon, what's this, the line to see Santa Claus or something? Move it." He hears nothing. Mustn't hurry it. He's past me now, but still looking back over his shoulder. One more time, five minutes to breathe. This time I flash him a smile he can take away with him. More brilliant than gold or pearls put together. Merry Christmas to you too, California.

3

What does she know about danger? Ah, she can feel it in her bones. If the junkies don't get me, the police will. What would I do if the cops came snooping around? Boom, boom, open up lady, we can't wait all day. Coming, officer. I rub off my make-up and limp to the door. I am bent double like a Jewish lady Rumpelstiltskin. Okay, lady, we only want to ask you a few questions. Hands on their hips, hats pushed back. I put a hand over my chest and demonstrate a convincing wheeze. Emphysema, officer. Okay, lady, take it easy. You ever hear of a guy called The Butler?

Butler? You think this is such a fancy establishment I got here? They roll their eyes at each other and shrug their big blue shoulders. Arrowcross, cops, gangsters: I know how to treat men who carry their brains between their legs.

Some of my best customers have come out of the New York Police Department. They still come for a drink, a game of cards, a quiet *tête-à-tête*, a little relaxation from the cares of the street. No, my new hobby won't interest them in the least. I explain to Rella the facts of life, to put what she calls her mind at rest. Fact number one: the Mafia protect me under their big black umbrella. This is part of my deal with The Butler. Fact number two: the Mafia and the NYPD also have an understanding. Fact number three: the NYPD will turn the other cheek in any case because of services rendered to its members. So, you see, all my bases are covered, I'm quite safe. It's no accident The Butler came to me with this job.

But what about the junkies, the addicts, she moans. Suppose they find out I'm sitting on hundreds of pounds of heroin? Suppose, suppose. Who does she think I am, Little Miss Muffet? Where I sit, I sit and no undernourished spider is going to frighten me away. She tries another strategy: Dope kills, she says. It's wrong to deal in dope. Who deals? I only babysit.

But they're desperate, she says, that makes them strong and dangerous. One day she'll come in and find me laid out on the kitchen floor, my lovely throat slit from ear to ear, Vitez with his nose floating in his plastic water bowl. I tell her she's been watching too many crime movies on the Late Show.

"If anybody climbs in the window Vitez will chew their heads off," I say.

"Dogs get shot," she says.

"They'll have to shoot me first."

She doesn't fool me, I know what's what around here. I know which men stroll past my windows taking in the scenery. What do they see? Me in a filmy nightgown reclining on my green chaise. Let them look till their eyeballs drop out onto the sidewalk and smash. But if those eyes roam anywhere else, let them beware. My precious Dusty I guard with my life. No one, but no one, knows where he sleeps. If anyone is keeping an eye on Gerda, Gerda is keeping an eagle eye back. I know which cars cruise past at two in the morning taking in the lie of the land. I know who sits in a parked car for too long, watching my windows and smoking. I do my homework. I have ears and eyes, nothing escapes me. I could always get down on my hands and knees and put my ear to the ground like an Indian. You never know, somebody might be nosing around down in the cellar, looking for a way in.

But danger? Worry? These are *her* wild exaggerations. If the police don't come to arrest me or the dope dealers don't shoot me in the head, or if I don't light myself up like a Buddhist monk with my own cigarette in the middle of the night–then the oil burner will blow up and shoot me through the roof like a rocket at Cape Canaveral. "Good," I say. "When I go, I'd like it to be with a bang."

She rocks and watches. She collects fears the way other people collect antiques. Do I know there are people afraid of string? Trees, fur, flutes? Do I know about the lady who was so afraid of balloons she broke off her engagement–in case a balloon should come uninvited to the wedding party. Hah! Balloons and flutes–the more the merrier for me. I have lived through too much to be afraid of such things. If she wants something to worry about, I can let her in on a private secret: Pssst, it's the men who are most dangerous. Little, big, skinny or fat, smart or stupid, once that thing stares you in the nose or bumps you in the belly, you're wise to be afraid. If it doesn't work properly, if it breaks down half-way through, if Old Faithful goes off with a bang and then hangs down like an old banana skin–then you worry. Not now. Not over an innocent little white lamb.

4

A Raoul made of silver–or gold? What magic have we here? Some days he stares out at me pale as a moon shining on her flat valley of a chest; other days he seems to burn like the sun nestled between two recently risen hummocks. Maybe my eyes, like my skin, deceive me. I use Eterna three times a day, religiously, but great miracles don't happen overnight. These curious changes I cannot fathom. She is the believer in miracles, maybe she can explain it. Ah, yes, that *he* is alive. She believes, she prays, she wears him on a chain around her neck; any day now there will be a visitation to her virgin bed–or mine. Ooh la la. Does she imagine he will come to me in the night on Soviet manufactured wings? The Swedish Pimpernel– released at last–flies non-stop to see his long-lost lady. The photographers and reporters wait to see the battered butterfly. I hang on his arm in my green gown from Lord & Taylor, hiding my wrinkled eyes behind dark sunglasses. I could swear she wears different medals on different days.

When will it be *my* turn to become a *cause célèbre*? Maybe I'll go to Stockholm too. I would not be ignored. I'll arrange to send pre-publicity materials–a picture of myself and a statement telling everything. They'll be waiting for me at the Hearings, the press from all over the world begging for interviews, fighting over exclusive rights to my story. The official Hearing will be totally eclipsed by me, dressed from head to foot in black with a black veil over my face. At last, the mystery mistress of Raoul Wallenberg is revealed. The beauty in black. No, this conspiracy against me cannot last forever. Someone must listen.

Jack-be-Nimble will escort me. He'll arrange details of the flight to Stockholm, the hotel; our meals, naturally. I can rely on him for these things. Rella can tag along too, if she wants; between the two of them I'll be safe. How long up in the sky? Twenty hours, ten hours–who knows? What's the difference? Once you're up there . . . you have drinks, you go to sleep, you wake up and there you are with your feet on the ground again.

If only this had happened thirty years ago. The photographers could not have kept their cameras from my face. Who is this great beauty? They would have asked this, fighting to get closer to me. The travelling would have been more dignified, too.

Now there could be questions. Why didn't you come forward earlier with this bombshell? Because I wasn't ready to drop it in your laps, I say into the microphone, in a husky voice. Maybe they laugh: how 'bout a little peep under the veil, Grandma?

Oh, it is a sinister plot; they're all in it together, including my besotted middle-aged teenager and that four-eyed fruitcake from the turret. He is alive, they swear, here is the proof: smell. I say it stinks. They say it is only a matter of time before he is released. Ah, but what do they know? Do they imagine after spending thirty-five years in a prison cell he's going to fluff up his feathers and come flying out like the angel Gabriel, blowing his horn? Fly, they say in chorus. Now, fly. But the wasted old bird only flaps his wings and croaks.

And after him, will it be my turn? By hook or by crook, to get me out of here as if I too needed liberating? What new technique has she got up her sleeve? Am I to be wired up to a machine operated by an upstate New York doctor who was a *maître d'* on a cruise ship before he went into the biofeedback business – a job my father would have relished? Oh no, the former Greta Garbo of Budapest will not be manipulated like a space dog by a *borscht*-belt mechanic. Not on your life, my little T-bone. They will have to do without me in Stockholm.

Jack

1

As a boy I lay on a dark pew stippled with sunbeams and watched the stained glass fishes of the Lord jumping out of their baskets. Now, in this room where Rella and I sat and waited, the light came from the bodies of golden fishes, only these were quite real, and as they flicked back and forth they shone upon us like miniature flashlights with tails. The smell of high churches drifted to our noses from oriental carpets and the sound of a musical instrument – like pearls dropping onto a jade platter – emerged mysteriously from behind the swiss cheese plant. It was an unusual atmosphere for a dentist's office.

A young woman in a white coat, with the healthy skin of a honey loaf, came in and took Rella's hand. "Hi, how are you. Nervous, I bet?" She smiled down at her. "Just relax. Breathe deeply and evenly. Experience your own body. Listen to the lovely harpsichord music. Watch the fish swimming round and round. Come, let your legs flop, your arms hang loosely at your sides. That's right." She manipulated Rella's stiff limbs until she lay like a dough doll on her leather pallet in the middle of the room. "Now we're going to give you some gas to breathe. You won't feel a thing, I promise. Take a big breath, that's it, fill your lungs all the way up to the top. Now just let your mind wander, relax, have a nice time, think about something pleasant, somebody you really like. Smile, that's it." Rella put her hand automatically in front of her mouth. "Just think, you won't have to do that for much longer," said the nice lady dentist. "Come, open up, I'm just going to swab your gums with this stuff to make them numb."

She swabbed and then she poked. "There, you didn't feel

anything, did you?" she asked, peering round at Rella. Rella shook her head. The instruments disappeared back into a compartment in the wall; perhaps she was not a dentist at all but a kind of magician. "Now you can rest," she said. "Just let yourself go with whatever is happening in your head. You'll start to feel a bit lightheaded soon, maybe even silly, but that's okay. Press this buzzer when you want to start. That way you control the situation. We don't start until you're good and ready, okay?" And she passed out of the room like the shadow of a fish. A few minutes later Rella picked up one of her own fingers and stared at it. Then she held it for a moment above the buzzer and let it drop. The dentist came in and said, "You're ready, that's fine." She asked me if I would like to stay or wait in the waiting room, but before I could reply Rella said "Stay" and giggled. "You can hold my hand," she said. I felt a hard candy lump in my throat; I swallowed again and again to melt it. No, I would be brave, I would not leave her. The dentist smiled at me and winked. "You can leave at any point if you have to," she whispered, pulling a spotlight down from the ceiling to shine on Rella's mouth. A stool was brought for me. The dentist said, "Open wide for me," and I picked up Rella's hand. It was like a cold fork and I closed both my hands around its tines like a pair of warm hungry lips. "Suck," said the dentist to her assistant. I looked up at the ceiling and saw a photograph of a laughing chimpanzee with a set of enormous teeth.

I let my own mind wander back, back to review the dedication ceremony of the new Raoul Wallenberg Playground that Rella and I had just come from. It had become a sort of craze: schools, parks, theaters, streets – all being named after him, or changing their names to his. Hundreds of people had gathered into the little square in Queens to pay tribute to the Swede. A concrete slab with a brass plate like a saddle had been engraved with his date of birth; the space for death was left optimistically empty.

A light hand touched my sleeve: "I think you're squeezing a little too hard," said the nice dentist, and I saw how I had been crushing poor Rella's hand in mine. "Oh, I am so sorry, excuse me," I whispered, and straightened and caressed her folded-up fingers.

218

I thought of Gerda's smiling teeth and the skin around her mouth which looked to me as if it would jump back to the touch as a sponge should do. And then I imagined how Rella's mouth would look without teeth: like a puckered pastry bag. But it would only be temporary, this state of toothlessness; eventually she too would have shining teeth like Gerda's. I heard drilling and sawing and chipping and in spite of all the exotic modernity of the dentist's office, I smelled the smell of hot powdered bone and felt quite ill. I wanted to put my hands over my nose and ears but I could not remove my hand from hers, so tightly was she holding on.

Eventually it was over, the extraction of I do not know how many teeth. The dentist massaged Rella's jaw, very gently, from side to side and gave her a little paper cup full of pink water to rinse her mouth, and a big white napkin to wipe it with.

"Well, that's all for today," said the dentist, whipping away the protective sheet from Rella's front like a conjuror. But what was revealed? Only the unknown daughter of a missing hero, toothless and bloody, who seemed to me so small and bruised I felt I must pick her up and put her in the pocket of my apron for safe keeping. "See you in a couple of weeks," said the kind dentist.

2

Her cold bones were running with sap once again; my tree was warming up. I imagined melted honey – in places dark and thick as molasses, in others pale and thin as wildflower syrup – running up through her branches and down through her trunk to her roots. But which way did the digestive system of a tree flow? I told myself to forget such questions, for what mattered was that she was coming to life again after her long hibernation. I too could feel a tingling in my toes; for it was spring.

It was happening to all the trees, of course, but this tree was special to me. I was like a proud papa observing his pleasingly mature daughter: what have we here? Ah, today she wears a new green cotton dirndl with laces and frills. Who could have chosen a fashion more perfect for her innocent charms? Yes, I approve. I nod my head in appreciation of the new mode; perhaps here and there a bit short for my old-fashioned tastes (How I loved a long skirt of leaves trailing to the ground, as in the willow!), but not tasteless like the mini skirt, God forbid.

No, my tree had a style quite individual and complementary to her graceful limbs. It was a relief her naked winter crotch was no longer exposed to view. But her poor twisted roots were another story. How unfair, I thought, that she should be so marred, like an angel with a club foot. But never mind, I reminded myself, rescue must soon come; spring is the time for repairs to those who suffer from cruel winters. My tree would have to wait her turn, but they would come to her soon, they would come. And she would be restored to perfection.

And then I thought of Rella's poor mouth, of her gums which were as bare as the branches of a tree in winter. Such strange timing it was; when everyone else in the world was dressing up. With such a warmth in the air, with so many buds fat and sticky as *Schaumrolle*, it seemed to me quite wrong for her to go toothless and in pain. But soon she would be perfect too; yes, very soon.

The day after her second extraction she had chocolate crescents under her eyes and her mouth was puffy and shiny with ointment, like a plum dumpling coddled in butter. "You are not working today, of course," I said, but she let her head roll weakly forward. "No," I shook my head quite firmly. "You must certainly not work today. Today you must go to bed with the painkillers the kind dentist gave to you. Besides, today is not a day for work; it is a holy day–Good Friday. It isn't your holiday, I realize, but never mind. You must stay and keep me company while I fast. And rest. Come," I said, and led her by the hand to my couch. I tucked her feet up under a blanket, gave her a hot water bottle to cradle against her face, put a soft pillow behind her head. "We will listen to music together," I said.

They were broadcasting the *Johannes Passion* of Bach,

played on authentic instruments of the eighteenth century by the Concentus Musicus of Vienna and the Vienna Boys' Choir. Vienna – city of music and fine pastries, home of the sweet tooth and the saving glass of cold water. But today was not a day for sweet teeth. Together we would listen to the *Passion* and in the spirit of pain and sacrifice I would bake nothing and we would eat nothing (not that Rella was in the mood for eating). I opened a new box of Earl Grey tea, dried the warmed teapot inside to receive the leaves. Everything would be dark and solemn and simple for the duration of this dark day; only the ears would feast. I wore for the occasion blue trousers and my new French beret which I had bought from a special shop in Greenwich Village. I felt myself becoming thin. But how stupid of me to forget, to think everything in springtime is yeast-risen. How could I forget the *Passion*? How?

The first chorus set my own teeth chattering. Rella's cup and saucer rattled on her pointy knees and when the chorus entered suddenly, some of the hot tea jumped out and burnt her hand. "*Herr*," shouted the strident young voices in chorus, which I translated for her: Lord. We listened after that, holding onto our cups until the organ sounded a dreadful note and the Evangelist spoke: Jesus thinks on his mother; he is unhappy about forsaking her. I thought on my own mother; where might she be after so many years? Probably safe inside her coffin under the dark wet earth, iced over like a chocolate *petit four*. Or perhaps safe behind the counter of my father's bakeshop – those two old people still satisfying the rich tastes of Viennese society. One day, I thought, I should like to take a trip to visit them; or write. Yes, why not? People live for a long time these days.

I thought on Gerda: Gerda getting fatter and shinier all the time, wearing earrings like a gypsy fortune teller and a white turban *geschnörkelt* with bright disks called sequins which flashed in the spring sunlight as she leaned on her elbows, looking here and there from her famous window, sniffing at the world under her nose.

Rella saw through other eyes. The painkillers seemed to be taking effect but she was breathing hard; listening and watching for some invisible evil, I surmised. What?

Perhaps this man known strangely as The Butler – Gerda's new boss – was the source of her worry. I knew only that Gerda was hiding something valuable for him, perhaps something illegal. And there was only the dog Vitez to guard her.

The organ sounded high up in the vaulted roof of the magnificent church where the music was coming from. I saw it so clearly, the organ pipes climbing to heaven, the gold swags, the symmetrical cupids on top of the console conducting music up to God with their chubby little fingers, one fat dimpled foot each sticking out behind. Rella held her face and rocked herself, with tears streaming down her cheeks; hers was not the face of a cherub. Then came the moan of an instrument not from this earth, reminding me of the two trees of my childhood, holding each other in the wood. *Es is vollbracht*, said the Evangelist. It is finished. The deed accomplished. And He bowed his head and gave up the ghost. And the viola da gamba wept.

Her lips were cracked like the texture of a muffin beaten too long. Why did she weep? She was perhaps over-excited from the combination of pain pills and Bach's moving music. I realized she had misunderstood the Passion; thinking only on Gerda, worried only for Gerda, imagining terrible possibilities. I tried to disabuse her of these strange imaginings, but she became more and more convinced some disaster was soon to strike. I put a cold cloth on her forehead to calm her but she continued muttering about danger.

Now she was telling of the boy who sat on the cold tiles of the lobby of our building, palms turned upwards to the world as if begging for something he could not name. I myself had wondered about him: Why does he sit there all day and all night? Where is his bed? Where are his parents? Why do his eyes roll up to heaven and his head keep nodding onto his chest as if it were filled with an over-heavy custard? Sometimes a needle would be found near him, a puddle of urine would escape from between his legs and run in a thin stream towards the door. People stepped disrespectfully over him, this human impediment, this limp gargoyle growing out of the woodwork. Once, on my way home from work, I offered my bag of bialys to him, but he hid his head in his hands.

Yet what did he have to do with Rella's worry for Gerda? "The Butler," she began to explain. "She mustn't do it – it's wrong, dangerous, bad."

"What must she not do?" I asked, but she couldn't find the words. "Don't worry," I said, "now you must rest." I stroked her forehead until she was quiet, and eventually her head fell sideways and one thin arm trailed along the floor. The comparison was inevitable. Soon, I thought, soon. Next week He will rise and she will get her new teeth, and Bach will compose a joyful oratorio and the tree's leaves will be heavy and full as with stout petticoats. Spring will make you beautiful.

Gerda

1

Late one night they come to take away the white powder: it
could be a consignment of ladies' bloomers. The next day
The Butler himself comes with a black leather case stuffed
with delicious green leaves. Spring is here. Welcome, make
yourself comfortable; stay awhile. The tree has a head of
pincurls. Soon they'll fluff themselves out into a magnificent mane, like mine used to be; only green, of course, the
color of money. Certainly, I tell The Butler, I would do it
again, willingly; why not? It's as easy as pie, as Jack-be-
Nimble might say.

Toothless Annie is busy being a new woman. Her head is
a cloud among clouds. She has got herself one of these new
hairstyles they call natural – though what it has to do with
nature I do not know except that, like a disease, it is
catching. Balloon heads, clouds of elbow macaroni, piles of
limp corkscrews. Natural, ha! The only place for a good
corkscrew is in the fragrant cork of a ripe bottle. I should
know. I lean out my window to take in the warm spring air
and Rella's head rises before me like a mushroom cloud
over Hiroshima. It makes my toes curl; my heart grows
hairy. I look down and see worms crawling up from the
cracks between her feet. They are fat and juicy and curly. I
think: they turn your guts to sauerkraut. Raoul went bald
at thirty.

When does she get her new teeth? The fancy lady
dentist in Greenwich Village is taking her sweet time.
Soon, she says. I remember how she looked after the first
operation. Her face was like a cockeyed omelette with
melted Velveeta and ketchup oozing out. I have a weak
stomach, I cannot tolerate the sight of blood. Better let

Mother Jack nurse her back to health, I thought; it suits him better than it does me. Afterwards, she insisted she had felt nothing; she had laughed and dreamed her way through the extractions. What kind of hocus pocus is this? Am I to believe one wave of the lady dentist's magic wand, a shot of kickapoo joy juice, and those old cocker teeth of hers bailed out one by one waving their withered root stumps in the air, yelling whoopeee? Hah! A good story.

But who am I to deny her a new image? I, Lady Bountiful, pay the dentist bills, hairdresser's bills, bills for clothing, jewelry, shoes, make-up–send them all to me. I am the one with the attaché case filled to bursting. Furthermore, I am the one who wished her different; I should be thankful. But with her tight-in-the-crotch yellow overalls, she looks to me more like a pregnant broom handle than a dream come true. Can it be that she and her fat friend finally figured out how to do it? All I can say is if a little Kraut should be cooking in there, she can raise the bastard down in the cellar next to the boiler, overseen by the rats; she can suckle it on the remnants of a coal heap in the corner, like a crone. Blankets I can provide. But I remind myself: how can she be pregnant when she has not had a period for the last twenty years? Too thin, says the doctor. No, the beautification program is distinctly otherworldly; Mother Nature will not play midwife to the laborings of that crimped mind. She prepares herself for the second coming of Raoul–the grand and glorious reunion between father and daughter. She is saving herself.

He is alive, he is about to be released–any day it could happen. (She's been saying it for years.) This time it's for real. He comes straight here, *directissimo*. She waits for him in her rocking chair, chewing gum with her new plastic teeth. Chewing and rocking and waiting. She is prepared. She fluffs out her hair with her monstrous Afro comb. Knock knock; she opens to him. What does he see? A skinny woman with false teeth and too much make-up; a strange, bulbous hairdo which makes her neck look as thin as a nail. Mutton dressed as lamb.

2

She goes out to clean the halls while I am having my beauty rest. Two seconds later my curly witch flies back in on her broomstick. I open one eye; what can it be that she should disturb me so early in the morning, a time when I am not at my best? A body, she says, a *dead* body. How does she know it's dead, there are so many drunks and addicts lying around these days? She knows, she says, because he's gray and cold and his tongue and eyes are bulging out of his head. He's fallen sideways onto the marble floor and cracked his skull and blood is trickling from it. Such appetizing details; she absorbs them like a mop. She's as excited as the night she flew in to tell me about Jack-be-Nimble dressed up as Adolf Hitler. In these moments of death and destruction her eyes are at their brightest; maybe these things run in the veins after all?

I don't wish to hear the gruesome details. I put my new pale blue mohair blanket over my eyes and ears – a present from Texas, recently returned from Scotland. Why should I lose sleep over a dead boy who was a dead boy even in life? A hopeless dope addict. People stepped over him, cursed him for being in the way. He was a terrible eyesore. All he could do was nod and beg and pee in his pants. Rella had to mop up around him every morning.

"He's better off dead," I say from under my pretty shroud. "Now leave me in peace." I watch her with one eye. Her false teeth are chattering in her head and she's pointing at me with her chicken-bone finger.

"You look like a pregnant blue whale. You have no feelings," she hisses, leaning her jaw against her broom handle to stop it shaking. Angry? My plucked pullet is angry? This is an interesting development. Perhaps a magic ingredient in the tooth cement has caused a change of personality?

"Now will you stop?" she shouts. I don't recognize her in my sleep.

"What are you talking about?" Can it be the shock of seeing a corpse? "Go and have a drink of water and put your head between your legs," I say.

"I don't need water. That boy died from an overdose of heroin – the stuff you're dealing. You're responsible."

"Me?" I sit up and laugh. Such an absurd suggestion, she must be losing her marbles. "Did I sell it to him? Did I shoot it into his veins? Did I force him to become hooked? No. He was a weakling, he liked the way it felt, like a warm blanket over his head. If not heroin, it would have been whiskey. His death has nothing to do with me." A pregnant whale indeed. "Go blow it out your own spout," I say.

The Butler tells me it isn't safe here for storage operations. The police are busy snooping around asking questions about the boy's source; for my sake and his, I must be clean, he tells me. Later, maybe, he says, when things cool down, but I can see in his eyes I'll be a bad risk for some time. He'll take his business elsewhere.

Hot, hot; it's already feeling like summer. I roll around the apartment like a stuffed derma in a pot of boiling water. I must think of some other way to earn a living. The $10,000 will not last forever, especially at the rate Rella spends it. No, I must have another source of income. Let me think. Prisoners are fashionable nowadays. Central America is big right now, with its disappeared ones, and Russia runs a close second, especially here in New York. There is much interest in the Jewish scientists and writers, the so-called dissidents. Yet who is the most glamorous of them all – Prisoner of the Year, Hero of the Century? Correct. She wants me to stop selling dope. All right. I have no choice in the matter. I'm too old to sell my body. What does she suggest I do? Go straight, she says; how straight, like an arrow? Like a girl scout? It's too late. There's only one thing left to sell and that is my life. That will open those saucer eyes of hers even wider. But she's a new woman now, she can survive anything. She doesn't need my protection anymore. Now I can tell the truth.

But who wants to hear? The voice of Mrs Kornblatt comes back to me: "Sell it to Hollywood, it has nothing to do with us." Hollywood; why not? Of course they may have thought of it already; one of their fancy writers concocting a sexy saga. What can I lose? Only the price of a long-distance 'phone call.

Get ready for a big catch, Hollywood.

3

Finally they have decided to fix the sidewalk. Ahahah-ahahah—those pneumatic drills go up and down between their legs. They're removing the old sidewalk square by square around the tree, the tattoos on their arms doing a fast hula hula. Oh they are enjoying themselves, these workmen, showing off their sweating, dancing muscles. Things would have been different ten years ago, twenty. But never mind. Soon they'll push the exposed tree root back under, where it belongs, pour in a fine new bed of concrete so smooth no one will ever trip again. I can still appreciate a polished technique.

The end is in sight. They've done their excavations, now they're shovelling cement to fill up the hole, swilling it around, slapping it and chopping it with the ends of their shovels. It'll be quick to set, they say, in this warm weather. It will be hard within the hour. They make their lines and rope off the area so the kids don't make a mess, clean up their tools and equipment. Peace at last, I can hear myself think again. Bye bye, boys. Just then, Jack-be-Nimble turns the corner into our street, carrying a big bag of groceries. (He feeds Rella these days, his mission in life.) He tiptoes over to investigate, as if the tree were his private property. He looks down and shrieks: "What! What are you doing? What are you doing to my tree, are you crazy?" He drops his bag so that glass, milk, eggs and who knows what else spill over his feet, but he doesn't notice. He's busy climbing over the rope barrier; soon he's down on his hands and knees digging like a dog at the concrete around the base of the tree. "Please," he cries, "you cannot do this. It is murder. You will kill the tree if you do not leave space around it. This way it cannot breathe. Don't you understand?" He is hugging the tree and crying and pulling on the workmen's cuffs the way people on the death marches pulled at the Arrowcross. All they got then was a boot in the face. "Okay, Mac, you're getting knee marks on the fresh concrete. Move it." But Jack is sitting up now, begging, like a child saying his prayers. "Please, just look, I am telling you, I know what I am talking about. If you let this material harden around the tree, it will die, as surely as I am sitting here." His voice is calmer now, he's trying to reason with them, use psychology. "I know about trees, you see. You must not do this, you must allow a small space all round, just a gap of a few inches, I will help you, not so much, just so it can breathe." He is rolling up his sleeves, trying to grab for a shovel. "It is as if you were putting a copper band around its trunk. Or like a snack around a person's neck." A snack? Ha ha ha, they laugh, such a joke, such a crazy foreigner. "How would you like it, a snake [he corrects himself] wrapped around your neck until you cannot breathe anymore? You are gasping for breath. How it hurts you. You pull at the snake with your fingers but it gets tighter and tighter until you are dead. Don't you see that is what you are doing to this tree? Can you live with this terrible act on your conscience?" And he reaches again for the shovel. The workman pulls it out of his hand and it catches him on the side of the head.

By now he's scratching at the concrete with his nails; his fingers are torn and blood is pouring from the wound on his temple. "Get a soap box, Mac, we're only following orders. You don't like it, complain to the City. See how far that gets you." He's holding onto the tree and weeping. "Only following orders? You dare say such a thing to me?" I call for Rella to go out and take him away before the cops come for him, or an ambulance. If they catch him doing this he'll be locked up again, this time for good. She runs out after him, flings herself over the rope and kneels down next to him. She takes his hand and lifts him to his feet, wraps his handkerchief around his head and helps him over the rope and the mess of groceries. He is blubbering like a kindergarten child who has lost his mother. His apron is filthy. I wave to Rella with a gesture for her to bring him in to me. I lock Vitez in the back room. It is too far for him to crawl up to his turret: I will nurse his wound.

He can rest here until he comes to his senses. I try to comfort him but he's in no condition to listen. He's still talking to his tree. The workmen are cursing him for getting blood on their new concrete. I tuck him up in my bed, under the salmon satin bedspread.

Jack

Where was I? I opened my eyes: two glacéed fruits surrounded me. One was a whole red cherry, the other a sliver of green angelica. I thought I must be reincarnated into a fruitcake. There was no air to breathe. So this is how it is in a bread tin; I gasped: air please. The angelica kindly loosened my tie. Better, much better; thank you. I was able to breathe again, and think. (Do fruitcakes wear ties?) Perhaps I was not baked after all. I felt the tie with my own fingers to reassure myself; yes. Please, a light, I heard myself say. The glacé cherry switched on a lamp which had as its base naked figures disporting themselves around a tree. A tree–was I lost in a forest? Or *en route* between heaven and earth? Now I was being licked by a huge tongue–about to be eaten by a wolf, help! The red cherry stood looking down at me (I seemed to be lying on a bed) with her hands on her great hips, smoking and, yes, laughing at me. Was I her prisoner? What did she plan to do with me?

"Well, well, so it's you at last. Jack-be-Nimble, pleased to meet you."

Nimble, nimble–how nimble when prone? "Excuse me," I said, trying to sit up and present myself. "My name is Jack Baum, like the tree, and I also am happy to make your acquaintance. However, I regret the unusual circumstances. Could someone please remind me what reason I have for lying here in your bed. Am I ill, please?"

The cherry laughed, "Nothing to worry your head about, Jack, just another one of your little fits. We brought you inside for a rest instead of letting you drag yourself up five flights of stairs."

And so it came back to me, how they were murdering the tree. I thought: I survive but the tree will not. I shook my head. I could taste death in the air, death by asphyxiation. "Please, could you open a window?" I begged, because the air was thick with cigarette smoke and I was having much difficulty breathing. This is what it will be like, I supposed, dying a little each day, gasping for a chocolate curl's worth of air. I felt my own neck, how it would be to have a concrete tie being pulled tighter and tighter as it dried until ... No more, I closed my eyes. I reached out my arm towards the tree but the frolicking porcelain figures did a turn and the light went out again.

I woke up; when it was, I do not know. Again I did not remember where I was. Then the dog Vitez licked my face and the cherry Gerda blew smoke into it. I made an attempt to get up. "Stay, stay," she said and sat down on a piece of me. "Please," I said, "I must go now to my own apartment." I remembered where I was and I felt a strange panic to get away, I did not know precisely why. She sprang from the bed and went to the door and Vitez began to bark at me. He knew she had been insulted. I was to be thrown out by both for my ingratitude. I tried to explain, to correct this mistaken impression. I said how much I was obliged for the care she had bestowed upon me, but I simply must return to my own safe nest. This I hoped she would understand. I promised to come back again when I was feeling stronger. Yet she was not much pacified by my speech. "Go," she said, like an SS officer, while Rella lurked in the background, rocking and hiding her head.

I climbed the stairs to my turret, one step at a time, my legs heavy as loaves of whole wheat *anise kuchen*; I leaned on the banister to rest. Christ suffered – he rose. Wallenberg spent thirty-five years in prison – they say soon he will be free. Rella is risen from the walking dead. There must be payment for these resurrections. Gladly would I have paid with my own sad and guilty life; yet an innocent tree has been chosen? Why?

2

I was invited to contribute $500 for a wheelchair (or if I preferred $2,500 for a bed), for the new Raoul Wallenberg Medical Clinic in Ma'alot, Israel; tax deductible. I was invited to sponsor a page in the historic "Chronicle of Courage" – A Major Pictorial and Archival Documentation of Wallenberg's Life – and to attend a Tribute Dinner in Los Angeles ($500 reserved seating for two; $1,000 for two seats in the Diamond Circle; $5,000 for two seats in the Diamond Circle plus a Private Cocktail Reception). The guests were to include members of the Wallenberg family and a generous sprinkling of Hollywood celebrities. The invitation, which was printed on heavy hand-woven paper with a glossy photograph of Wallenberg on the cover, also with a reproduction of his signature and the Legation stamp from Budapest, told me I should become a "Humanitarian" with such-and-such a contribution.

Already I had a box full of invitations to dinners, concerts, memorials, christenings, tributes, demonstrations. These events were supposed to be for the purpose of honoring the Swede, or protesting on his behalf, or raising money towards his release; but somehow they seemed to me to have a life of their own, quite separate from anything to do with him. I imagined him alone in his cell: would it please him to imagine people in elegant clothes, glittering in jewels and conversation, on his behalf? Perhaps. He was a man once used to the fine things of life. But such events had nothing to do with me, a poor bialy baker who had already given enough of his own memory. I put the invitation away into the box along with the other mementos.

On the day he was to be made an Honorary Citizen of the United States, I invited Rella for a private celebration in my apartment. I dreamed of serving something light and cooling, for it was already early summer and getting to be quite warm at night in my kitchen under the eaves. I decided on white chocolate as the main ingredient. White chocolate has a pleasing creamy taste and great potential

233

for cool, magnificent desserts. It wears its pale color in elegant confusion, for technically it is not chocolate at all but is made primarily from cocoa butter without the characteristic heavy chocolate liquor. But never mind. I made a light frozen mousse using the white chocolate, egg whites, sugar and whipping cream. I served it in mounds, sprinkled with fine strands of orange peel. I christened this creation: White Chocolate Clouds. Then I decided to add a batch of *Lebkuchen*, made also from white chocolate, to be eaten alongside the clouds. White Clouds and White Hearts in my white kitchen, to celebrate Rella's new white teeth and the hero far away in his white exile. The first honorary citizen of the United States had been Winston Churchill; Wallenberg would be the second.

I turned on the television set. The President of the United States stood at a lectern in the Rose Garden of the White House. He was smiling. There was a breeze but his hair did not blow in it; perhaps it was a wig – his teeth also looked false. I imagined the audience of roses, listening solemnly. Would there be a Wallenberg rose some day – white as the snow outside his safe cell? In due course the President made a speech about planting trees under which Wallenberg could not sit. He said he was going to do his damnedest, however, to make it possible. And with a great flourish of his pen he signed the bill. Raoul Wallenberg – Honorary Citizen of the United States of America. I switched off the television. I set the table with White Clouds and White Hearts and one long-stemmed white rose in a thin silver vase.

Rella and I took our seats, facing one another. She was beautiful now. She was wearing a red dress. Her skin was no longer brittle and transparent as dried strudel leaves and the bones no longer protruded from her wrists in such an alarming way. She was quite filled out. The shape of her face was transformed by her new teeth and the curly golden hair was the halo of an angel. I could hardly eat, torn as I was between the beauty of her and the deliciousness of the Clouds. The white nothingness slipped between her lips, floated easily down her throat and into her stomach. There was no pain. Her eyes glowed, large and golden brown as two Hungarian coffee rings filled with sweetened cream cheese and topped with drizzled melted chocolate alternating with spokes of apricot jam. I thought at any moment she might float away out of the window. She was so sure everything would come to a happy conclusion. Wallenberg would be soon free – perhaps in a matter of months, weeks, even days – released like a *torte* from a springform pan. Citizens of the United States do not remain prisoners of the Soviet Union, she assured me. But I could not share her confidence. To make him a citizen seemed to me a great gesture for causing oohs and aahs, as is the presentation of a flambé. But when the flame dies away the show is over; so with Wallenberg's citizenship – an empty gesture. If the Stockholm Hearings did not bring him freedom, why should this?

Rella was also happy because Gerda had given up her dangerous business, or had been forced to give it up. She suspected Gerda might still have "something up her sleeve," but she did not know what it might be since Gerda was so good at keeping secrets. There was still one remaining thing to worry about and that was an attaché case filled with money which she had discovered in a drawer. She had tried to persuade Gerda to put the money in a bank, but Gerda had refused. She said she did not want her money locked away behind bars where she could not get at it. Suppose it became known she had a large horde of money in the house, Rella challenged, but Gerda dismissed these qualms as foolish. Nevertheless, she had ordered a gun from a mail-order catalogue, just to be on the safe side.

I myself was afraid for Rella. I did not know why, but I felt a sore place in my heart when I looked at her. She was so fine now. Too fine? Perhaps. I told myself it was an old man's superstition and I was being both silly and wicked to think such thoughts: why should anything happen to her? I watched as she picked up one of the white heart-shaped cookies and bit into it with her front teeth. Yes, the kind dentist had done a wonderful job, the teeth looked quite natural. I wanted to say I did not love her more now that she was beautiful, but instead I dipped into a White Cloud with my white cookie heart.

As the days floated past I heard the tree gasping for air. It could not get out of its concrete straitjacket and I could do nothing for it but bear witness to its agony. By late summer its leaves became dry and shriveled and then they fell off and its branches were quite bare. I became cold each time I went near it and I had to protect my ears against its strangled gasping and wheezing.

I ate many ice cream cones. I worked my way through every flavor in the shops regardless of quality: Butter Brickle, Raspberry Ripple, Green Mint Fudge, Fresh Peach Melba, Chocolate Cake, even Bubble Gum; single scoops, double scoops, chocolate dipped, sprinkles. They made my teeth and my heart cold; I tasted nothing. Rella, for whom I feared, ignored my silent warnings and smiled at me from far away with her beautiful new teeth; and Gerda, whom I feared, beckoned to me from her window.

Gerda

She does herself up like a poodle bitch in heat, topknot cut and shaped; but to which dog does she run at five in the morning? I stick my head out the window but all I can make out are cats screwing under the cars. Let them come near me and I will pour boiling water on their greasy backs. I spy a boy sitting on the stoop: "Have you seen Rella anywhere?" I ask, but he shrugs. "Maybe she fell down the cellar steps and broke her leg?" he giggles. Very funny. I tell him to go down and look but he shakes his head and runs away, the miserable coward. No, it is more likely she is with Jack-be-Nimble. He is in love. No more yellow bag of waxy bones with rotten teeth in the head; now she is a beauty, a hot number. New sensations come awake in the old boy as she flounces her pom pom at him. Pink short shorts! Long tanned legs like crusty French sticks, lovely to nibble with unsalted butter; delicious! He is hooked, the lovesick dachshund.

He serves her a luscious strawberry shortcake and a chilled hock. Perhaps with a little wine to loosen her, she will look more kindly upon him. It is beauty's turn to pity the beast. He stares at her. Her tongue is up to the hilt in whipped cream. She licks her lips, cuts another piece of cake and raises it slowly to her lips, uses her tongue to scoop up more whipped cream, then pops a whole strawberry into her mouth, which is itself like a wet strawberry. Before he knows what he's doing he's staring at her chest, imagining hidden beneath her brassière two perfect, pale wild strawberries, the kind he used to find as a boy – if he was very lucky – in dark moist corners of the Wienerwald. She walks around the table to him, sits on his lap and places

237

one of his hairy, sweating paws on her chest. Feel that, she says, teasing him. He looks up into her face and the tears roll out from under his glasses and ski down his cheeks. What can he do? There there, she takes off his glasses, wipes his wet eyes with her lips. Her breath smells of strawberries, her lips feel slippery and rich from whipped cream. He closes his eyes; let her do what she will with him. But what is this raising up his apron? Jack-be-Nimble, Jack-be-Quick, Jack where is your candlestick? Oh, but not so fast; these Europeans don't rush to any conclusions. Slowly, slowly, he peels away her clothing like the skin of a grape. He lays her down on his white sheet and kisses her palms, her toes, her knees, the nape of her neck, her armpits, her navel, and last of all, the special place at the base of the spine. Finally he flips her over like a pancake and puts his head between her legs and sniffs: mmmnnn, strawberries. He takes off his own clothes and is ashamed of the smell which comes from down there: onion bialys.

Who is this witch telephoning me at five in the morning, interrupting my sweet dreams, telling me a riddle: what goes down and doesn't come up? I hang up but the 'phone rings again. Rella in the cellar. Now a nursery rhyme; the woman must have loose screws. Wait a minute, what is she trying to tell me. It's the mother of the cowardly boy saying she heard from her son Rella is missing. So? So she saw a man follow her down into the cellar late last night, then she saw him come up again a little while later carrying a briefcase. But no Rella. She says maybe I ought to call the police. I tell her maybe she ought to go back to bed and mind her own business.

No, I will phone the baker, she must be shacked up with him; why didn't I think of it before? I let the phone ring fifteen times, finally he picks it up. I ask to speak to Rella at once. "Excuse me, I do not understand. I am just leaving for work, how should Rella be here with me at this hour?" Simple Simon couldn't tell a white lie to save himself; it must be true, clear as the morning sun coming up. I tell him she is missing. Daughter of the missing hero, also missing; maybe she has gone to look for him over the Russian steppes in her hot pants? I tell him a neighbor informs me a man followed her down there late last night.

238

"Oh, *mein Gott*," he says, forgetting himself.

By this time Vitez is behaving like an SS bloodhound, growling and whining and trying to squeeze himself out between the bars; he will never make it. What is happening? Why is everyone getting so excited? A minute later, Jack-be-Nimble is down in the street in his white work clothes. "A flashlight, quick," he orders, not even a please or thank you. Has he gone mad again? I notice there is sweat on his forehead although the morning is cool. He grabs the flashlight from me and rushes away; never have I seen such a fat little dumpling move so fast. Vitez lets out a high-pitched yowl which hurts my ear-drum so much I crack him across the muzzle. He snarls and goes wild, hurling himself onto the windowsill, clear over the bars and onto the sidewalk. He skids over to where Jack is, at the top of the cellar steps, leaps onto his chest and licks his face (Nice buttery crumbs?). The baker wraps his arms around the dog (he must be thinking of me), buries his face in his fur; this seems to calm them both. But Vitez gets a whiff of something more exciting than the baker, a smell which drives him nuts. "All right," says Jack, "come, now we will be brave," and he follows him down into that black hole. Good, now they are gone I can go and check on my loot; that briefcase the witch saw, whose was it? I go to my dresser drawer to say good morning to all those fresh green babies. As I suspected; gone.

I want to yell from the rooftop how my fine Goldilocks has robbed me and run off with a Mafia drugs-runner. Where? California, Budapest, Russia? Off with her new teeth in her mouth paid for by me to search out her long-lost papa. Well I have news for my curly-haired Nazi, a special SOS. I fling open the window as wide as it will go but it is not wide enough; the message I have for her ears must carry over continents. They are such fools to look in the cellar. She is gone, gone, taking my money with her.

Outside, the first time in thirty-five years, in my bare feet and transparent kimono. How does it feel to be out, free? Cold, my feet are not used to it; I am shivering. The air, all around me, is a shock. It gets me in the back of the neck, up between the legs; I am tingling all over. I would like to spread my arms and dance but I hear Vitez howling down in the cellar as if he were being tortured to death. What is Jack doing to him? Why don't they come up? They're wasting their time down there. More howls, to which I add my own special one: Eichmann. Adolf Eichmann. Do you hear? May those words float away on the morning's summery breeze and grab you by the back of your scrawny neck, wherever you may be, my chickadee. Listen again to those sweet lyrics: not Raoul Wallenberg but Adolf Eichmann. Do I make myself clear? Take that and run headless, flapping your see-through wings, you thief.

Jack

It is not possible, it is not possible, it is not possible there is
no God. I prayed and mumbled to myself like a crazy man,
and beat against the wet walls of the cellar with her shoe
which I found stuffed into a pile of coal from the old days. I
squashed a water bug with the shoe to see if any red blood
came out but it did not, I knew it would not, the red blood, a
thin trail from the coal pile, was only human. The trail led
... I knew where the trail led but I kept my back to the
monster, I could not look him in the eye with my horrible
accusation. I must be certain of my charge. How could it
have been that she had forgotten him for nearly twelve
hours in this heat? But the people needed only hot water,
no heat; perhaps she thought it was not necessary for him
to drink so often. But still he works to make hot water,
generates a great thirst, still needs cooling down or over
the top he goes and burns himself out. After all, everyone
else on this block slakes their thirst: Italian ices (lemon and
chocolate flavors), Cokes, juice, lime Rickeys, seltzer;
everyone walks around sucking on ice and pulling drinks
through straws to keep the fire in their own bodies down.
But him, the boiler monster, did he become so dry, so
feverish, his thermometer red (the danger zone), that
when she finally appeared, late last night, in her shorts, all
he could see with his burning eye was a cool glass of beer
with a head of delicious froth and he was tempted to slake
his thirst on *her*? When she got too close – with her saving
funnel of water, just about to satisfy him – did he reach out
one of his pipe arms and take her in one great gulp into his
mouth and rub his belly afterwards with satisfaction? At
last I turned to accuse him and saw by his horrible grin that

indeed he had been greedy, he had eaten far more than oil and water. I thought I heard the crackle of human bones in his jaws. Oh, but there are some things not for eating, not bodies, no, please no, I prayed, and backed away from the rude sounds of his indigestion. I ran from him and lost my stomach in the alley. But what was here? Under the tree I saw Gerda and she was yelling the name Eichmann and Vitez was howling at her. Was I again going mad? I leaned my head against the building and closed my eyes for a moment. When I opened them she had reappeared at her window. Her eyes were almost as red as the boiler monster's, and she belched smoke. She believed Rella had stolen her money and run away. Oh no, oh no, I could only shake my head and point to the cellar where the unspeakable crime had taken place.

She would not believe me. She insisted Rella had run away with her money, that she was by now out of the state, perhaps out of the country with some man, with *her* attaché case. But when the police came, as they soon did, I showed them the blood and the Devil Dog shoe and they shook their heads and at last shut down the boiler monster. He heaved a great sigh and all his black bones rattled and after many hours the great fire in his mouth and eye went out and we could see the charred leftovers of his wicked meal. What were her new teeth made from that they did not burn? Oh what have you done, you greedy beast, I wailed, but got no reply from the dumb creature, no reply at all. I beat my breast, remembering other hungry ovens. I tried to understand but I could not. The tree, all right, some injustice I could accept, but why also Rella? Please why, I do not understand. Help me.

In the church there were old women dressed in black in spite of the hot weather. I kneeled forward and looked up at Christ and the red glass behind him reminded me of the boiler monster so that I was stricken with fear. Still I prayed and asked my simple question, but I received no answer. I put a handkerchief over my head and entered a synagogue; perhaps Rella's God would speak to me. But the only voices I heard were the chants of old men and I smelled the smell of hot black cloth.

I went out into the white hot street. I took the uptown

train to Manhattan and then I walked until I came to the most famous of all New York bakeshops. This is my church, I thought, these are my gods, I will pray to *them*. And I dropped to my knees on the sidewalk outside the shop and pressed my forehead to the cool glass, for it was in the shade. I addressed myself to the *petits fours*, the *Sachertortes*, the strawberry shortcakes. In each of their respective languages I asked them: *pourquoi, warum,* why? But they only stared uncomprehendingly at me, or winked, and the proprietor came out of the shop and told me to get a move on, and kicked me in the side; this was no place for drunks, he said. I staggered away and realized with great shame that I had not prayed at all, but stared at these objects with desire, with my tongue hanging out, drooling like a pervert. I deserved to be kicked, and worse.

There was nowhere left to go with my empty question, my empty stomach. I passed the window of an ordinary bakeshop which had such a dirty window I could hardly see its wares. The cakes inside sat on plastic altars and looked so dried up and dumb I knew it would be useless to stop and ask them anything. How could such poor creatures have answers? Muffins with weary peaks, cracked and wobbly; a chocolate cake going grey at the temples, wearing a shriveled and lonely off-center cherry; a practically bald coconut cake, its desiccated hair dropping onto its plastic doily; *langues de chat*, the very tips of their bright yellow tongues bright green with icing. Poor tongues, they babbled nonsense at me as if poisoned, I could not understand a word they said. There was an angel cake standing guard over the others with shoulders stiff as a soldier's; it might have been made of cardboard. For a moment I saw it transformed into a real angel with fluffy white wings, but when I blinked the wings collapsed and the angel stood stiffly as before. It reminded me of Rella and the miracle of her pearly teeth and angel's hair. And then the cake spoke to me. It said: Do not ask. Go home to Gerda and comfort her. I went into the shop and asked to buy this wise cake, but they said it was a dummy and not for sale.

Gerda

No, I do not want to go down to the basement to identify an empty briefcase and a set of half-melted dentures. Vitez is mad, chasing dustballs, his tail; maybe he can smell her blood. My money gone and my daughter gone; how? I must figure it out: she goes down into the cellar to do her boiler feed and he's waiting for her. (It must have been one of The Butler's men who knew about our deal.) He holds a gun to her skinny ribs and tells her to get the briefcase. Like an idiot she obeys, runs upstairs in her short shorts, steals the case while I'm asleep and runs back down and hands it over. Thank you, ma'am, he says, and knocks her over the head with his gun. He rapes her limp body, then throws it into the furnace. He thinks he's so clever, getting rid of the evidence, but he's forgotten her shoe and the trail of blood and the briefcase. How stupid can you get? But she is the dumbest of all. Was. She knew I had a gun hidden under my pillow. All she had to do was wake me up and I would have protected her, and the money, and Vitez. All that dental surgery for nothing.

They bring Jack home in a police car, he has been found in front of a bakery somewhere in uptown Manhattan, God knows how he got there, they think he's drunk with the DTs. I tell them to bring him into my house. Now we're both alone it is only fair we should look after one another. I rehearse my plan while he sleeps. With Rella gone, his salary will be very useful. In return, I provide room and board and a little spice to his life. He bakes for me and I reward him with a smile. An artist needs an audience at certain times in his life; a *bravo*, an *encore*, to tell him he is appreciated. Rella could never provide that; she didn't have the appetite. We must stick together in our hour of need.

Jack isn't listening to me, his eyes are rolling in his head like a dog with distemper and he's mumbling about cakes and pastries and God. He believes the boiler monster gobbled her up. He keeps saying: Why? Why? Why? I hold his head in my lap and give him a shot of brandy. It brings tears to his eyes and he says, "You must not be so kind," and then, "What have they done with her?" He means what is left of her. "Gone," I say. "The handsome detective carried her away in an asbestos bag when her bones were cool enough to handle. Vitez and I watched from the window, we waved goodbye. I cannot bear funerals, but this was tasteful and simple. In my opinion, the only way to go. You would have appreciated it, I'm sure."

"I'm hungry," he says, whimpering, but when I try to stuff a chocolate-covered mallomar into his mouth, he spits it out, like a baby who does not know his own mind.

Jack

There was no funeral. A policeman carried her bones in a plastic sack to the trunk of his car and drove away. The daughter of a famous hero would have had a polished coffin with brass handles, wreaths of flowers, celebrities and socialites dressed in best black, a solemn clergyman; afterwards, cold cuts from the delicatessen. Perhaps it was better, as Gerda said, to exit in a simple sack.

I held my own service. I visited a cemetery where many roses grew; I examined and picked a dozen of the most perfect leaves I could find and took them home in a plastic bag. I spread them out on Gerda's kitchen table and stared at them, wishing I were in my own white kitchen instead of this one, which was green and black and got very little daylight. But no matter. I found a white plate amongst the collection of variously patterned ones and placed the most perfect of the leaves on it. I washed them one by one with the utmost care, patted them dry with a paper towel and laid them to rest. Then I placed a bar of best bittersweet chocolate in a bowl over boiling water. When it was melted I brought it to the table. I held the first leaf up to such light as was available, feeling gently with my fingers for its veins. On the veined side I then spread a thin coating of chocolate with the handle of a wooden spoon. I spread the chocolate as carefully as I could to the edge of the leaf, trying not to let any of it overflow to the other side. After painting it in this way I laid it gently to set on a piece of waxed paper. Thus I painted a dozen leaves and left them to harden. When they were ready, I separated the rose leaf from its chocolate coat, quickly before the heat of my hand could warm and melt the chocolate. The real leaves I discarded, and set the thin chocolate ones – which had dried with the pattern transferred onto them – on a white plate, and put them in the refrigerator to cool. Later that night I made an offering of the leaves to Gerda. She nibbled around the edges of one while I said a prayer to myself: These leaves, with the imprint of life, are in honor of Rella, may she rest in peace. Amen.

"Delicious," said Gerda and she smiled her *Windtorte* smile that swirled around my head and took my breath away.

Part VI

1986

Dear Rella,

I don't lift a finger anymore, Jack does everything –
errands, shopping, cleaning, cooking; baking, naturally.
Since your time his artistry has flowered; I am his
inspiration and his muse. How unlike me not to have seen
love staring me in the face, ever since those days at the
Majestic half a century ago. Who would believe I am the
same woman? But to Jack I am as beautiful as ever. Of
course that's partly because the eye doctor gave him a pair
of tinted glasses – rose-colored in gold frames. Sometimes
he tells me I am too fat, but I tell him it's his own fault. How
do I become thin when he stuffs me with pastries? He
doesn't criticize, you understand, his concern is strictly for
my health. It doesn't matter how I look to other people, to
him I'm still a svelte young woman in a red dress.

There is nothing between us *that way*; he sleeps in your
bed, I sleep in mine. We are both of us too old and set in our
ways to change. I never could tolerate a man in my bed for
more than a few hours and Jack, well, I always knew there
was something queer about him in that department. But
I'm not complaining, with so much *crème chantilly*, who
needs *that*? Vitez still keeps me warm at night, but he's lost
most of his teeth and tends to dribble. He reminds me of
you, before your new teeth. Each day he gets skinnier and
skinnier. Jack says soon he will die, and I am preparing
myself. I have my eye on a Great Dane puppy.

Not everything is a bowl of glacé cherries, so far as Jack is
concerned. I watch him with an eagle's eye, you never
know when he'll have one of his mad spells. So there is one
tree less in the world, so what? He should worry more

about people. But you know how he is, the way he talks to them as if they were human. This Hallowe'en, let me tell you, he baked a bunch of brownies. Naturally they were gourmet brownies, made with pure butter, stuffed with nuts and raisins and whatnot, and the children were lining up outside our door like it was Nathan's. He baked batch after batch; they kept coming back for more – I think they brought all their little friends from other neighborhoods to join in the queue. I told him he should go into business. But getting back to Hallowe'en. The next morning we heard the news that some poor child had perished from eating a brownie with a razor blade stuck into it. Cookie, brownie, nobody knows exactly what it was, but it didn't take two shakes of Vitez's tail before the fingers were busy pointing at Jack: Jack the foreigner, Jack the crazy man – why not Jack the child killer? It was the logical conclusion. The irony is how terrified he is of razor blades – he runs away when I shave my legs. I suppose you know what happened at Buchenwald? I can remember how the kitchen staff at the Majestic gossiped about the infamous Hanno Baum who escaped from Buchenwald by putting razor blades into the Nazi high command's dessert. I also remember how disappointed I was to meet him, a little round tub of a man. I thought: this is a hero? He didn't look the part to me. Anyway, you can imagine his reaction to *this*; that he, Jack Baum who couldn't hurt a fly, should do such a thing. He could not believe his ears, he swore they were playing tricks on him. It was a lucky escape for him when they caught the real culprit; he would have been lynched. It was a close shave. Hah! As it happened, he had to be put to bed for a week afterwards, he was so upset by the whole episode. He kept imagining he had committed the crime, everything became mixed up in his mind. He woke up screaming, thinking he was back at Buchenwald, confessing his guilt. I assured him he was quite innocent, but after a time you start to wonder yourself. It isn't every day you meet someone who has the idea of escaping from a concentration camp by putting sliced razor blades instead of almonds into the sweet. I tell him next Hallowe'en he should turn out the lights and go to bed until it's all safely over. "You're better off letting them play tricks on you," I say. "What will they do to me?" he asks, cowering like a round mouse in the corner. I laugh at him but that's how he is. My hero.

As for the movie, it's a tragedy you missed it. Jack tells me it brings tears to his eyes. This is no reliable measuring stick since he would cry over a wounded onion. But everyone in the neighborhood says it's a breathtaking spectacle, a glorious panorama of Budapest in all her pre-War glory. How these Hollywood people do it, I don't know, but they work miracles. Everything is larger than life on these big screens.

Jack says the heroine of the movie looks nothing like me, she has a long snout like a collie dog. Can you explain to me this fad today for ugly actresses? They think they are being realistic, but is it not absurd to make me appear *less* beautiful than I was in reality? Ridiculous. Perhaps there doesn't exist in all of Hollywood an actress with talent *and* beauty; it's asking too much. At least she can act; her accent is perfect Budapest, she studied a year to get it just so. She should have come to me, I could have taught her a thing or two.

But how did it happen? You are dying to know. Or perhaps you know everything where you are? I will tell you, anyway. It was all very simple. I sent my story to this big film studio in Hollywood and before I could say Jack-be-Nimble, the big boss was calling me long-distance offering me wine and roses. What's this, I asked myself, and then the truth dawned. It came to me how just then Raoul Wallenberg was a prime investment, a hot potato. So I asked for double what he was offering me for the rights to my story. He offered to meet me half way and I refused, and so we did a dance back and forth for the next half hour until we came to a deal. Do you know how much we settled on? Come closer, I'll whisper it in your ear: $200,000. Well, you can imagine how pleased I was. The timing was perfect. The heroin business was long *kaput*, at least for me, and you had just disappeared as my only remaining source of income. Jack was waiting in the wings, but the salary of a bialy maker is not exactly princely. No, to live in comfort, I needed more. The ingredients for his concoctions alone would have broken me. Things are so expensive now, a chocolate chip is like gold. So now we are set up for life, Jack and I. I pay him a salary so he doesn't have to work any more. It's much better for both of us that he should stay and bake for me.

I could have asked for twice as much, who knows? But that's life, I was innocent. They were in such a hurry to get this movie into production, you wouldn't believe it. They had everything figured out, they were pulling strings everywhere, it was incredible. Don't ever let anyone tell you Washington has the power. Wrong, Hollywood has it. Not that all this makes any difference to Raoul. The Russians are still keeping him "safe and sound" as ever. They could pronounce him a god and the Russians wouldn't change their tune; how could they after so many years? It would be such an embarrassment. Naturally they call the whole show a propaganda exercise. Whatever it was, people went in droves to see the film, there's been nothing like it in the history of the cinema since *Gone With the Wind*. It won every academy award, including best actress to the collie dog. She was called Greta in the film. As you know, they have to change the names to protect the innocent.

They sent the script to me for approval. I approved. It's full of sex between the signing of *Schutzpasses*. Tip-offs, bribes, counter-bribes, rescuing of Jews, screwing – it is all there – while the sky is bursting with Russian gunfire. Even the salmon satin bedspread is there. These are the things that make it seem true to life. Of course I didn't see it myself, why bother? It is my life, I can remember the real thing – although after so many years, even I must admit to forgetting certain details. My neighbors inform me "Raoul" is very handsome – much thinner than the real Raoul and with a full head of pale hair.

Eichmann is portrayed as a devil, that's good. It shows how I agreed to have relations with him only to obtain information for Raoul and the rescue mission. A little exaggeration here and a small omission there and I am as heroic as Raoul. My becoming pregnant is not mentioned. It would have made a sloppy ending, I felt, not knowing who the father was. Besides, the public would never tolerate such a monstrosity. Imagine, even the *possibility* of a child by Eichmann! You don't mind my saying these things, I'm sure; I suppose nothing can hurt you where you are. According to the movie, Greta does what she does for the sake of saving Jews and for love of Wallenberg. Wallenberg does what he does for the sake of saving Jews and for love of Greta. It is very pretty and precise, not like life at all in that respect. But it proves the end justifies the means, thank goodness.

No, I do not go to the Russians in the end, Hollywood wouldn't hear of it. They make a movie like a stew: a pinch more salt, a cup of hot paprika to disguise a bitter taste. They said the movie-going public would find such behavior unacceptable; the heroine betraying the hero to gain her own release from the Russians – impossible! Furthermore, they said, it would play into Russian hands by planting the idea that Wallenberg might, after all, have been a spy for the Americans.

The end of the movie shows Budapest deep in snow. Raoul and Greta are in the back of his chauffeur-driven car, saying their farewells. The Russians are standing by with their arms crossed, waiting to take him away. He gives her the diamonds and she opens the door of the car and makes her way through the deep snow in a pair of big black boots. (Did I actually own such a pair of sensible boots, I wonder?) She walks in one direction and the car drives slowly away in the other, its tyres slipping on the ice. She keeps walking without looking back, so he cannot see her face with the tears rolling down. Still he watches her back through the rear-view mirror. More snow is falling, the Russian motorcycles are gunning their engines. This is the end. Some writing appears on the screen, saying, "Raoul Wallenberg is still believed to be alive and a prisoner of the Soviet Union." Or some such thing. There is not a dry eye in the house.

Jack is the same, of course; he knows everything but he says nothing. His motives are as pure as his ingredients. He answers hundreds of telephone calls and guards the door against curiosity-seekers, reporters, troublemakers, and those who would wish to be rude to me for one reason or another. I don't need to go into details, you must use your imagination, such as it is. Between him and Vitez I am well protected. He will hear no evil about me from any source; whatever he may think I did he keeps it quietly under his beret.

We are very safe in his pudgy hands. Raoul and I are his little mannequins. He picks us up and places us with great care at the top of a white cake with many tiers like the lobby of the Hotel Majestic in its heyday. Raoul calls for a taxi – up and up we go into the sky. We get off on the roof garden and there we stand together, arm in arm like bride and groom, looking down at poor Jack-be-Nimble, standing with his turned-out feet planted on mere flat earth. We are smiling at him with our perfect white teeth: such a handsome couple. I am feeling very safe up here, wearing the lovely coat of white icing he has made for me.

That's all for now. Hope you are fat and healthy wherever you are. I suppose your false teeth don't trouble you.

Au revoir,
Gerda

Dear Rella,

My life is very fine. I do not work in the bialy factory anymore, for Gerda is so generous as to give me a free room and board plus a small salary. In return, I do her shopping and baking, but this is more a pleasure than a chore. To have such a boss. She is to me the *Reine de Saba*, an unusually rich French chocolate cake, distinguished by a center even slightly underdone: a toothpick inserted comes away sticky. It is a joy to watch her eat – the way she licks her fingers and lips; the more elaborate the creation, the better. She has gained weight and that is not so good. Sometimes I pluck the courage to tell her she must go on a diet, but this makes her angry and, to tell the truth, she frightens me. And she is right, it *is* my fault; if I did not bake fine desserts each night, she would not become fat. I am myself not so fat anymore. I bake but I have little appetite for eating; I prefer to watch her. She says I should have been an artist, I missed my true vocation. With all due respect, I wish to say, I *am* an artist, working in the medium of the edible. Each day I create something different. I lie in your little bed in the morning, pulling my feet back into the warmth of the covers, and I think what to bake today. I have been making the Viennese classics – the strudels, *Gugelhupfs*, *torten* and so on, but I also add to my repertoire the French pastries so as not to become stale. You would not believe the miracles: babas imbibed with rum, *crêpes chantilly*, fruit charlottes, soufflés – and there is no end in sight. One day I made *Mille-Feuilles*; these are layers of puff pastry interspersed with pastry cream and iced with fondant and chocolate. They took me most of the day to make and I became quite flustered and dirty, which is unusual for me. They are also known by the name *Napoléons* and there is a wicked story which says Napoleon ate so many of these pastries on the eve of Waterloo that he lost the battle. This I can well imagine. I also made a *Pithiviers*, which is almond cream baked in puff pastry; buttery, flaky, tender; in short, one of the most glorious uses to which one can put the common puff pastry. I served it with a sparkling Vouvray and together we drank a toast to your memory.

There was *Le Succès* – light yet rich, innumerable layers of baked meringue mounted one upon the other with buttercream, nut frosting and filling. I suppose you know the occasion for which this was made? Yes, the signing of the contract with Hollywood, Gerda's great success. You see, she is quite rich now. One day she telephoned a message at the bialy works to say, "Hand in your apron, Jack, we're in business." I was quite bemused, but I obeyed. That is how it is with Gerda. She shines down on me, like the bride at the top of a wedding cake, so that when she says do this or that, I am creamed butter in her hands. I am her groom. Of course her rewards are generous, I never regret doing something for Gerda. The sight of her smile alone makes it worthwhile.

I had no idea she had written her memoirs and sent them to Hollywood, so the whole thing came as a great surprise to me. She is very good at keeping secrets. But these Hollywood people were apparently so impressed by what they read – and also Wallenberg was by this time considered a good box office investment – they settled quickly and generously with Gerda, and that was that. I am sure she drove a hard bargain, as they say. Sometimes I think about borrowing money from her to start my own bakeshop, but I am too old, it is too late for me now. Sometimes I miss my apartment up in the turret, with its light and air; but Gerda also makes up for that.

I went to see the film which was based on her story. She made me promise to give her a detailed report of the actress playing the starring role, which I did. In my opinion she was really rather ugly, with a long nose like a bread stick. She could never in a hundred years compare with Gerda for beauty.

People are still talking about the film, although they don't always say kind things about it. I heard someone say the only good part was when a fat English actor brought an elaborate cake into the dining room of the Majestic for Wallenberg, Greta and Eichmann. That was me, had you guessed? Imagine a famous actor playing me! He had just the correct number of chins. At least for that scene I can vouchsafe a certain likeness. For the rest, the kindest one can say is that it was beautiful to look at. But I have heard people say rude things about it. They say it is a distortion of the truth, a lie, Hollywood propaganda, irresponsible romantic junk – that sort of thing. But what is truth, that they should know it when they see it?

The fact is, the film has been criticized rather severely in serious circles because of this nagging question: why did no one know of Gerda's relationship with Wallenberg? Perhaps it never really existed at all. I am myself somewhat confused. I saw them together the night of the dinner party at the Majestic, but I knew nothing more. They might not have been so close after all – or at least not in the way Gerda told it. Of course she would not speak about it; she would not read the reviews which were unfavourable. I hope you are not offended with me for telling you these criticisms, and the questions about Gerda.

Today I made her a *Windtorte*. Not since I was challenged by the manager of the Majestic (Gerda's father) have I tried to capture the extravagance of this cake. This time I put all my powers of artistry and imagination into its creation. The inspiration was Gerda herself in her white turban; the cake a sculptural dedication to her. Winter is the best time to make the *Windtorte*, so much whipped cream does it require, in designs of lace and eyelet and snow waves. However vulgar, it is nonetheless a baroque triumph in conception, design and execution, and tastes of heaven. Gerda was asleep by the time it was cooled and iced and stylishly decorated with candied violets and tiny pink rosebuds. I left it for her in the refrigerator with a note, so that she would find it when she awoke.

Perhaps you wonder how I can live with a person who

may have betrayed Wallenberg to the Russians? This, by the way, was not included in the film. Is it true? Yes, I believe it *is* true, as are other things which are not so flattering to Gerda. Perhaps it is just as well you did not know everything. She does not know I know, and I am quite willing to protect her secret with all my heart. To me it is well worth it. Why? I do not think she is a bad person. She did what she did to save herself; is that so bad? I believe the Russians would have arrested him anyway. It is not so nice, any of this; I do not congratulate her, but also I do not condemn her. Her crime, in my opinion, was her great beauty; for this she cannot be blamed.

Last night there was a demonstration for peace in San Francisco; it was on the television. People were dressed in strange costumes, some of them walking on tall wooden stilts. One was dressed in a long white gown with a shaved head wearing little silver spectacles: Gandhi, I suppose he was meant to represent. Next to him was an Uncle Sam in his stripes and top hat and big cowboy boots. And coming behind these stilt figures came the trees—yes, trees, human trees dressed from head to foot in pine boughs. A reporter put his microphone into a tangle of branches and one of the trees spoke: "Since the trees can't be here for themselves today, we're speaking for them." The reporter asked him what his name was. "Doug Fir," said the human tree. "Thank you," said the reporter. "That's all for now from San Francisco."

Later that night I had a dream about the demonstration, only things were rather different. Walking next to Doug Fir was *my* tree, the one which used to grow outside The Bridge Arms and was choked to death, you may remember. In my dream it walked in great beauty and dignity, its leaves just turning to rich autumn colors. Next to it came a stilt figure of Raoul Wallenberg, and next to him was the Uncle Sam. They made a strange collection of figures. I could not tell in my dream if the Wallenberg was real or a dummy. People were throwing confetti and flowers at him and that was when I became convinced he was not real, because he did not shy away but remained stiff on his stilts. When the camera came close up to his face, I could see he was made of flour paste and wire, his skin was shiny and glazed like French pastry. In place of his eyes were glass marbles, and when he was made to bow to the crowd I saw he could not bow from the waist. How can he sit beneath the shade of the righteous trees, when he does not bend, I wondered? It was only a dream, but everyone knows dreams can be quite revealing. When I told it to Gerda she said, "Not so crazy, Jack, they were as thick as thieves." Wallenberg and Uncle Sam, she meant.

As for the real tree, it died a little more every day until it became a grey scarecrow. I do not know if it frightened any birds, but I myself was frightened. The children broke off its arms and carved initials and dirty words into its drying flesh. Then one day some workmen came along and chopped what was left of it down, leaving only a pile of sawdust and the roots in their concrete grave. I am glad you didn't live to see that sad sight. Where it stood is now bare as a desert. Recently I saw a newspaper report: TREES CAN TALK. It said trees can transmit information, or warnings, from their roots through the soil to other trees. Perhaps Gerda is right and I am not so crazy after all.

Vitez – I am sorry to have to tell you – is failing. He has lost many teeth, his eyes are covered in a cloudy film like melted cornstarch, and he does not hear except for sudden noises, like the snapping of fingers, which seems to frighten him almost to death. Yes, he will be with you soon. I suggested to Gerda she feed him fewer sweets, but she told me to mind my own business. "What else does he have to live for?" she asked. I suppose the strain of too much weight, and perhaps the lack of air and exercise, have taken their toll. And then – he looked for you everywhere – out the window, even under the furniture, sniffing here and there. He still looks; he seems unable to accept that you have disappeared forever. He keeps hoping; perhaps the disappointment is too great for him.

He gets little rest during the night, so busy is he pacing back and forth between our bedrooms, guarding us. Gerda, as always, is still his first and last love. When he does sleep, he has terrible dreams, shaking all over like an epileptic. I pray he will one day soon have a dream in which he is running hard across an open plain, against the wind, both his noble ears blown back, his face in a big smile, and then not wake up.

It has been snowing all day today, white blankets are covering the city. The wind has blown the snow into drifts here and there; they are very deep. Now the wind has died down and the stars are coming out. Perhaps it will freeze tonight. It is very beautiful and quiet as we walk round and round in a small circle with our signs and our candles glowing in the white darkness. We continue to make our demonstrations here in front of the Soviet Embassy each year on the anniversary of his disappearance from Budapest; a few people still have the heart left to do it. I feel you are here with us in spirit. Most people passing by hurry on with their hands in their pockets and their noses tucked into their coat collars for warmth; a few turn to yell angrily at us, "Go back to Russia." They do not understand.

It is snowing again. Our hands are becoming frozen stiff around the signs we carry. Soon we will be covered in snow and we will resemble perambulating snowmen and snow-women. I can still wiggle my little toe. The snow has made designs on the buildings like thick white icing. I am happy to think of Gerda safe at home, eating.

And you? How are you? Often I think of you as I lie in your narrow bed. In the darkness I can see your face, sometimes with your new teeth and sometimes without. Always your eyes stare through the empty space at me. I hope you are safe where you are, and warm tonight. I hope it does not keep you awake at night, worrying about Eichmann. This was another thing not in the film; of course Gerda could never really be sure. But what does it matter who was the real father? The truth, so far as I am concerned, is that the Swede will always be yours. And you are you, the *biscuit à la cuiller*, the unpretentious ladyfinger; oldest of the French *petits gâteaux secs*. Remember that.

Love,
Jack

KING PENGUIN

☐ *Selected Poems* **Tony Harrison**

Poetry Book Society Recommendation. 'One of the few modern poets who actually has the gift of composing poetry' – James Fenton in the *Sunday Times*

☐ *The Book of Laughter and Forgetting*
Milan Kundera

'A whirling dance of a book . . . a masterpiece full of angels, terror, ostriches and love . . . No question about it. The most important novel published in Britain this year' – Salman Rushdie in the *Sunday Times*

☐ *The Sea of Fertility* **Yukio Mishima**

Containing *Spring Snow, Runaway Horses, The Temple of Dawn* and *The Decay of the Angel*: 'These four remarkable novels are the most complete vision we have of Japan in the twentieth century' – Paul Theroux

☐ *The Hawthorne Goddess* **Glyn Hughes**

Set in eighteenth century Yorkshire where 'the heroine, Anne Wylde, represents the doom of nature and the land . . . Hughes has an arresting style, both rich and abrupt' – *The Times*

☐ *A Confederacy of Dunces* **John Kennedy Toole**

In this Pulitzer Prize-winning novel, in the bulky figure of Ignatius J. Reilly an immortal comic character is born. 'I succumbed, stunned and seduced . . . it is a masterwork of comedy' – *The New York Times*

☐ *The Last of the Just* **André Schwartz-Bart**

The story of Ernie Levy, the last of the just, who was killed at Auschwitz in 1943: 'An outstanding achievement, of an altogether different order from even the best of earlier novels which have attempted this theme' – John Gross in the *Sunday Telegraph*

KING PENGUIN

☐ *The White Hotel* D. M. Thomas

'A major artist has once more appeared', declared the *Spectator* on the publication of this acclaimed, now famous novel which recreates the imagined case history of one of Freud's woman patients.

☐ *Dangerous Play: Poems 1974–1984*
Andrew Motion

Winner of the John Llewelyn Rhys Memorial Prize. Poems and an autobiographical prose piece, *Skating*, by the poet acclaimed in the *TLS* as 'a natural heir to the tradition of Edward Thomas and Ivor Gurney'.

☐ *A Time to Dance* Bernard Mac Laverty

Ten stories, including 'My Dear Palestrina' and 'Phonefun Limited', by the author of *Cal*: 'A writer who has a real affinity with the short story form' – *The Times Literary Supplement*

☐ *Keepers of the House* Lisa St Aubin de Terán

Seventeen-year-old Lydia Sinclair marries Don Diego Beltrán and goes to live on his family's vast, decaying Andean farm. This exotic and flamboyant first novel won the Somerset Maugham Award.

☐ *The Deptford Trilogy* Robertson Davies

'Who killed Boy Staunton?' – around this central mystery is woven an exhilarating and cunningly contrived trilogy of novels: *Fifth Business, The Manticore* and *World of Wonders*.

☐ *The Stories of William Trevor*

'Trevor packs into each separate five or six thousand words more richness, more laughter, more ache, more multifarious human-ness than many good writers manage to get into a whole novel' – *Punch.* 'Classics of the genre' – Auberon Waugh

KING PENGUIN

☐ *The Pork Butcher* **David Hughes**

War crimes, secrecy, and a brief, voluptuous love affair are all preying on Ernst Kestner's mind as he drives back to the French village where he spent the summer of 1944. 'An unforgettable experience' – *Observer.* 'A true and illuminating work of art' – *Scotsman.* Winner of the W. H. Smith Literary Award

☐ *1982, Janine* **Alistair Gray**

'This work offers more hope for the future of fiction, considered as art and vision, than the vast majority of novels published since the second world war' – *Literary Review.* 'Bawdy and exuberant . . . he is in love with the power of language to encompass life' – Robert Nye in the *Guardian*
